THE CALL OF FREEDOM

HIDDEN HEROES SERIES BOOK 3

SARAH BLYNNE

SARAH BLYNNE WRITES

CONTENTS

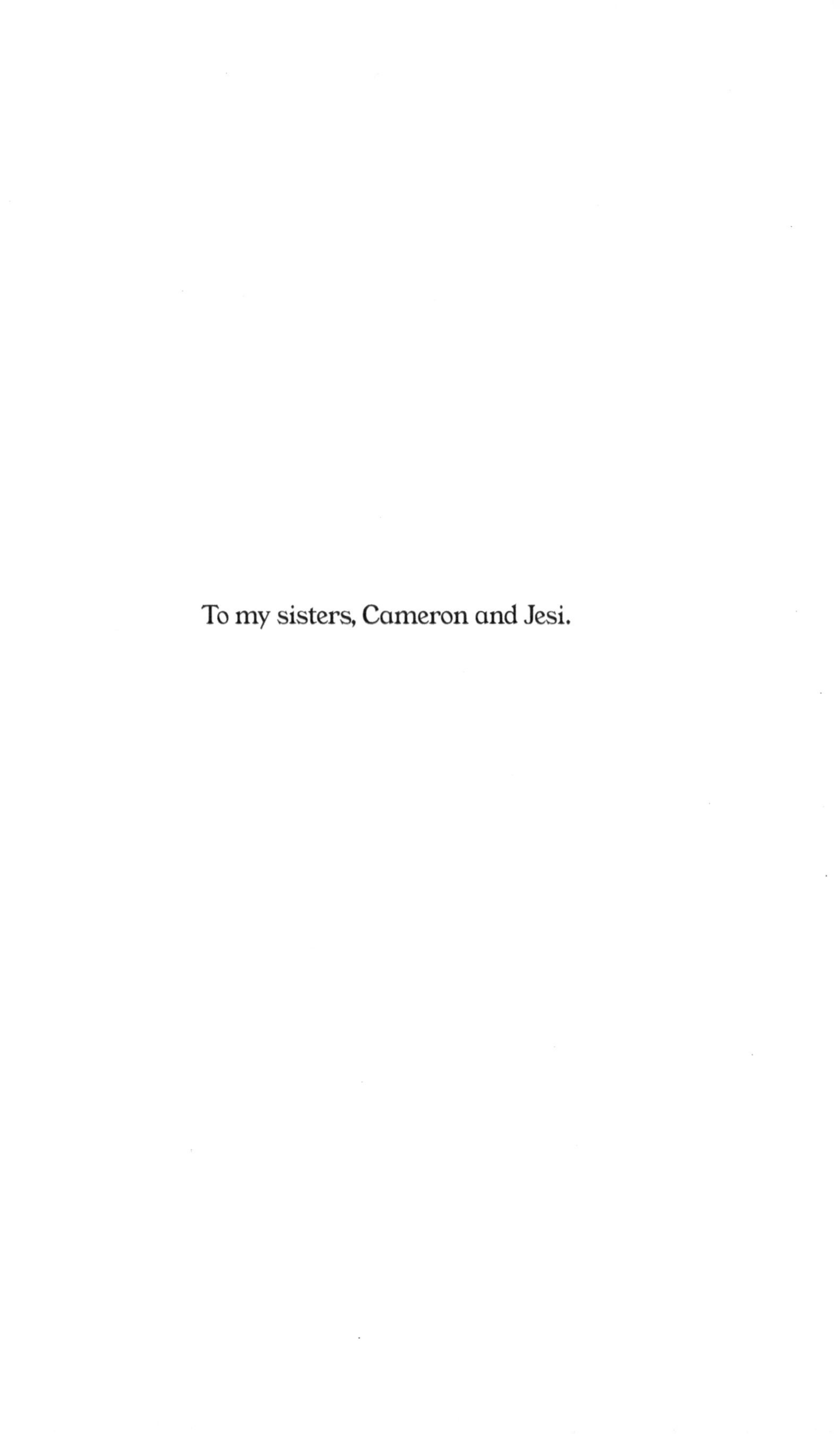

To my sisters, Cameron and Jesi.

CHAPTER 1

ANARA

After falling for what felt like hours, I'm engulfed in water and I'm struggling to reach the surface. Thank Halivaara I didn't land on solid ground. This landing is painful enough as it is.

I kick my feet to find the bottom of whatever I landed in, only to find it's a pond about three feet deep. Once I wipe the water off my eyes, the darkness convinces me that my eyes are closed.

No. It's truly that dark. A mist in a purple hue somewhat illuminates my surroundings—the ground, the water, the thin clouds in the sky, even the mysterious fog squeezing itself between the blackened, dead trees around me. It's the same shade of purple that ignites the tree symbol in the Dormant King's hand when he uses his abilities. There's no possible way I'm still in Petros. It's eerily silent; so much so that my breaths could be heard a mile away. There are shadows of tiered, rocky cliffs off in the distance, and to the left is a wide-open field with the blackest grass I've ever seen. Everything is still, not a breeze in the air. The air is stuffy, the way the eatery in Macaphin Village is when there's wall-to-wall people smoking Bamboo Rollies.

This has to be the other dimension. The Dormant King's home for the last five centuries.

And I'm realizing that Wave is missing.

"Wave?" I call out weakly.

No sticky frog legs on my skin. No low growl or fur against my leg. No gusts of air from flapping wings. He's stuck with Quill and the Dormant King, and I'm here in a completely strange land teeming with Dormants all by myself.

I'm so screwed.

Above me, where the "sky" is, must be what serves as the barrier between this dimension and Petros. I have no clue how high it is, and there is no easy way to figure out how to get up there.

The water sloshes around my boots as I trudge out of the pond, each step as cautious as the next. I'm dehydrated, and I don't have a ton of water left in my last bottle. My trident is the only trusty thing I have in protecting myself. The lack of any sign of movement whatsoever—save the crunching grass under my boots—has my grip on the trident tighter.

It's a whole new world down here, and much more humid than it is on the other side, which actually bodes well for the water that courses through me. The Dormant King thought he was so clever putting me here. He's a moron.

I was so sure we had a chance of winning this war. Four Descendants and five Bennarus should have been sufficient. He was just too good. He copied my powers and we were doomed. Then I felt a force of air tugging me backward, everything went dark, and I knew we were the losing side.

But nothing beats the feeling of helplessness, being alone without the friends you've come to know and love. I had just gotten closer to Ender, and now he's not with me.

I have to get back to them. Back to *him*.

Suck it up, Anara. You're smarter and tougher than this. You knew what you were getting into when Havanna found you in Macaphin Village.

I return to my careful steps toward the open field on my left, dirt rolling under my feet. For a world dominated by Dormants, it shocks me that I have yet to come across any.

A footstep and a low growl have me freezing in place. I may have spoken too soon.

I swallow hard, wondering if staying silent will deter whatever made that noise, or if I've just become an easy target for a predator. Sweat covers my palms as my grip slips from my trident. I wipe my hands off on my skirt and grab the last bottle of water that does little to quench my thirst. I'm thrown into a small fit of apprehension. I need to refill my bottles. I don't know where I am or how to get out. I don't know how long it will take to escape. All the problems filled with uncertain solutions have my breaths quickening, desperately seeking a way out.

Knock it off. There are much worse scenarios than this.

Shadows move and create shapes within the purple mist, and I'm surer than ever I didn't just imagine that menacing growl.

I poise my trident. Focused. Ready for anything.

Icicles and fire shoot my way. Thankfully, with Upsurge, I can control ice, so I use my hand to make a sweeping motion and the icicles fly off. I drop to my knees and roll to the side to avoid the fire before it hits the grass and bursts into flames. The source of the footsteps emerges from the mist, the notorious tentacles waving about around its neck. I take off in a run with the Dormant following suit.

I peer over my shoulder to see how close it is to catching me. That's when I see two others show up on both sides, and now three are chasing me, roaring mightily. I make sure to run in a zigzag pattern to avoid their numerous attacks on my back and feet. I frantically examine the area around me. I need elevation, something they can't climb. They're gaining on me and fear is preventing my legs from moving faster.

For the love of Halivaara, why do the cliffs feel so far away?

The mist clears slightly and I find another puddle of water straight ahead, just beyond a small, rocky protrusion. I use Upsurge to dehydrate the ground, then form a rope with an extremely sharp point. I run over the protrusion, jump, and turn, aiming the rope toward the Dormants. It skewers each one, going in one side of the neck and out the other, and it's over in two seconds.

I managed to get out of that one easily enough; surely, I can handle myself while I figure out how to get out of here.

All hopes are dashed when something wraps around my shin and yanks me down on my stomach. Dry grass and dirt scrape my arms and thighs along the way. Thankfully, I still have my trident in my hand. I turn myself over just before I end up in the Dormant's mouth and stab the prongs in the tentacle. It screams and loosens its grip, giving me time to regain my footing and run again. Up ahead, I finally find shadows of what looks like tiered bluffs reaching higher and higher toward the sky. My legs are tired, but I run faster. With the land being this flat, the bluffs are farther away than they appear. It feels as if I'm running against a moving belt. The cliffs get bigger and bigger, but in small increments.

To my right, the ground rises into a large lump that moves straight toward me. I have seconds to figure out how I'm going to climb this extremely tall rock wall to the first bluff with no holes or ledges to help. I round the rock formation, looking for anything that can make climbing easier while also trying to not die at the hands of this underground monster. A few tall trees, a few bushes, and—

A small lake.

I use Upsurge again. The lump is gaining on me and the water rises slowly. I'm getting dehydrated again and it cannot be at a worse time. I focus harder, sweat beading my forehead and my hair sticking to the back of my neck. I'm not dying a humiliating death in this stupid place. My death will be graceful and it will be in a comfortable bed, just like everyone else.

The water rises high enough to move toward me in a stream. It gathers beneath my boots and lifts me up just as an enormous, snakelike Dormant bursts through the ground, mouth open and fangs flashing. Thankfully, the stream is faster than the creature and I allow it to carry me to the top bluff before I collapse and catch my breath. My head aches intensely, but I have to push through. I'm so close.

I stumble upon rising to my feet and look down at the land I escaped from. A lot of the trees are small dots beneath me and the lake that helped me get up here is the size of my thumbnail. The sky, though, still looks to be much higher from where I am. How did the Dormant King ever manage to simply walk through the portal I opened on Luna Island? The hole was standing upright. He didn't spring up from it, as if the ground spit him out; he *walked* through it.

I hold out my hand and open a portal in the sky above using the rest of the strength I have. Water pours in a nonstop gushing current. It feels like an answer from a deity I never knew about. The entire surface of the cliff is soon covered in inches of water in a torrent stronger than the waterfall over Voda Cave, and shows no sign of stopping.

The water pools around my feet, fully at my mercy. I command it to lift me through the opening, working against the force trying to push me out. Soon, I'm enveloped in lukewarm water. Small bubbles tickle my face. A dull drone of emptiness fills my ears. Opening my eyes, the water is bright and blue. A deeper blue than the tropical waters in Macaphin Village. I swing my arms about, trying to reach for air with each stroke. My racing heart is stealing my breath slowly until I break through the surface.

It's the ocean. A vast, endless ocean.

I spin around to gauge where I am. It's not Agura Ocean, because I don't see Macaphin Village or Luna Island in either direction. On my map, I remember that there is a cluster of small, uninhabited islands on the eastern side of Petros.

The very ones that present themselves in front of me.

Remos Islands in the Volare Ocean. The side of the kingdom I've never been to before, but have always been curious about.

I swim to the small, rocky islands and drag myself to salvation, lying face down on the flat surface like a beached whale. I chuckle to myself in disbelief that I made it here, but I'm also physically drained. My mouth is dry, I'm out of water, and my clothes are drenched, potentially making it harder to move quickly if I need to.

Just to test it out, I lick the water droplets on my forearm. Plain and fresh. Not saltwater, which means I can drink it.

I don't know what kinds of creatures the ocean makes a home for, but I'm too desperate to care. I inch closer to the edge of the rock, dip my bottle in the water, and gulp it down. I didn't realize how thirsty I'd become *and* don't focus on the fact that I'm likely drinking unclean ocean water.

Shivers course through my body, goose bumps covering every part of my exposed skin. Growing up in a tropical setting, I've become sensitive to cold, even if it's not cold to others. A soft breeze over my wet skin and clothes only makes it feel worse, so much so that I can barely bend my fingers. The only reprieve I can find is a break in the clouds that lets the sun beam onto a patch of rock. Even the water feels warmer than the air itself. I down another bottle, then think of my next move when I refill it. The coast isn't that far away, less than a mile if I had to guess. The extreme height of the cliffs is a huge disadvantage, though. I'll need an intense wave to get me to land and I'll need to drink more water.

So I do.

Something slimy slithers around my arm that makes me jump. The texture reminds me of Wave's tongue when he licks me, and it brings unwelcome shivers all over my body. The creature's snake-like form curls around my arm and makes its way up my bicep at an alarming rate. Its golden, sparkling eyes are innocent as a Winged Wolf cub's, but hides devious plans behind them. The sunshine reflects on its slimy, wet skin, crawling across my arm with suckers along its belly that propel it forward.

Trying to scratch it off with my other hand isn't enough. Neither is beating it against the rock to break free from its grasp. I resort to swinging my arm up and around, doing everything I can to make this thing leave me alone. My frustrated whimpers are pathetic, even to me.

My heart lurches to my throat when I see its golden eyes turn a deep red, similar to Dormant eyes. Its mouth opens, the corners curving upward in a wicked grin, and shows me two rows of black, razor-sharp teeth. Before it has a chance to bite into my flesh, I grab it and squeeze its neck as hard as I can. It seems to work when its grip loosens on my arm and slips off. I throw it with all my might back in the water and breathe to bring my heart back to a normal rate.

That was disgusting.

Then the same, slimy feeling makes its way from the ankle of my boot to my thigh, my heart rate accelerating again. Another one of those nasty monsters decided to make me its home. The eyes will turn red at any moment. It's all a blur when I grab its neck, yank it off my leg, and hurl it in the water. But that isn't enough because I see three more coming dangerously close to my foot. I shriek and run across the length of the rock, but they're nearly as fast as I am. It becomes a crowd of red eyes and flashing black teeth.

"Oh, *come on!*" Can everything just stop attacking me for more than one freaking minute?

I make it to the end of the island chain with no other way out and am now cornered by these sneaky aquatic snakes. I make quick work of using Upsurge, turning a wave into a sheet of ice, and crushing them with a motion of my hand.

I need to get out of here, whether those things can swim or not.

I focus on forming a wave. It increases in height every second, testing the limits of my abilities. The water level under the rock drops drastically, revealing a whole world beneath the islands I stand on. Textured rocks, barnacles, and starfish are exposed along the underwater cliff.

Focus. You're almost there.

I raise the wave until it blocks the sunlight and casts a shadow far over the ocean behind me. Just when my head starts to ache, I make the crest drop and slide toward me. It scoops me up and carries me toward the cliffs at a speed that blows my hair back. Rushing, powerful water fills my ears, a reminder of what I'm truly capable of.

The water rises high enough that I can finally see what lies on the other side of the immense cliffs along the coastline: a layer of white brighter than my hair. So bright that I have to shield my eyes from the daylight beaming on it. Sand can be white, but it's never *that* white.

The wave releases me onto the white land and recedes to the ocean below. After a huge crash and rush that lasts for a few seconds, it calms down, pretending that no one had mastery over it just seconds ago.

The powder under my boots melts in my hands and becomes excruciatingly cold water. It slides off my fingers, leaving trails of wet as I regain my footing. The air itself is crisp, clear, and fresh. Combined with the mild warmth of the sun, it's still cold and uncomfortable. Very different from the humidity I'm used to. I take some time to survey the endless expanse of the substance. It's nothing but white for miles, save for the huge mountain right in the middle of the open space, and a line of rocks that show a sign of depth below. I have no sense of where to start my journey. Nothing is pulling me in any one direction.

I suppose I'm left to my devices. I'm now a wanderer.

I take my trident, using it to hold me upright. The only thing that seems to appeal to me is the formation on the way to the mountain. Even if there's nothing there, I can find a way to make it a resting place. Or a place to die. Either way.

One step after the other, using my trident as a walking stick, I start my new journey.

CHAPTER 2

Havanna

I open my eyes, surrounded by the warmth of a roaring fire in close proximity to my face.

The fireplace is inside a brick hearth, just the way it looks back in my house in Ketra. I weakly skim my hands along the inside of the heavy, thick fur blanket wrapped around me. I'm still cold, but both the blanket and the fire are doing wonders in bringing me back to life.

I examine my surroundings and see lots of wood paneling. The walls, the rocking chair beside me, the kitchen area—all made of polished panels that creates a rustic, cozy environment. My heart beats harder and harder as confusion and panic sets in.

Then it comes back to me, stealing my breath.

I was fighting off the attacks of a man who was actually my father.

"Warrioress? You're alive?" my father had said breathlessly. He looked just the same as he did the last time I saw him ten years ago, only now wearing a beard with splashes of gray. He began to cry and took me in his arms. The woman standing outside the door of the cabin, who I then recognized as my mother, came to join in the reunion. I don't remember what was said because I wasn't paying attention to that at all. Disbelief, rage, and joy meshed together in a messy knot of emotions.

That was all I remembered before everything went black. Now I'm here in what I'm assuming is their log cabin. The home they made for themselves. Without me.

My parents are *alive.*

They have been here, hiding in the Paluso Mountains. They have been alive, yet they never came for me after I settled in Ketra. They promised me. Instead, they left me there until Jael had no choice but to take me in.

I remember Bolt isn't with me—no thanks to Quill. I will never forgive him if something happens to my Bennaru on his watch. I will never forgive him for being such a traitor.

Anger boils within me. I missed my parents. I'm worried for Quill. But I'm angry at both. The internal conflict has me quivering in rage at myself, and at my heart for not being able to decide which emotion is a valid emotion to feel.

"Oh good, you're awake," my mother says as she walks in with black clothes draped over her arm. Her blonde hair is a little drier and the corners of her eyes are wrinkled with crow's-feet, but I know for a fact she's my mother. "I washed your clothes for you."

My clothes?

I lift the blanket just enough to see that I have no clothes on, except for my bra and underwear. "You took off my clothes." It's more a statement than a question.

"You were freezing," she says with concern. "You passed out. When your father brought you in, you were so cold. We were surprised you were still alive. Your clothes were wet, which makes it harder for the body to keep warm."

After ten years of never seeing me, she decides to act like a mother again? Where was she when I was ten and scared out of my mind?

Looks like anger is going to be the main emotion here.

"Here, Warrioress," my father says behind me. "I made you some stew with Midnight Pig and a side of Petros Rice. It's very hot. Should warm you right up."

Jael earned the right to call me Warrioress because she became my new mother. It irks me that my father ignores the bull in the room and still calls me that. They only know the ten-year-old version of me, not the woman who became a warrior and is on her way to taking down the biggest enemy for the Descendants. At this moment, I'm their houseguest, not their daughter. They don't really know how to treat me.

"I would like to put my clothes on."

"Of course." Mama points down a short hallway with two other bedrooms. I don't really know who they were saving the second bedroom for. Perhaps for strange wanderers like me? "Right down there."

I clumsily hold the blanket close to my body while I come to stand with one hand, then take the clothes from my mother with the other. I shut the door behind me and take a deep breath. I have to be in a reverie. This is all a hallucination from being so cold and exhausted. I stumbled upon a hospitable couple in my journey that I've never met before. That couple just happens to be my parents. I must be losing my mind.

I change into my clothes, dry and warm, and emerge from the bedroom. Papa holds the bowl of stew and plate of rice in his hands. The heat of the plate nearly singes my fingers, and I welcome it. This, indeed, is not a hallucination.

"We have so much to ask you," he says, "but I know you must be starving with the shape you were in when you came here."

Another snide remark stops at the tip of my tongue, something in regard to how much I enjoy feeling more like a stranger than their daughter. He is right—I'm starving. And thirsty. The reply dies on my tongue and I snatch the plate and bowl from him. The last thing I find myself caring about is how sophisticated I appear shoveling food in my mouth and drinking water so fast that it dribbles down my chin. I don't even know if the food tastes good. I don't care.

"How did you end up here?" Mama asks once I've finished.

They have the nerve to ask their questions as soon as I'm barely well enough to talk. I'm not going to play along with this one. I don't owe them answers.

They owe *me* answers.

"That is a long story," I reply, "but first, I want you both to tell me why you never came for me when you promised you would."

My parents eye each other, unsure of who should primarily answer the question. Mama raises an expectant eyebrow to Papa, validating my reaction. They knew this reunion would trigger me at some point, but it didn't stop them from leaving me behind.

Papa clears his throat. "The night the Backers began raiding our street," he begins, "and we put you on Bolt and sent you to Ketra, the Backers saw you. They started following you."

I dig deep in my memory of that night, and I don't recall anyone trying to follow me. I was too distracted and distraught with the fact that I was alone, starting then.

"Your mother stopped them with Gridlock and her electricity, which made her—and us—a target. We had to escape right away. So, we ran through the trees and hid just until we knew we lost them. We both knew that staying in Cal-léa was out of the question. We left that night and ran as far away as we could."

Mama made herself a target . . . to protect me. It's a fleeting moment when I feel some appreciation for that.

"Why didn't you send a message to Ketra?" I ask, raising my voice with each question. "Didn't it occur to you that your daughter would want to know if her parents were still alive? Perhaps you could have written a letter to explain why you weren't going to make it to Ketra?"

"It was much too risky to have anything tied to your location, and ours," Mama explains. "We were doing our best to make decisions that kept everyone safe, even if it was painful to know we wouldn't see you for a long time."

You could have made an exception, I wanted to say. *You could have tried harder. There had to be other ways to reach me.*

They were just doing what any other parent would, making painful sacrifices for the child's benefit, Jael would have told me. *That's what I did, in case you don't remember.*

I do remember. She lost her life to save mine.

Perhaps I have to change my perspective. My parents' hearts were in the right place. Mama and Papa's hearts were in the right place. They were trying to protect me, and it caused a lot of anger and regret.

"We are so grateful to the one who raised you and kept you alive," Mama adds.

Being grateful is not enough. If only Jael felt appreciated before she died.

"She did it at the cost of her own life," I say with a low voice. "She died in front of me."

The looks my parents give me say more than words can. Ones that say they realize I've been through way too much in a short period of time.

"That's why I'm here, and not in hiding. Backers killed her, and I'm taking down the Dormant King." I square my eyes directly at them. "I found the other Descendants."

The shocked expression from Mama makes me think she'll pass out at any moment. "The Dormant King." She gasps, hand clutched to her chest. "The Descendants. Has the time come?"

I run my hands through my hair and sigh. "It sure felt like it when I left Ketra."

"What happened?" she asks, barely able to swallow through the shock.

I tell them everything, starting with when I left.

They let me tell them the whole story and only interrupt with a question as to why I came to certain conclusions. Truthfully, assuming the Dormant King was in the middle of the map was *not* mine, but that was beside the point.

When I tell them about Quill—when we met, how he saved me, and helped me escape—an aching weight crushes my heart. Despite the circumstances at the time, I consider them wonderful memories. Remembering how the blood thundered in my veins when I first saw how beautiful he was is still a feeling I carry with me. Then I remember what he did—the way he made me feel means nothing and the bubble bursts.

"I found out the poem you made me keep all these years was the key to finding the Descendants," I tell them, explaining how I held the poem over the fire and figured it out. Then I told them that Cal-léa now has a lantern festival to commemorate the night they were attacked. Mama's eyes swim with tears, reflecting the exact feelings I had at the time.

I go into the parts when Quill and I found the other Descendants, then officially found the Dormant King back on Luna Island, and because he stole Anara's Gateway ability, he scattered us, which is how I got here. Bitterness coats my tongue and my words when I tell them that the Dormant King is holding Quill and all the Bennarus captive.

Neither one of them speaks for a while. Papa shakes his head in disbelief and Mama wipes at her eyes, sniffling with a silent heartbreak for the trials her daughter has gone through. Without her.

"I . . ." Papa stutters. "I don't know what to say."

"I'm so sorry." Mama's voice comes out strained as she holds back her sobs. "I'm so sorry you've been through so much. I have no one to blame but myself."

Seeing her now, heartbroken and guilt ridden, I feel myself soften. They not only did what they could to protect me at their own expense, but Mama had to use her abilities to throw off the Backers. To make sure nothing happened to me. They may very well have killed her had the Backers caught them.

I slide off the sofa and kneel in front of her, gripping her shoulder with a half smile. "I've been through a lot," I affirm, "*a lot*. I've been mad and confused for a long time, but I never understood it to be for my sake." I run my hand up and down her arm. "Thank you."

Papa rubs my arm with his hand, but I'm more focused on Mama when she runs her fingers through my hair, just as she did when I was young—as if nothing has changed. "You've turned out to be an incredible woman. And we're thrilled to know that you're all right."

I scoff, sitting back on my heels. "I'm not quite all right. The Dormant King is at large. My friends are missing." I shake my head and focus on my hands in my lap. "I was so sure we were enough to defeat him. I was wrong. And I'm so . . . lost."

"What exactly is causing you to feel lost?" Papa asks.

That was the question of the day. One I didn't have an answer for.

Everything that I believed to be right about the Dormant King was wrong, including his abilities. I underestimated him. We all did. And I don't know where to start. I don't know if I need to find my friends first or find the Dormant King again. Or find my Bennaru. I need Bolt by my side.

"All of it."

Mama comes to stand and guides me back to the sofa, Papa sitting on my other side. "Perhaps you should stay here for a while," he suggests. "We can keep you safe. We've missed so many years with you. Perhaps we can start over?"

"Yes," Mama agrees.

Being with my parents again, as one, is a comforting image. One that I've pictured for a long time. I envisioned reuniting with them one day and having them join me in finding the Dormant King. But their idea to keep me here is a testament to the fact that they haven't changed. It's a solution that fits them best. It's what they always felt was best.

Jael did the same thing.

No. I can't go back to that life. Not when I've come this far and made friends with the Descendants. I was the one who decided to change the narrative for us when no one else did.

There is a way to be able to keep my family and still work toward my goal. A solution that serves us all.

"I can't stay," I say softly, "I need to find the Descendants. I still need to save the kingdom." I lay hopeful eyes on them when I add, "There's room for both of you to join us. You have skills with the sword, and you have abilities."

Mama shifts uncomfortably. Papa stiffens. A rejection of an idea if there ever was one.

"I don't know if that's a good idea," Papa answers with a cringe. "That is quite a heavy task."

"Especially if there's no plan in place yet," Mama adds.

My heart sinks at their responses. "I may not have a plan, but perhaps you can help me come up with one," I suggest. "Either way, I'm still going to do everything I can to save Petros."

"You're the only one who knows more about the Dormant King than we do," Mama says. "I don't know how I would be of use."

"I just need to know how to defeat him," I state simply with heavy despair.

"There's one thing I remember when I was a knight in Cal-léa," Papa starts. "When travelers came and went, we had to observe closely in case we needed an easier way to capture them if they caused trouble." He gestures excitedly, using a teaching voice. "Everyone, villain or not, has a weakness—a vice—that ultimately brings them to their knees. Once you pinpoint it, success is guaranteed."

My weakness is the desire to be free. Water is my vice. Quill's weakness is a desire to feel understood, hence his nearly siding with the Dormant King. Anara views vulnerability as a weakness, although Ender seems to be reshaping her thinking. Ender's weakness is laziness—a desire to be taken care of. I wrongly assumed that the Dormant King was too weak to fight against all four of us.

I analyzed everything else about the Dormant King, *except* for his weaknesses.

I turn to Mama. "Did your family ever tell you what the Dormant King's weaknesses are?"

She shakes her head, much to my disappointment. "Based on the story of the Ancestors, it's hard to deduce." She peers up thoughtfully, chin on her hand. "The obvious one is the lust for power, considering how he copied the Land Ancestor's abilities, and your friends'." She wrinkles her face as she thinks harder. "If I knew more, I would tell you. I'm sorry, Havanna."

"If we were in Cal-léa, I would say to simply find any old records of the Ancestors, and see if the answers come to you," Papa says. "Cal-léa had quite the library, from what I can recall."

The library in Cal-léa is huge. With its dome ceiling and wall-to-wall books, I never felt so small. Mama would take me there sometimes when she wanted a break from the crowds and the noise from being in the middle of the city. It was quiet—the perfect place for a scholar or an avid reader. I didn't read all that much; I was satisfied enough to stare at the architecture of the ceiling all day.

"I don't want to go back to Cal-léa," I voice my decision out loud, and I don't feel the need to delve into the reason behind it. "I don't have time for that kind of research. He's at large and so are the Dormants. I need to find my friends first before more innocent people are killed."

My parents nod reluctantly as I rise from the sofa and head to the door where my shield and sword are leaning against the wall. I proceed to strap them to my back.

"Havanna, perhaps you should stay and rest," Mama practically begs of me, a last-ditch effort to return to my old life. "It may be a long journey."

I give her an apologetic smile. "I have to do this." I walk back to stand in front of her. "I need to finish what I started."

She purses her lips, a whimper of distress in the back of her throat. "Please. What if we lose our chance to be a family again? What if we never see you again?"

"You will," I reassure her, whether I believe it myself or not. "When the war is over, we will have all the time in the world to make up for everything we've lost."

Mama sniffles, nodding to a situation she doesn't want to accept. She pulls me in for a hug, tightly embracing me from my neck. "If you ever need to, you're always welcome to come back here."

I find myself hugging her back. In some way, I have their support, even if it's minimal. One more reason to fight for my life in this war—to reunite with my parents. I'm determined to stay alive. I'm determined to win. I'm determined to come back for them.

Papa approaches me when Mama lets go and hugs me too. "No matter what happens, know that we are so proud of you. War-rioress."

I haven't been hugged by my parents in ten years. This may be the last time I get to do so. I let myself sink into the warmth of their embraces, enjoying it while it lasts.

"At least take this," Mama says, going to a small closet between the bedrooms. She pulls out a coat that's long enough to reach my knees, made with soft fur mixed with black and white colors with hues that blend into gray in between. It's not a thick coat, but it will be better than wandering through the snow in short sleeves. "You're going to be cold."

It's a miracle I didn't die from hypothermia, or simply froze to death. I happily take the coat, closing it taut around my body. It's as warm as their ten-year delayed hugs. "Thank you, Mama."

I purse my lips, studying both of them, how much they've aged since I saw them last. Papa, who was once a knight in a fortified city, had black hair that converted to gray and showed in his beard with strands of white. Violet half-moons under his eyes and the wrinkles on his forehead and cheeks show his age even more so. Mama, thinner than she used to be, kept the white olive branch tattoo on her forearm.

They've changed so much, but also have stayed the same.

"Wait," Papa says just before I open the door. He goes to the kitchen and pulls out a few small pieces of paper, the same color as the parchments I have. "If you ever need help, or you're in danger . . . write a note and have Bolt deliver it, when you can find him again. This time, we *will* find you, wherever you end up." He hands me the paper, his eyes imploring me to take them. "We want you to feel you can still count on us, even if we disappointed you in the past."

I turn my gaze to Mama, who nods. If I had a chance to make things up to Jael, I would take it in a heartbeat. My parents want to make up for the time that was lost between us. Perhaps it's time to let them.

So I take the papers and hide them in the sheath of my sword.

"Be strong, Warrioress," Papa encourages me. "And don't ever give up."

Those are the last words spoken before I walk out their cabin door, back into the snowy mountains.

Back to the search for Bolt.

For Anara and Ender.

For Quill.

For salvation.

For freedom from the Dormant King and his vile grip on the world.

Back into the fray.

Back into war.

CHAPTER 3

ENDER

Wherever I am, it's hot. Not just the dry air in my face, but this beige-colored powdery stuff I'm lying in is nearly as hot as a cooking pot. A welcome relief, actually. The sky is clear and blue, and everything is so bright that I wish I had shade just for my eyes.

I lean up after being on my back for a few minutes and scan the area. There's nothing for miles. Just this weird, pebbly powder everywhere. I take a handful and let it rest in my palm. I draw circles in it with my finger, studying it closely. It doesn't dissolve. Simply tiny pieces of rock pulverized into a smooth texture. I saw substances similar to this in Vulca Mountain when I mined stones. Aanu told me this stuff is mostly found in beaches and the desert.

This must be the desert.

I have no idea where to go. No direction to turn.

I come to stand, wiping the sand off my bodysuit. The one that Anara made specially for me.

Anara. My compa. Who's missing, along with my friends and my Bennaru. No thanks to the Dormant King. Even my unusual strength wasn't enough to take him down.

It all makes me angry, anger that I really wish I could unleash on him or the Dormants. With none around me, it stays contained within, with chances to grow into an unbearable ball.

I suppose the only choice I have is to go forward, so I do.

The heat is so intense that there are waves above the ground, creating illusions of water that appear to be close by, but I know it's just tricking me.

I already hate this place. Not because of the heat, but because I'm by myself. I'm not used to being alone. I always had my aani, and as of recently, my compos. On top of that, I'm hungry with no one around to make me food. There's nothing to indicate I'm close to finding anyone.

Step after step, I let those negative thoughts feed the ball within me. Thirsty. Alone. Hungry. Powerless. It all bubbles up and comes out in a throat-splitting, thunderous roar that could scare creatures within a mile radius.

If I have, it means I still have something left that isn't a blow to my self-esteem.

Unlike Havanna, none of that inner rage is geared toward Quill. He's my compo. The Dormant King appealed to whatever weakness he had, which speaks volumes to his power. Quill righted himself before he fully succumbed to him and fought alongside us. Havanna was furious with him, understandably, but she needs to get over it. There's no need to hold a grudge against someone of our own just because they're not perfect. In my tribe, there is no room for grudges. We work things out. We stick together. Always.

I've walked for what feels like millions of years. For all I know, I'm walking on a rolling ball that takes me nowhere. My tongue sticks to the roof of my mouth, my throat parched and drier than the sand itself. I wish Quill were next to me, laughing at my commentary and giving me advice on girls. He's good at helping us forget how dire our situation is, even just for a moment. He'd be a helpful asset right now, because life sucks.

That is, until I see a structure. Among a flat land of sand, there's something more elevated. They look like they could be rocky cliffs, but I'm still too far away to tell.

I increase my pace. I need somewhere to rest, and I want it now. I want a heaping pile of steaming, charred meat. I need a barrel of water, as long as I don't have to use Blaze anytime soon. I want someone to give me a bath. It's been hours, and I've been alone far too long. I need to regain strength and go back out to find the Dormant King and kill him. He's gone too far, separating us and proving his arrogance with stolen power.

He's going down.

Those thoughts have me running faster, the sand caving beneath my feet and creating divots. Running through sand takes so much effort and leaves a deep burn in my thighs. It slows me down, though, and makes me angry again, but I push forward. My back aches, and sweat beads on my forehead and gathers underneath my suit. I always loved getting a good sweat out of genuine effort. It told me I worked hard, and I accomplished what I needed to. It told me the effort was worth it. This effort is wearing me down rapidly, to the point where I'm unsure I'll make it there without passing out.

The structure gets bigger, and I hear the hum of voices talking over each other. Sandstone buildings rise above the walls of what appears to be a civilization. One building on the other side of the wall gets my attention. It's taller than all the others, with open windows where the observer gets an incredible view of the entire desert. At one of the entrances, two women stand guard with curved, knifelike weapons attached at their hips, their hands always on the hilts. They stare straight ahead, masks covering their faces from the nose down, their ankle-length panel skirts billowing in the breeze. They look as fierce as Anara did when I first met her.

I swallow, but I have no moisture in my mouth to coat my throat. I don't know if I'll be able to speak, but I have to try.

I come closer to the guards, who finally turn to address me. "Need. Meat. Sleep. Now."

My knees buckle and bring me down. I lose the will to stand back up, so I settle for a pathetic crawl, using what little strength I have left in my arms to slide myself forward along the piping-hot sand. Once my arms stop working, I just let the sun beat down on my back, allowing the heat of the sand to encompass my cheek without a care.

"Oh!" they shout, immediately coming to my aid. They smell of citrus and vanilla, intoxicatingly beautiful. I must have arrived in heaven. "What happened to you? Are you all right?"

All I manage is a groan. My jaw is too tired to form words.

"Let's bring him to the infirmary," one of them suggests.

They grab hold of my ankles and hands and attempt to lift. They strain and grunt to the point where I could laugh. No mere person has successfully been able to carry me. It's not much easier with my axe attached to my back.

"He's too heavy," one of them says. "What do we do?"

"Go fetch our king," I hear one guard say to the other. "I can stay here with him."

Heaven has a *king*? Thank Halivaara. Everyone here must live in comfort and wealth— just what I need.

"Can you tell me where you came from?" the woman guard asks, shaking me by the shoulder. I don't budge. "Are you injured?"

I ever so slightly shake my head. I don't want to talk. My story is much too long to tell.

"Our King." I hear urgent footsteps approaching and the sound of dangling jewels. "He appeared here like this. He's too heavy for the two of us."

"What happened to him?" an authoritative voice asks.

"We don't know. He can't talk. All he said was that he needed meat."

"He may have passed out."

"With the shade of his skin, he appears to be a Mulhutna," he remarks with a thoughtful tone. "How did he end up here?" He says this more to himself than to the women. "Very well. You both grab his feet and I will take his arms."

Good luck.

To my surprise, they lift me, but not without more loud grunts from all of them. My torso skids against a more solid surface, perhaps a type of smooth stone. It's not much longer before my body plops on the ground.

"He's too heavy," the man says, catching his breath. "Grab someone to help us."

Soon enough, another man arrives, and now four people are carrying me. I float for a while and it's relaxing. I must have fallen asleep, because the next thing I know, water is tossed in my face.

"Anara? Compos?" are the first things out of my mouth because water to the face is exactly the kind of thing Anara would do. It brings me out of my deep sleep and into strange surroundings.

The washroom I'm in is huge and practically sparkling with a bright, clean vibe. The white tile has a glossy surface, with a ceramic basin sitting on a white stone countertop, and the bathtub I'm lying in is much more comfortable than the one I used back home. White polished stone surrounds my whole body in one full circle, big enough to fit at least three more people. Everything is so clean, even the towels that hang on wooden hooks at the end of the tub.

"I don't know who 'Anara' and 'compos' are—"

I shriek at the sound of a sultry woman's voice to my right, sitting in the middle of the washroom on a chair, flanked by two other women. If they were the ones that helped me, I have no idea.

"—but I'm Calista, Queen of Sabbia Desert."

She's a beautiful woman, a golden crown of the sun on her head, her hair falling off her shoulders in subtle waves with a golden spear upright in her right hand. Seems as if this entire town is full of stunningly gorgeous women.

"I know seeking parties are a favorite among men," she continues, "but I never expected one to suffer to the extent you have just to attend. The party isn't till tonight anyway."

I quirk an eyebrow and sit up straighter in this fancy tub. "Seeking party? What is seeking party?"

She's the one to quirk a curious eyebrow now. "Surely, you've heard of them. Seeking parties are a nightly affair meant for men to be better acquainted with the Sabbian women."

I am *so* confused. "What is Sabbian woman?"

Calista studies me as if trying to understand a unique and odd specimen before her. The ladies beside her roll their eyes, something else that reminds me of Anara. "Wait. You—" She wiggles a finger at me. "—you didn't come here in search of a mate?"

"No!" Then I look at the three of the women standing before me. "But now you mention it, I no object." I wink at one of the women with a flirty smile, which she returns. For a place that hosts seeking parties full of men, these ladies must have never seen a handsome man before. I'll fit in nicely here.

"Then what are you doing here?" Calista urges.

I was raised to never answer questions that involve my background as a Descendant for fear that it was always possible it was for the Backers' benefit. My first instinct is to lie—also what I was raised to do in this scenario. However, the Dormant King is going to make an appearance here at some point, and he'll bring his Dormants with him. Anara brought him out of the other dimension. He's not going back. No point in lying anymore.

"I in war with Dormant King. Then he sent me to land of sand."

Calista stiffens, her eyes turning cold at the mention of the Dormant King. The two women also seem baffled as they turn to Calista for a response. She sits up a little straighter, gripping her golden spear tighter. "War?" she says with an eerie calm that sends a shiver spiderwebbing down my spine. "With the Dormant King?"

"His name Alaric." I don't know why that's important. "As you see, I Mulhutna. I strong. My fire no beat him. He copy Water Descendant power, use on us, and I here."

She swallows nervously. "Are you telling me that . . . you're the Fire Descendant?"

"Yes, compa."

"She is Our Queen," the woman to Calista's right rebukes. "You must address her as such."

"It's all right, Zena." Calista waves her off, then releases a nervous, quivering breath. "Where are the others?"

"I too hungry to talk. I no know," I whine. "I need bath. And meat. I tell you more when fed and clean. I miserable too long."

Calista breathes out slowly, her lips in a tight line, seemingly considering whether or not to cave to my wishes. If she doesn't, I will die. I will shrivel up and die right here.

She finally turns to the women beside her. "Give him whatever he wants."

CHAPTER 4

QUILL

How did everything get this bad?

That's all I can think about as I watch Dormants surface and reach the coastline. My friends are gone and all their Bennarus are being held hostage with me here on Luna Island, relying on me for a plan of escape. Even Kane, whose evil owner is standing in front of me.

I don't have a plan yet, I tell them, *the Dormant King is a tad strong.*

I watch in horror as Alaric aims his hand at the ocean, making the water rise, higher and higher, testing the new abilities he copied from Anara. Remembering how he pretended to be dead, then waited for the precise time to grab her by the neck and use Usurp just makes me angrier by the second.

The wave rises five feet, then ten. He ushers it toward him, forming a puddle within the sand. He stares at the result of his newfound power with satisfaction. He creates another stream from the puddle and sends it back to the ocean. All proof that he is more capable now than he was before.

"You know, ally, I was thinking," the Dormant King says with such an air of arrogance I want nothing more than to plunge a knife into his heart. He turns to me, a sly smirk playing on his lips. "Perhaps you can help me make a decision."

I say nothing.

"I could kill you and the Bennarus, which will lure the Descendants back to me so I can finish them off," he says with deep thought, "or I could keep you all alive, and make the Descendants come fetch you after trying to fight through me. And they will, because apparently, you mean *so much* to them." His last sentence is spoken in a mocking way that has me releasing a low growl. "In reality, you mean nothing to them. You nearly betrayed them. How will they ever trust you again? Face it, Descendant, we're allies. You have no choice. I healed your arm wound, something Havanna couldn't do. What use are she and any of the other Descendants? I can kill you just as fast as I can heal you."

The slam on Havanna and my friends cuts deep. Ender is the first male friend I've had since I left Arbol Village. Havanna was the first friend I made at all, and the chemistry was an immediate thunderstorm. I tell myself that I don't want to go further with her, but every time my heart beats, it nags me to change direction. For that to happen, I need to stay alive. I need *her* to stay alive.

He may be capable of killing me in an instant, but his threat remains empty. If he truly wanted me dead, he would've killed me by now.

"We're *not* allies," I growl.

"As I said, you have no choice," he remarks over his shoulder, and turns back to the water with Upsurge at work. "What do you say, ally? Will you head back to the coast with me and make this kingdom the way it was meant to be?"

I say nothing and stare at his back. As long as he's turned away from me, I have an opening to form a plan out of this. I still have my bow. I still have the knives around my legs. The Bennarus have their abilities to take on their larger forms within seconds.

With much at my disposal, I have to be cunning. I have to think fast because Dormants have climbed the cliffs to land and they're minutes away from creating disaster on the closest civilization.

I tell the Bennarus my plan with Transmission, and they agree when all but Koa crawl into my quiver or my pockets. Koa remains on my neck as a small bird, waiting for my signal.

With careful precision, I reach for the knife closest to my hand, eyes locked on the Dormant King's back to ensure that he won't turn around. He will at any moment. This has to be done perfectly.

I only have one shot, otherwise it's a fight I won't win.

"Just think," Alaric says, tranquil and calm, "the inhabitants will never know what they have coming. They will have no choice but to bow to their new leader. Their new king."

"You don't know what you have coming either."

It all happens in seconds. Just before he turns to inquire, I flick my wrist and throw the knife at his midsection. The moment he doubles over, I run as fast as possible. Koa sprouts into his hawk form from my shoulder and grips my arms with his talons. He tosses me in the air and catches me on his back.

I can't believe it. It worked. The coastline is so close now.

That is, until Koa turns back to the island and returns to the Dormant King.

You're not the only cunning one in this place.

Transmission. He's using Transmission to control Koa.

I should have thought that one through.

Koa makes his way back to the Dormant King, who is just a black dot in the ruins of the island. I already know this battle for control is going to be a tough one.

I softly touch the back of Koa's neck. *Koa, turn around. We need to save the others.*

At my command, he turns around again and heads back to the coast. Just when I think I have him, he circles back again.

No, Koa. Don't listen to him. He's just using you. Remember, he's using you to destroy us.

He turns back to our destination, but barely has enough time to flap his wings before he's aiming for the island again. He caws incessantly, frustrated and confused. His swinging back and forth has me getting dizzy and nearly falling off him.

Koa is not yours to control.

Well, he is listening, is he not?

Time to show him who has the upper hand.

Koa, listen to me. Now.

His caws turn into high-pitched shrieks that have me covering my ears. He's aggravated, doesn't know who to listen to, and he's going crazy. He twists in one swift motion and I slide off his back and off the side. I grab onto his talon for dear life, grunting and yelling loud enough for him to notice his master is in danger.

If I can control your Bennaru, everyone else will fall into submission to my power too. All will fear me. You must stop fighting it, Descendant.

I hate him as much as my parents now. I will prove him wrong, just as I did with them.

Desperate, I grasp Koa's neck and give him all I have.

Koa. You know me. You know my voice. You were there when Indy died. You were there when my father hit me. You were there when Nyx and I became friends when we were young. Don't listen to anything or anyone else. You. Know. Me.

Something changes in him. He stops flapping. He just glides there, the breeze carrying the burden of keeping us afloat. He knows he is being played, just as I was when the Dormant King relayed his past to us.

He relaxes, loosening up beneath me. In one calm, seamless turn, he heads toward the coastline, ashamed that he fell for the Dormant King's control. The same shame that's coursing through me.

"It's all right, buddy," I console him, patting the top of his head and ruffling his feathers. "He almost had me too."

Koa caws in agreement, flying more determinedly and flapping his wings with such force that my hair nearly comes loose out of its tie. The Dormant King loses this time.

Just as we're almost crossing over land, shrieks reverberate behind us, closing in. Dormants fly in our direction, tentacles waving around and throwing ice. The Dormant King is relentless in gaining our obedience. The whole kingdom submitting to him won't be enough. He needs the Descendants' obedience too.

I turn around on Koa's back and nock an arrow. I fire, then nock another in one smooth motion. Each Dormant plummets to the sea before they can reach us.

He's such an idiot, using them as a last resort. I never miss. Me and my bow never fail.

Finally out of danger, we cross over Petros.

CHAPTER 5

HAVANNA

My face is numb. But thanks to the coat Mama gave me before I left, I'm much warmer than I was when I showed up at their cabin. It's a wonder that I even survived walking to Paluso Mountains.

I've been walking through Paluso Snowfield for what feels like days. I lost my sense of time the second I woke up in my parents' cabin. I have no idea where to go, but the positive twist is that I get to see much of Petros that I never had the chance to explore. With way too much time to get into my own head.

The reunion with my parents certainly didn't go the way I imagined it for so many years. I'm disappointed that they're continuing to hide while their only child fights the battle that should have been their own. At least they didn't leave me completely on my own, for once. They made themselves available to help, just within the confines of their home. I would have asked them to do research on the Dormant King to find any patterns that lead to a weakness, but they wouldn't have recommended the library in Cal-léa if they had the means to research in their home.

They'll be my absolute last resort, if I need it.

As much as I'm glad to see what this kingdom has to show me, I'm still so angry with Quill for being responsible for all our Bennarus getting taken from us. Had they not been held hostage, Bolt would be with me. I wouldn't need to walk for miles in the middle of nothing on foot. In the cold. Alone.

Being mad and staying mad is proving to be an exhausting feat. Instead, I repeat Papa's words in my mind.

Everyone, villain or not, has a weakness—a vice—that ultimately brings them to their knees.

I think about the battle on Luna Island. The Dormant King's weaknesses didn't blatantly reveal themselves. He was all strength and used it to his advantage. He was impeccable with multitasking. One hand to move us around while deflecting attacks with the other. Using Transmission as mind control.

Conniving snake.

Quill could use Transmission on him too, but it ends up being a battle of minds. Even one strike of my lightning and Ender's fire wasn't enough. Perhaps it's not an elemental power that will bring him down. For Quill, it was something that hit home for him: his relationship with his parents. But there's no easy way to find out more about the Dormant King's life prior to his banishment. He hated the Ancestors. They must have known why his heart turned to ice, surrounded by a wall. Nothing can bring the Ancestors back to help us.

According to my nearly destroyed map, I'm getting close to Snake's Canyon. From a distance, I can see the jagged line of rocks—two of them, in fact. Meaning there must be some space in between those rocks, whether it's filled with water, dirt, or more rocks.

I increase my speed to get there faster. I'm unsure if I will find salvation there, but there's nothing but snow and some hills beyond the canyon, and I need to find a place to sit without getting wet.

A slim line of blue appears under the edge of the rock outline the closer I get. The water is a beautiful, glorious shade of emerald green that sucks me in like a moth to a flame.

A body of water lies at a low elevation, calling me to come closer, the way water always does. The cliffs are steep, from what I can tell within the shadows. More than the water, something else steals my attention.

A bright light so white that it seems blue explodes out of one wall of the canyon, not even trying to hide its beacon of salvation.

A cave.

Thank the heavens. A place to rest.

I'll have to do some rock climbing downward to get to it. There is no paved path leading to the maw. Luckily, I'm not a stranger to climbing rocks. While Jael trained me to run up Montanha Peak and go back down until I vomited, I practically had to climb some of the way because parts of it were steep. She took me to other parts of the mountain and showed me how to climb. She also used the rocks around Ketra Falls as beginner's practice. The hardest part was climbing downward, since it was impossible to not peer over my shoulder to gauge the next step below.

This is going to be a nightmare to climb back up.

I make it to the edge of the water within fifteen minutes or so. With just a dip of my fingers, the water is ice-cold from being a drop-off for melted snow. I balance myself between the rock and water's edge toward the cave, and look closely at the particular curves and protrusions that will steady my feet and give me a good grip. Then I leap toward that spot.

My hands hold tightly while my feet rest on the parts that stick out, and I move sideways. The tips of my fingers quickly start going numb from the cold and the amount of weight I'm putting onto them, but I push myself, inching closer to the entrance of the cave, then finally drop.

It's more of a tunnel than a large, inverted hole. Patches of algae and moss spread sporadically around the walls as I proceed down the path. Curiosity urges me farther down the tunnel toward the blinding bright light's source. It leads me to bank a sharp right and then bluntly stops. The temperature here is slightly warmer than it is outside, a respite from the never-ending cold.

The reminder of all the traps I've found myself in has me reaching for the hilt of my sword as I move closer to the blinding-white illumination. The reflection against the wall flows in a circular motion, smooth and nonthreatening, yet so very odd. Not just a single light. It's thousands of threadlike lines broken up into sections, all moving clockwise as one unit around the rock walls. A living being.

The cave's end hosts a small pond, the same emerald hue from the water outside.

"What is this place?"

My voice thrums within the walls louder than I like. The light keeps moving. Then a deep, womanly voice cuts through me and makes me tremble.

"Havanna. Descendant of Voltana, the Ancestor of Lightning. Blessed by none other than me, Halivaara."

Halivaara.

I found *Halivaara.*

I'm speechless. Never in my life would I have imagined coming across the one who gave us powers. The one responsible for the very existence of Petros.

Halivaara has been *here*.

I finally manage to swallow. My voice is a strained whisper. "You're . . . Halivaara?"

"I am the entity to whom you speak."

The depth of her voice is similar to Calista's, one that is soothing and brings fear to nothing. "What do I call you? Since you're an entity."

"Halivaara will suffice."

"How do you know who I am?"

"Your abilities hum through your very being. I sense them. After all, I am the one who blessed your Ancestor with it. I am the entity who responds to the needs of the land. I am glad you found me, my dear Descendant."

Halivaara responds to the needs of the land. Perhaps it can respond to what I need to beat the Dormant King. It *created* the Dormant King, after all. Halivaara may be my only hope. Otherwise, all hope is lost.

That and the pure mental exhaustion of this entire mission has me dropping to my knees, right next to the pool. I swallow down the tears that beg to build up in my eyes.

"I need help," I explain in hopelessness. "I've tried so hard to beat the Dormant King, and I've failed. Every single time. Everything I've fought for has done absolutely nothing. He's too powerful for us."

There is a pause, as if the entity needs to think of the right words to reply with. "You have been through many tribulations. That much I can see. But you have far from failed, my beloved

Descendant. Hope remains, and you shall attain it. Your loved ones will be redeemed by your determination and vigor, and the strength of your kind."

I scoot closer to the edge of the pool, desperate for answers. A sense of tranquility washes over me. I'm communicating with the very source that can help me. "But how? What do I need to do? How do I defeat the Dormant King? You know his weaknesses better than anyone else. Don't you?"

I still can't seem to wrap my mind around the fact that I'm talking to Halivaara. *The* Halivaara. Its delayed pause has me doubting my reliance on it. What if Halivaara is just as lost as the rest of us? What if the Dormant King, the Power Descendant, is so far gone that Halivaara sees no way to salvation?

"Greed is poison to the heart," the voice says. "The power and authority he claims will be his demise. There is always a limit to be reached. That limit, my beloved Descendant, will be what breaks him."

The satisfaction in that response feels . . . empty. In fact, it's not an answer at all. All it does is take me back to what the Dormant King's weakness is, one I haven't pinpointed. This frustrates me even more, combined with my own mental and physical exhaustion.

Before I can respond, the light detaches from the walls, combining midair above the pool in one large atom of energy, brighter than it was as threads along the rock. Slowly, it floats toward me in an ethereal way. "In the meantime, may you have the strength to keep fighting. You have my backing. Never give up."

The energy sinks straight into my chest. The light explodes and splits in all directions of my body. Gentle heat and stimulating vibrations carry through my arms and legs. A comforting, strengthening warmth encompasses my heart, the way Calista's hugs feel, but more invigorating. All the hopelessness, exhaustion, and defeat I've felt evaporates. My strength and body temperature is revived. How long that will last, I don't know, but Halivaara itself helped me, and gave me something to ponder over. Even if those things leave me with more questions than answers.

The light travels out of my body and soars back into the rock walls. Darkness envelops me, as if the light were never there at all. The only guide I have to lead me out is the moonlight at the maw of the cave.

I asked Halivaara for the answers with no breakthrough. But I have one answer I can take with me as I leave this place.

Halivaara rekindled my fire. I can't let it die.

I *cannot* give up.

CHAPTER 6

Anara

I've officially made a decision about my feelings toward snow.

I hate it.

However, the only perk to this substance is that it turns to water when it melts. I even succumb to scooping some in my bottles and waiting for it to melt as I walk. A few drops of water at a time are better than nothing at all.

I finally reach the canyon after trudging through a million miles of snow. At least, I believe that's what I'm seeing. I can't tell now that it's dark outside. The faint glow of the moon is all I have to guide me. This would be the perfect moment to have one of my iced Twinkle Fireflies help me, even if their glow will only shine a few feet in front of me.

It's going to take me a long time to get down those jagged, steep cliffs. I'm hungry, thirsty, and so cold that my skin is sensitive to even the slightest touch. That's enough reason for me to try.

I find grooves within the rock deep enough to step on and very slowly work my way down. My boots were not built for climbing, yet here I am, nearly sliding off the stupid cliff. I skim my feet over the rocky texture to find something to hold my weight with each step I take. The moonlight on the water dances among the ripples and another dim light presents itself at the mouth of a cave. Relief blossoms within me. I'm going to be too exhausted to carry on after fetching some water. That cave is the only source of refuge I've seen so far.

Legs and knees cramping from my calculated steps, I finally make it to the water. I find a rock to sit on as I grab my bottles. I barely let one of the bottles fill up before I bring it back to my mouth. I gulp down its contents like a dying plant, water dribbling down my chin and onto my skirt. So cold and so refreshing, reviving me with every sip. My head starts to hurt from how cold it is, but I ignore it. No amount of water will be enough to satiate my thirst with the way my mouth still feels dry after every drink. When I finally start to feel hydrated and ready to burst, I dip the bottle two more times and keep drinking before I fill up the others.

I come to stand and head over to the cave, taking my time, arms held out to my sides for balance. I stumble slightly as my boots topple off the uneven path, my heart lurching to my throat, but keep focused on what lies ahead. I have no idea what to do or where to go from here. My drenched map doesn't help. All I've been focused on is escaping the dimension and finding water, hoping to find my friends along the way. *How* to find them remains to be seen.

Something about that changes when I hear the echo of footsteps about a dozen paces away from the cave. I solidify my footing before I reach for my trident. My body is fatigued and cold has reached the marrow of my bones, but I will fight whatever is in there if I have to.

The noise changes from a soft echo to pronounced steps as a figure emerges from the cave. To my relief, it's not a Dormant. It's a person. A woman. A thick coat drapes to her knees that I'm sincerely wishing were mine, and her legs and feet camouflage with the dead of night. Which means this figure is wearing black. I only know one person who always wears black.

Holy Halivaara, it's *Havanna.*

I can't believe I found her.

"Havanna!" I shout with relief and excitement, waving in her direction. She turns toward me, and I swear I hear her gasp.

"Anara?" Her shout reverberates back to me. I race toward her as fast as I can as she tiptoes along the level rocks to meet me. I launch at her and hug her tight, much to my own surprise. She hugs me back with a relieved laugh, her body surprisingly warm. It's only after about two seconds that I realize I'm doing something completely out of the ordinary.

I shove her off me. "Wait, wait. Did I just hug you?"

Havanna gives me a sideways smile. "Yes. Yes you did."

I clap my hands together as if dusting them off. "Let's pretend that never happened."

She pats me on the shoulder with a chuckle. "Glad to see recent events haven't changed you too much."

We both crouch to sit at the water's edge, letting this moment sink in. "How did you get here?"

She lets out a bitter laugh. "That is a long story. But . . . you're not going to believe this—"

"Highly possible."

"—I met Halivaara."

This woman *must* have smoked a Bamboo Rolly. "What?" I ask, incredulous. "You . . . met Halivaara? *The* Halivaara? Where? In that cave?"

She nods, wide-eyed and excited. "I swear to you. It was just a light in the room, and it spoke."

She *definitely* smoked a Bamboo Rolly. "It spoke," I deadpan. "What did it say?"

Havanna stutters, trying to find the right words to begin this story. "It knew who I was. It said I was the Descendant of Voltana, the Ancestor of Lightning. When I asked how to defeat the Dormant King, it just said something about him having a limit and once that limit was reached, it would break him." She waved her hands around in exasperation. "Before I could ask more questions, it disappeared. It didn't help at all."

I roll my eyes. "You're telling me." I lean in closer, getting ready to mock her. "Were you just so hungry and thirsty that you were hallucinating and most likely talking to yourself? I can see you doing that."

It was her turn to roll her eyes, followed by a harsh sigh. "I wasn't hallucinating. I would drag you in there to prove it but—" She shrugs. "—it's gone." She releases a satisfied breath, her attitude confident and hopeful. "But I know one thing. We're not alone." She turns to face me with a side smile. "We never were."

I was feeling at a loss the moment I ended up in the other dimension. I had no solid plan after I arrived at Snake's Canyon. Just when it seemed like everything was falling apart when we all split up, Havanna shows up with energy and vigor. Perhaps she *did* meet Halivaara and gained strength from it.

Staying true to myself and denying how I really feel, I scoff. "I knew that, Electric Doofus." I stand, my butt officially numb from sitting on uneven terrain. "Now the question is, where do we go from here?"

Havanna pulls out the near-ruined map from her pocket. Her squinting is an indicator that she can barely see anything on it in the darkness. Eyes locked on it, she takes her left arm and points straight ahead. "That way."

I lend a hand and help her to her feet as she packs the map in her pocket. "I suppose I'll follow your lead."

"As if you have a choice," she quips. Then she stops and shucks off her coat, handing it to me. "Here. I'll be fine. I think you need it more than I do."

I don't hesitate to take it and squeeze it around my body as tightly as possible. I can literally hear my teeth chattering. A light wind whistles through the canyon and numbs my skin with the chill. "Thank you," I say with shivers behind each word.

It's a steep hike back to the snow and neither of us speak until we find our breaths. Walking side by side, together once again.

"Now, tell me what happened to you," I demand.

Havanna chuckles sarcastically. "Oh, do I have a story for you."

CHAPTER 7

QUILL

Can anyone hear me?

After a few minutes, I still get nothing.

I ride on Koa's back, flying over the expanse of green that is Petros. With the nighttime air, it's more different shades of black with the bluish white of moonlight on it.

Tell me where you are. All the Bennarus are with me.

A few more minutes. No response. They have to be around somewhere.

It's all my fault everything turned out this way. One moment of weakness was all it took to bring me down. On the other hand, perhaps we were simply not strong enough to take him on.

Perhaps we should have prepared better.

I'm sorry, I tell the Bennarus huddled in my shirt. *I'm doing my best to find them.*

Collectively, they crawl to my neck and nuzzle it, showing their forgiveness. Flame burrows himself in the waistband of my pants for warmth, not used to the coldness of the sky. It brings me relief to have their approval, but not enough that I can forgive myself. I didn't fully turn against my friends, but the possibility was there if no one talked some sense into me.

Another hour passes as I scour the land below for any travelers that could potentially be a lead. A few lone travelers, specks of black moving about in the night, but no Descendants. This search could take days. They could be anywhere.

My first priority upon finding them is making amends with Havanna. I screwed things up before the events on Luna Island, but even more so *on* Luna Island. More than anything, I need Havanna's trust. I can't allow her to be anything more than just a friend, but I don't want to lose her in any capacity. She means way too much to me.

The dark landscape brightens to a faint beige as we enter unknown territory. I pull out the map from my pocket and study it, the wind from Koa's flight bending the parchment so much that I flatten it along his neck. Sand and small hills for miles. The only sign of life is the occasional cactus.

This looks like Sabbia Desert.

The cold, however, is nothing I've ever experienced before. Arbol Forest became frigid at times, but the type of cold in the desert is much more intense. The thickness of my pants and my long-sleeved shirt do little to keep me warm and the wind from Koa's speed just makes it worse. I'm pretty sure the cold has seeped deep within me because I can't move my fingers and my cheeks are numb.

Just when I'm at the peak of misery, I see two dots walking on the sand below, surrounded in moonlight. The first sign of life since I entered the desert about fifteen minutes ago.

I have Koa dive slightly so I can get a closer look. It would seem peculiar that there are travelers just taking a stroll through the desert. Unless there are still stray Backers wandering around that were not at the Fortress when we destroyed it.

One of the figures is a bright blonde whose hair is a beacon in the darkest of nights. A trident hitched on her back is a dead giveaway. The other person, clothed in black, is the one person I could pinpoint anywhere.

Anara and Havanna.

I found them.

A large lump in the sand charges toward them at lightning speed. They stop and get their weapons ready. Havanna's electricity glows in the night and makes it easier for me to see.

Another lump in the sand makes its way. Then another.

I swoop farther down to meet with them, and the Bennarus emerge from my clothes, turning into bigger versions of themselves. I almost tell them to wait, until I see a few more lumps swimming toward them. The Bennarus get to work shredding them to pieces, some as large as a tree. I nock Pineapple Shell arrows and shoot them directly at the lumps closing in on Havanna and Anara. The explosions cause the Dormants to spring free from their hiding places, then land back on the sand with a thud. One lands in front of Havanna, and it looks like a vastly enlarged version of a snake, fangs as long as I am tall. A single strike of lightning may not be enough for that one.

"Hang on, Havanna!" I shout. Koa circles around for me to get a better angle as I get another arrow ready. The arrow explodes on its body, and the next few moments occur as an unspoken plan that works in beautiful succession.

Havanna connects her electricity to the lightning in the sky and throws it down on one Dormant. Anara forces water to twirl around her trident, turning it to ice as it progresses, and stabs another Dormant with a swing of her weapon. I make sand rise, forming a fist with it, bigger than the three Dormants combined, and throw it down on another monster. They all turn to dust, and our job is done.

Koa lands in front of them just as Wave gallops toward Anara and Bolt practically dives for Havanna. Whines of desperation to reach them fill the air. Kane comes to my side, then crawls on my shoulder as a shrew, no owner in sight. His tiny, sweet whimpers against my ear make me feel sorry for him not having a master. I reach behind me and pat his head with my finger, the only way I can be consoling.

I approach the girls as their Bennarus go insane over them, soaking in their praises and happiness.

"Bolt!"

"Wave! You're a butt for making me worry so much!"

Anara and Havanna embrace their Bennarus for a long time, and they have no qualms about receiving return affection. Wave licks Anara's face while Bolt nudges his bird head against Havanna's chin repeatedly. I let them have their moment before I make them notice me, to notice that I managed to escape the Dormant King's grasp and saved them.

"Quill! You idiot wrapped in a moron!" Anara screams while she launches herself with her arms spread. "I'm going to hug you and I need you to pretend it never happened. But *man,* am I glad to see you!"

She hugs me tightly and I wrap my arms around her waist, equally relieved to find almost all of my friends. I glance over Anara's shoulder and I'm met with Havanna's fiery glare. Anara lets me go and Havanna's derision drives into my soul. Her feet stay planted in the sand, making no moves to greet me and staying silent. Anara clears her throat, the tension palpable between all of us.

"Havanna," I regard her, trying to sound cheery but coming out nervous, "I'm glad I found you."

Her already disgusted look turns into a near snarl. "I'm sorry, do I know you?"

Oh boy. This is going to be harder than I thought. Perhaps this is a valid excuse for me to not pursue anything. "You should. I sacrificed my arm to save you. Remember?"

She tilts her head to examine said arm. "Where's the wound?"

I grimace at the thought of telling her the truth, but I suppose there's no other logical explanation. "Alaric taught me a trick," I tell her, which is somewhat true, but I also wanted to break the tension.

"Oh yes, I should've expected that since you guys confide in each other and everything now."

"Oh for crying out loud, enough with this crap!" Anara groans obnoxiously, addressing Havanna in particular. "Quill knows he screwed up. He never actually turned against us, and never planned to. He fought the Dormant King with all of us and even escaped. Give him some credit, Doofus."

I point a finger at Anara while looking at Havanna's beautiful but angry eyes. "What she said."

Havanna folds her arms, her lips forming a tight line. She knows we're right, but I also know that she's stubborn. Sometimes more than she should be.

She shifts her weight from one leg to the other as she fights with herself. I don't understand what debate is going on in her head. Just as Anara said, I never fully betrayed her or anyone else. Why is she holding on to this with a death grip?

She takes a few steps toward me, her face a mask. Then she pats my cheek. "I'm glad you're all right."

It's a small win, but I have a long way to go. "Have you seen a lot of Dormants so far?"

"Not until now, but the dimension is full of them," Anara answers with that trademark sarcasm.

"Dimension?"

She waves in dismissal. "I'll tell you about that later."

"What's going on?" Havanna asks.

My throat bobs. "After we all got separated, he summoned all the Dormants in the vicinity. They were crawling up the cliffs to land. They're roaming Petros as we speak."

Anara mutters a curse while Havanna sighs heavily. The situation has just gotten worse for all of us, becoming bigger than the four of us alone can handle. I found myself unable to form a plan on how to stop them, but I had to focus on finding everyone first. Even now, I'm coming up empty.

"We're screwed." Anara flaps her arms. "We're going to need a freaking army for that."

"That's why we're going to Sabbia," Havanna says. "I know the best person to help us."

"Good. We'll get there faster if we fly." I jog to Koa and mount his back. "No sense in hiding our Bennarus anymore. You can both tell me what happened while we were apart."

Wave turns into a macaw while Havanna gets on Bolt's eagle form, and we head to Sabbia.

CHAPTER 8

ENDER

S abbia is fantastic.

I've eaten multiple servings of food until my belly feels good and inflated. My baths are given as requested, my clothes have been washed, and—because of my size—I've had the privilege of sleeping in the king's and queen's monstrosity of a bed. Vulca never hosted this kind of luxury, even when my aani did everything for me.

Even now, as I lie in the multi-person bathtub once again, Calista's servants, Freya and Zena, run a scrubbing brush along my feet and legs, giving me a foot rub that will surely lull me to sleep tonight. Their sighs and rolling eyes tell me they don't enjoy doing this, although I don't understand why. I thought they would revel in seeing a bare-chested man in a bathtub covered in bubbles. I'm getting the treatment of a king.

But I still miss my friends. I miss Anara.

Last time I saw her, she needed my support when she used Gateway to bring the Dormant King back. She was afraid, and it was shining in her eyes when the Dormant King threw her at me and Havanna just before the portals made us vanish. She was finally accepting me. Trusting me. Seeing me as a man, not a superficial boy. I miss antagonizing her and seeing her exasperated response.

I'll find them soon. I'm too comfortable here. I'm sure they're still alive.

Queen Calista stomps in with purpose, equally as irate as her servants. "All right, you've milked it for long enough." She regards me with a glare. "You. Get up and out of the tub."

I flap my hands, exasperated. "They not done," I explain, gesturing to her servants. "Can I have more Winterbulb Wine? Feel good with bath."

"No," she snaps, "I have met all your demands before you reveal anything about your kind and their whereabouts. You've had five heaping plates of meat. And you most certainly will not eat in the bathtub."

"But I a growing boy," I say, flashing my handsome, white-toothed smile of innocence.

Calista wiggles her finger and shakes her head adamantly. "No. No more. You have run Zena and Freya ragged with your demands of continuous food, sleeping in *my* bed, washing your clothes, luxurious baths, and foot rubs." She emphasizes her point when she gestures to me in the bathtub. "You've had more done in a day than I have done in a month, and I am the bloody *queen*."

"I guest." I shrug. "You take care of guest, no?"

"I don't enjoy taking care of *insufferable* guests," she comments. "Have you ever done anything for yourself?"

"Yes. I tribal chief of Mulhutna." I motion to my naked form. "I mine rocks, hence my body."

Calista rolls her eyes and sits in front of me at the end of the tub. "Zena, Freya, will you please excuse us? You are free to take the rest of the evening off."

They both heave an audible sigh of relief, then leave the bathroom. With no doors in this house, Calista waits until they're a safe distance away before saying with a glare, "You will tell me what you know. *Now.*"

I hesitate, simply because I'm getting a thrill from irking her. Prolonging the luxurious treatments is all I want right now. "I no know," I muse playfully.

Before the last word leaves my lips, Calista takes out a short stick that turns into her spear within seconds, and aims it at my exposed neck. "You have tested my patience more than my husband has in our entire marriage," she growls. "Talk. Now."

I fold my arms, my biceps no doubt bulging and accentuating my pecs. "Why you need know?" I ask. "You be trusted?"

She withdraws her spear, but remains alert. "More than anyone you've met in this kingdom, I'm sure." Her eyes turn distant as she stares at a nearby wall. "I met Havanna when she stumbled upon this town looking for the Dormant King. She was so . . . childlike. Scared. Angry. Hurt. But she also displayed more bravery than I could ever have imagined for anyone her age, saving me and this town from imminent peril. Since she left, I have worried for her. I've come to love her as my own." Her eyes shine with tears of concern, a look I've become accustomed to with Aani. "I need to know if she's all right."

Havanna. The closest thing to a child she has, as far as I know. This must be how Aani feels each day she has to live without my presence. Each day I don't return, her heart likely sinks a little more. She probably has no clue if I'm still alive.

I sit up straighter in the bath, my heart more compassionate toward her. "I understand. I sorry," I say softly. "I want tell you Havanna is all right, but, I not sure—"

Shouts of alarm interrupt us. Calista whips her head toward the doorway, clutching her spear tighter. "Our Queen!"

Calista stands in front of her. "Keeley? What's wrong?"

"She has . . . returned!" the woman says with joy between gasps for breath. Freya and Zena appear behind her. "The Lightning Descendant! She has returned, and has brought two others!"

The Lightning Descendant. Two others.

Havanna. With Anara and Quill.

She's talking about my friends. They're alive.

Happiness courses through me more than the hot bathwater ever could. Words fail to form on my lips when I rise out of the tub without a single thought about the fact that I'm still fully naked. "My compos! My compos are here!"

Freya and Zena shriek at the sight, shielding their faces. Keeley, on the other hand, rakes my body with her eyes, her smirk an indication of how impressed she is with the view. I place my soapy hands on my hips, forgetting for a few seconds why I stood in the first place.

"Grab a towel, you idiot!" Calista snaps, her cheeks red.

"I go see my compos!"

"No!" she shouts. "I will bring them to you in a moment. Stay here, and for the love of Halivaara, put some clothes on!"

Footsteps rumble across the room as the women leave and race downstairs to greet their guests. All I can think about is finding something to cover my body and reuniting with my friends. It's been two days, but it feels much, much longer.

I was getting the treatment of a king, but I still missed them. Especially Anara.

My clothes are nowhere to be found, so I grab the next biggest thing to cover myself with and race downstairs.

CHAPTER 9

HAVANNA

I hate my traitorous heart for flip-flopping upon seeing Quill. I forgot how strikingly handsome he is. How kind he is. How he is always capable of making me laugh. Perhaps I should have let down my guard and hugged him the way Anara did. I couldn't bring myself to express those feelings.

I have to remind myself of the root of my anger. He's done a fine job of pushing me away, but he has the nerve to seem disappointed that I'm not showing my emotions. He's making this much more complicated than it needs to be.

Standing between him and Anara at the front gates of Sabbia Town, I simply wish Quill was an ugly, dreadful being to look at. His gray shirt clings to all the corded muscles on his back and thick biceps that I have imagined having wrapped around my waist, especially at night. My imagination won't allow me to dream of anything worse, nothing that can ease the pain.

Returning to Sabbia is bringing back memories, both unpleasant and positive. Queen Calista is the only woman who welcomed me kindly. It took me almost dying to save the town to gain the respect of everyone else.

"Havanna?" a woman shrieks, heels clomping on the sandstone pathway to the entrance. "Is that you?"

Calista appears with a bright smile, as a mother would with her daughter, and all feels right in the world. I'm near happy tears when she pulls me into a tight embrace. "I've been so worried about you, my child. I'm so relieved you're alive."

I smile and hold her tight. "I missed you."

She takes me by the shoulders and pushes me back to scan my entire body, head to toe. "You're not hurt, are you? What are you doing here?" She eyes my companions and gives me a knowing smile. "And who might these be?"

"Quill and Anara," I point to each one. "Land and Water Descendants."

"Nice to meet you . . ." Quill says, and pauses as he waits for confirmation on how to address her.

She nods to him. "Queen Calista."

"Queen Calista," he repeats. "An honor to meet a gorgeous queen such as yourself."

I roll my eyes. Hard. I hate that that is the kind of charm that once worked its magic on me. Calista doesn't fail to notice my annoyance, but flashes a flattered smile at him.

"Well, aren't you a pleasant young man," she purrs. "Welcome to Sabbia. It's an honor to meet you." Her eyes rove Quill's body, then turns to Anara. "It's not every day that I have the privilege of meeting figures that will shape the future of our kingdom."

"No pressure or anything," Anara responds with heavy sarcasm.

Calista puts on a grimace, understanding immediately the kind of person Anara is.

"Don't mind her," I reassure her. "She doesn't really know how to mince words."

Anara doesn't argue, and instead shrugs in indifference.

Calista waves us inside. "Come. Your friend Ender is here. Do us all a favor and lift him out of my bathtub."

Anara gasps while I drop my jaw. "Ender's here?" she nearly shrieks.

"Yes, and he is insufferable." Calista rolls her eyes. "Please, for the love of Halivaara, take him with you when you leave."

Insufferable is, unfortunately for him, a very accurate word to describe his behavior. Quill hangs his head and chuckles as she leads us to her house. "That doesn't surprise me at all," he comments.

We walk across the sandstone pavement directly to Calista's house and throne. On the other side of the Reddawn Oasis, women arrange instruments such as a set of drums, a flute, and a very small wooden plank with strings attached. People gradually fill in the space around the oasis. Masks in all different colors cover their faces from the nose down.

"What is this?" Anara motions to the growing crowd.

"The seeking party is about to start," Calista answers.

"Seeking party?"

"It's a nightly party where men and women meet potential mates," I sum it up for her.

Anara's lips curl in disgust. "So, an orgy?"

Instead of being offended, Calista barks out a laugh. Quill snorts to hide his own amusement. "Far from it. It gives a chance for the ladies here to meet men from all areas of the kingdom. If they connect with a man, they are deemed worthy to take off the mask and see the woman's true, full beauty."

As Quill walks in front of me, I attempt to read his expression. His gaze is locked on everyone filling the town space—everyone but me. It bothers me beyond all reason that he pays no attention to me, and I'm positive it's showing on my face. With the women parading around us, of course I'm the last thing he's thinking about.

We make our way up the stairs to the throne room, sparking memories of when Calista first took me through here. Lost, alone, and out of my mind. When I descended those same steps, ready to strike, just before Calista's life was going to end. Remembering that time fuels me with a spark of vigor, ready for what the next trial holds.

On the dais is King Malik. I immediately smile upon seeing him.

"Havanna?" he exclaims. "How wonderful to see you!"

He pushes himself off his throne and makes his way to me. After an affectionate side hug, I introduce him to Quill and Anara, which leaves him so bewildered that he finds himself at a loss for words.

Ender's enormous form flies down the stairs in the back, bare chested and wrapped in nothing but a too-short towel that doesn't cover a whole lot. His powerful thighs reveal themselves to us with each step he takes. From the corner of my eye, Anara stares. Hard.

"Compos!" Ender shouts, arms wide open. I silently pray that his towel doesn't slip off his hips. "You alive!"

Just as he did the first time we met him, he hugs all of us as if we've been friends for years. Flame hops out of Quill's pocket and crawls along Ender's leg.

"Flame! You all right!"

Our chatter and happy laughs take up the space of the throne room as he envelops all three of us. Quill and I let go, but he hangs on to Anara a little longer, squeezing her close to him with one arm. "I missed you," I hear him mumble into her hair.

She turns her head away from him, flushed and awkward. They seemed to be drawing closer, even possibly in a romantic sense. If her face is any indication, she doesn't care for that notion.

"Are you all right?" Anara asks instead.

"Yes, I fine," he answers casually. "I treated like king here. Compas here beautiful, but mean."

Quill snorts.

"He's getting better treatment than I am," Malik mumbles. A corner of my mouth quirks up when I catch Calista glaring at him.

"Because he's lazy," Quill says to Ender with a lifted eyebrow.

Calista chuckles, pointing at Quill. "I like him."

I release a heavy, relieved sigh. I can't help but smile at Calista's approval of him, but I also can't let any of them think my visible happiness has anything to do with Quill. I turn my head to glance over my shoulder, hiding the relief that's so obvious on my face, until the room quiets and silence engulfs us all.

When I turn back to face them, we look to each other in hopes that someone will take the lead on the next steps from here. Calista sighs with the weight of having us together and what it means. "Now that you're all here," she begins, "we have much to discuss."

"How about some drinks?" Malik announces with a clap.

"Food first," Anara demands.

"Yes!" Ender points to her.

I, for one, could use a few drinks.

CHAPTER 10

ANARA

I missed you.

As the four of us recount recent events to Malik and Calista, Ender's admission sits at the forefront of my mind, a spinning wagon wheel that only says those three words.

I can't get over how his hands felt when he held me. My goodness, the warmth that swam through me with his touch was incredible.

I missed him too. That's the problem.

It reminds me of how vulnerable I've become to him. I've worked so hard *not* to be. To have it crumble because of a troll would be an insult to my character.

My chest nearly exploded when Calista said Ender was here. I felt even better when I saw him for myself, alive and unharmed. He's the reason I fought so hard to get out of the other dimension in the first place. He's the only good friend I have; I want to keep him in my life. Nothing can ruin that.

Ender has to be shoved to the back of my mind, where I put all emotional issues.

All of us crowd in the living room by the bar in Malik's and Calista's home. The Bennarus chow down on Petros Rice and Midnight Pig in their smaller forms behind the bar while we drink from expensive, shiny glasses. The stem of mine is made with braided cords that form a slope at the top to hold the rest of the glass. Beautiful, detailed work.

"I must say, I thought I could find the answer to all of this somewhere in your summary of events, but this one is a bit complex." Malik sips his whiskey. "I thought for sure the four of you together would have bested him."

"Thank you for the insinuation that we're weak," I remark with my mouth full of Dewey Fruit. I didn't realize how hungry I was when we got here.

Calista's simmering glare in my direction may as well have burned me alive. Just how Havanna looked at me when we first met. Who is now subtly shaking her head at me before she drinks Winterbulb Wine from a round, stemless glass.

The seeking party is in full force downstairs, the beating drums pounding out a rhythm that makes it hard to not dance to. The flute and stringed instrument combine to bring magic to the music, romantic and seductive. My hips involuntarily move side to side in my seat until I shift my focus back to the conversation at hand.

"No one is insinuating anything," Calista responds with a bite. "I am, however, in awe of the Dormant King's power."

"He's had hundreds of years of practice," Havanna chimes in, smacking her lips after another sip. "And we've had all of, what? A couple months?"

I scoff. "Speak for yourself. I honed my abilities when everyone in my village thought I was asleep." With another mouthful of fruit, my voice turns vile when I say, "If anyone had the potential to beat him, it was me."

It is Havanna's turn to glare at me. We're closer friends now, but it doesn't mean I have to stop being a dreadful presence. I know very well she still plans on making the final blow to the Dormant King. Doesn't make me any less powerful.

"I had the woods to practice on when I was younger," Quill remarks with a shrug, holding a mug of beer. "But with the Dormant King sharing my abilities, I was fighting against a shadow of myself out there."

"And now he knows what to do to bring you to your knees," Malik adds thoughtfully. "Perhaps it would be beneficial to figure out how you can block him from entering your mind."

"That I never did. Didn't think I needed to."

"Perhaps that would have made the battle easier for us to win," Havanna mumbles.

"It may be an essential skill for you," Calista suggests. "All of you, really, if he has the ability to control minds—human and animal."

"This will still be a tough one to win if Dormants are crawling through the land, regardless if the Descendants are at their peak power," Malik says. "You need an army for this kind of feat."

The music outside turns into a more emotional, heavy tone, but still laced with enough romance for couples to keep dancing.

"Our soldiers are a start, but not nearly enough," Calista remarks. She glances at Quill. "How many would you estimate were headed to Petros?"

He shrugs. "From the island alone, I'd say twenty or thirty."

The whole room groans audibly.

"And considering how many Dormants are still living in the other dimension, I would guess the number is triple," I add.

Calista frowns and turns to her husband. "I believe this will require the help of multiple cities and their forces," she says with dread.

"Where we start?" Ender asks. He's been a little quiet this evening too. Fortunately, he's now fully dressed in the bodysuit I made him. Calista didn't allow him to join us unless he was "in a modest state of dress."

Before anyone can answer, frantic footsteps ascend the stairs into the bar. "Our King! Our Queen!"

Malik and Calista leap to their feet, Calista's hand on her shortened weapon. The same Sabbian woman that was alerted of our arrival—Keeley, I think—races inside, eyes wide, alert, and urgent.

"What's the matter?" Malik asks.

"I just received word from male visitors that Solma Hills has been totally burned," Keeley answers in a panic. "Acres of land at the base of the Paluso Mountains have been torched. And to make matters worse—" She swallows deeply. "—there have been reports of the sand in the desert . . . moving. In large lumps. The males have stated that one of them chased him all the way here until he reached safer ground."

All of us shift in our seats to turn to her, practically frantic. "Has anyone been harmed?" Calista asks.

"The male visitors are well, but fearful." Keeley points with her scimitar to the walls on the west side of the town. "From there, I spotted large movements in the sand that didn't go in any particular direction. The males said that on the way here, they saw them head toward Vulca Mountain. From their observations, they had caused a large amount of chaos in Sabca Hot Springs. It's nothing but rocks now."

Ender shoots to his feet with accelerated breaths. "Vulca Mountain. My tribe." His panic sends him weaving between the furniture in the room. "I head back now."

"Ender," Havanna calls to him calmly, reaching up to grip his shoulders. "They're going to be all right."

He doesn't hear her with how much he moves about. He runs his hands over his bald head and blinks incessantly. Malik and Calista call his name to calm him down, but the voices drown into mumbles as I observe Ender. I know why he's terrified. His father was killed by Backers and he was powerless to stop it. The title of chief was passed to him, all while grieving his loss. The Mulhutna became his responsibility. His *people*.

Being here in Sabbia means he can't save his people. He couldn't save his father; he wants to be able to have the capability to save his tribe. However, he forgets that the Mulhutna have one asset that all other civilizations lack. He needs a friend to remind him of that. It's the least I can do after all the times he's been a listening ear for me.

I chase him down the hallway. I remain calm but firm as I grip his forearm. "Ender. Look at me."

"Aani need me. Mulhutna need leader."

"Look at me." My hands reach to gently hold his face. My eyes bore into his with great sincerity, and I can feel his pulse beneath my palms. "The Mulhutna will be fine. They're huge. They're strong. They have the Tyranodrake, remember?"

His eyes soften the moment I mention their guardian monster. I become hyperaware of the way his heartbeat feels in my hands. It begins to slow down in seconds.

"Besides, your mother is a Fire Descendant. They couldn't be in safer hands." I lean in so close that we share a breath. My whisper brushes against his lips. "I promise you."

His throat bobs as he swallows. He leans his forehead against mine, the heat of our bodies and heartbeats blending together.

His eyes flutter closed, a display of his ultimate trust in me, the reassurance in my words. "Thank you."

As I give him a warm smile, Malik declares his decision. I guide Ender back to where everyone is gathering by the bar, and sit back down. "Until further notice, we need to have constant surveillance. Keeley, warn your troops and assign their stations. Please be as discreet as possible so as not to alarm anyone."

"What about seeking parties?" Calista asks.

"Does this mean we're going to be locked in here?" I cry. Havanna and Quill say nothing. They avoid paying attention to each other, wooden and stoic expressions on their faces.

"Everyone, calm down," Malik says with authority, pumping his hands up and down to make a point. He puts a hand to his chin to consider the options. "As long as we have continual protection on our walls, there is no need to discontinue the parties for the time being." He nods toward Keeley. "If anyone raises questions about this arrangement, they can come to me or Calista."

"Yes, Our King." Keeley bows her head and races back downstairs.

"What exactly are you hoping this will accomplish?" Calista asks, leaning back on the arm that's bracing her weight.

"Our people will be safe and everyone can live as normal." He fixes his gaze on all of us. "Again, discretion is necessary. No point in causing stress if we can avoid it. Everything will be fine."

"They won't be enough if a swarm of Dormants show up," Havanna points out, voicing my own internal thoughts as she curls and uncurls her fingerless-gloved fists.

Malik sighs, the stress of it all becoming evident. "Keeley has plenty of strong women in her force. I trust she will handle it well."

His trust might be misplaced. There's only so much a small army of women can do against a flood of Dormants, should they make an appearance again.

"King Malik, with all due respect," Havanna starts, "we can't delay taking action here. Dormants are looming in the desert and destroying Petros as we speak. We have to do something before they move in on cities and villages."

"She's right, my love," Calista agrees softly, running her hand on his bare bicep.

"Very well. I will send a formal letter to King Aldous of Arythica and let him know we request his attention. Perhaps he already has the situation handled and has his army in the fight."

"We don't have time for a letter," Havanna replies with a cringe. "I suggest we physically visit the king in Arythica."

"And as a former citizen of Arythica," Calista adds, turning to her husband, "perhaps it will give the Descendants leverage if you go with them. Besides—" She eyes the rest of us. "—they need all the support they can get for something as serious as this. I will join you as well."

"Wait." Malik shifts in his seat. "Who will oversee the town in our absence?"

"Freya and Zena are perfectly capable of holding down the palace. Keeley will have forces all over the town. We won't be gone long. It will be fine."

Malik takes a deep breath. Silence falls over the room as he ponders this discussion. "A king and queen rarely leave their posts at the same time." His tone is laced with concern. I don't have room in my mind to commend him for his concern over the Sabbians' well-being. "Allow me to make sure everything is set in place and everyone is aware of their role. I will send a letter to the king alerting him of our arrival, then we'll head to Arythica the day after tomorrow." He slaps his knee. "For now, unless any of you are planning to go to the seeking party, I'm going to turn in."

Malik holds a hand out for his wife to join him, which she accepts with the softness of a woman who loves her man. "Let's get some rest, and we form a full plan tomorrow," Calista tells us all. "Good night, and it was a pleasure meeting you." She aims those words particularly at me and Quill. Enough proof that she's tired of Ender.

He can be insufferable, but he's taken space in a special place in my heart.

The place where my walls are crumbling.

CHAPTER II

QUILL

J ust when I thought the cold of night was unbearable, the heat is on a whole new level.

Fortunately, I'm not left without. Malik and Calista were good enough hosts to give me clothes to ward off the heat, not to mention I still have the Ice Stone I bought in Arythica before heading to Vulca Mountain. It gives me a chance to show off my bare, sculpted chest and torso. Havanna may not swoon, but the other ladies will.

Except she's the only one that I hope will look.

Ender sticks to the bodysuit Anara made him, considering no other clothes fit his massive frame. Anara's ability to create ice is sufficient for her to cool off.

Malik leads us to the eatery and treats us to breakfast. It is a bountiful feast, and I take advantage of stuffing my mouth with everything that is edible—Chill Grapes, Dewey Fruit, sweet flat cakes with a layer of sugary spread, and eggs that are perfectly seasoned. I don't care about my figure for a moment. It's been too long since I've eaten decent food. Ender keeps asking for seconds, thirds, fourths, to the point that the servers are groaning. A needy, lazy man indeed.

"Now that we've gorged ourselves—" Malik breaks our gluttonous silence. "—I would be remiss if I didn't warn you of what is to come when facing the king."

"Should we be scared?" Havanna asks.

"I believe 'careful' is a better word," he corrects. "King Aldous is a stickler for the rules and traditions of the court. He upholds them with utmost authority, and anyone who disobeys will be disciplined."

"Oh joy," Anara drawls as she drops a napkin a little too harshly.

Malik braces himself to give us his input, scooting closer to the table and hands on either side of his now-empty plate. "Immediately upon entering the throne room, it's vital that you get down on one knee and bow. It shows your respect for his authority. Keep your head down at all times."

My eyebrows furrow. Malik has only revealed one fact about the king, and he already seems to think much too greatly of himself.

"If you wish to speak, lift your head and make eye contact, but *do not* speak until he gives you permission to do so."

I spare a glance at Havanna sitting across from me, whose eyebrows are bunched with an incredulous expression, then returns my gaze. We are both in agreement with how ridiculous this is. Anara's face is unfathomable, and Ender doesn't seem to pay any attention as he continues to stuff his mouth with food. I wouldn't put it past him to have two stomachs.

"Once he gives you permission to speak, rise from the floor and state your case. Be sure your words are tactful and respectful." A pinned glance at Anara. "That is especially important for you."

Anara doesn't have it in her to look even slightly offended. She shrugs and lays her chin on her hand, fully embracing her bluntness toward others.

"Please don't screw this up, Wet Wench," Havanna begs to Anara sitting behind her. I smile at the acclaimed nickname, remembering the first time Havanna called her that. In the woods, where Anara saved us from a horde of Niminims.

"I make no promises," she responds in a bored tone.

"If you speak out of turn," Malik interrupts, "or speak without permission, you very well could be incarcerated. Or even executed."

Every pair of eyes casts a warning glance to Anara, the one most likely to be the first to be punished by the king.

"I love that everyone has such faith in me," she says, keeping her voice bored. "You have nothing to worry about. I'd rather not die."

"Excellent." Malik winks with a half smile. "I would rather you not die either. I don't wish for that burden to rest on my shoulders."

"Why rules?" Ender finally contributes. I'm amazed that he was even listening while he was reveling in gluttony.

"Arythica has always upheld high standards for royalty," Malik says. "It speaks to the status and wealth of the city, as well as recognition that true royalty and dominance is in our midst."

"You don't make us treat you that way," Havanna notes.

Malik smirks. "I prefer to rule by earning respect, not fear."

Ender points to himself, mouth full. "I do too."

Malik sits back in his seat, a mischievous smile quirking his lips. "Oh? Are you a king?"

"No king. Chief of Mulhutna."

Malik nods. "That explains the constant demands for service," he murmurs.

Anara barely cracks a smile at the comment while Havanna laughs lightly.

"What?" Ender asks, not hearing Malik's quiet retort.

"He said it explains why you're so strong," I tell him.

Pleased with this answer, he nods with confidence and agreement. To my surprise, Havanna smirks at me, even though she holds a grudge in those eyes.

That, in its own small way, is another win.

"Havanna," Malik addresses her, "would you like to be the one to state our case to the king? Simply because you've been deemed somewhat of a leader in this mission. I have faith that you have the right words to explain our desperation."

Havanna stills. The pressure of talking to the king—inquiring of him—with punishment always on our shoulders would be suffocating. "Yes. That's a good idea," she says with a lift of her chin.

"Now, be honest," Anara starts, regarding Malik and bracing herself for his answer. "Do you think this will go in our favor?"

He gives her a reassuring but calculating smile. "If he is truly the king of Petros, he will do what he must to protect any and all possessions that city contains. He won't have a choice."

After we spend a couple hours developing the right words to say to the king, Malik announces that he has matters to attend to with Calista. Havanna returns to the house to do some research in the library, and Anara declares that it is nap time for her—a time that Ender also announces—arousing suspicion from me and Havanna.

I take advantage of going for a dip in the Reddawn Oasis, as most of the people here enjoy doing. I trudge in with my linen pants, shirtless, and plunge my whole body in it. I've been so used to the Arbol River being the only swimming area my whole life. It was always freezing cold since the water came straight from Paluso Mountains. Now, I'm reveling in the warmer water.

The oasis water is, quite literally, an oasis.

A slight reprieve from the heat, with or without the Ice Stone. Clear as crystal. I can see to the endless sandstone bottom, at least twenty feet below. At the bottom of the funnel-shaped oasis appears to be a tunnel—a secret passageway to another part of this world.

I'm not brave enough to find out.

I'm not opposed to staying in the water all day. It soothes the muscles that worked overtime to fight the Dormant King, and escape him. The longer the heat seeps into my body, the more I realize how physically and mentally exhausted I really am. My eyes can barely stay open.

Anara and Ender were onto something with the idea of taking a nap.

It takes great effort to get out of the water and head back to the palace. But the effort is worth it when my head hits the pillow.

People are drinking and dancing around a bonfire in the center of Arbol Village.

Except me. And Havanna, who's staring at me.

A cold, icy stare.

I feel bad for hurting her. She doesn't deserve the treatment I've given her. I'm grateful for our friendship, and I royally screwed it up.

I step closer, holding out my hand to tell her I'm dedicated to working this out. Whatever this is.

Those stunning eyes turn dark when she switches her gaze from my face to my hand. Back and forth. Her lips form a thin line with this unpleasant encounter.

She turns away from me, my heart dropping to my stomach. She's leaving me, and it's my fault.

"Keep trying, brother. She'll come around."

My head whips to the left. Indigo stands beside me, alive and well. He was never killed after all. He was here. The whole time. The hole in my chest fills with relief. Then dissipates when I realize none of this is real.

I turn back to the space where Havanna was, only for it to be completely empty of her presence. Doubt creeps in without missing a beat.

"What makes you so sure?"

"When a girl has eyes for a man, she takes every bit of attention he gives her. They know you're serious when you don't give up."

I feel a hand on my right shoulder and I turn to find my best friend, Nyx, standing there with imploring eyes and a wry smile.

"He's right, you know," she says, the notorious know-it-all I always knew her to be peeking out in her tone. Her own eyes darken with a fury I didn't know she had. "But I hope she rejects you. That's what you get for leaving without saying goodbye."

I have no words for her. Because she's right.

I let her down, and I let Indigo down. There's no way I will fail everyone else in my life.

My eyes snap open. Then I remember I'm not in Arbol Village anymore.

I'm in Sabbia Town, lying in the bed that was surely made for royalty. Nyx and Indigo are nowhere to be found, and that's when reality sets in once again.

Nyx is still in Arbol Village, and she's probably stewing in anger from my departure.

Things with Havanna are at a standstill.

Indigo is dead. When I need him now more than ever.

The sound of clattering outside draws my immediate attention. My eyelids feel heavy when I slip off the bed and look out the open window, greeted with an evening sky mixed with pink, purple, and blue. A group of musicians are hard at work preparing their instruments, just as they did for last night's seeking party.

Seeking party. Meeting women with concealed faces. Not a bad idea. Havanna won't talk to me; surely, someone else will.

The party is in full swing by the time I have the strength to get dressed. I fully embrace the clothing of the Sabbian men when I put on clean, white linen pants, set just below the bright red scarf that hangs diagonally from my left shoulder to right hip. My sculpted chest is in its full glory—the whole reason why men wear these clothes.

I feel liberated. Confident.

Head held high, I traipse downstairs through the throne room and into the growing crowd around the oasis. The men have no problem gawking at the women twirling their hips to the music's rhythm. I don't see Havanna or Anara being one of the victims of those men, but Ender, a tower among the entire town, fully embraces the energy of the party. A horde of women surrounds him as he raises his arms and whoops repeatedly. The women are like needy felines, clawing their nails across his abs and purring. He swivels his body side to side, encouraging them to keep touching him.

Then, sitting by a box garden on the edge of the oasis, I spot Anara, cheeks red and blazing as she watches Ender absorb the nonstop attention. Her deep frown with her chin on her hand does little to hide how much she hates how popular he is.

I stalk around the crowd while I search for a dancing partner. The women seem occupied, either drinking or dancing with someone, never alone, with Anara being the exception.

Then I stop in my tracks. Havanna, the only woman without a mask, has her hands on a man's bare shoulder. A strikingly good-looking man with defined abs that could cut stone. His bronzed skin glistens with sweat as he twirls her around and she shakes her hips side to side with a flirtatious, seductive grin. He gawks at her figure as she brings her arms above her head and only swivels her bottom half in smooth, perfect circles.

I came to make company with other women, only to find I just want *hers*.

With a roll of my shoulders and neck, I move over to the dancing couple, blatantly squeezing myself between them. "Mind if I cut in?"

The man stutters and Havanna's jaw tightens with a promise of injury.

"I suppose, yes," the man finally says and steps aside.

I nod at him and give him a pat on the arm. "Thank you, good man."

I try to grab Havanna's hands, only for her to rip them away from me. "Are you serious right now?" she seethes.

"As serious as a stab wound."

The music changes to a song that sounds equally romantic, sentimental, and serious, perfectly reflecting this moment. I offer her my hand.

"What are you doing?" she growls.

"Trying to dance with you. What does it look like?"

Her eyes soften just a bit as she tilts her head to ask, "Why me, of all people?"

In her tone, she's not asking to get attention. She genuinely feels insignificant in comparison to the other women, and she's far from it. "Well, for one, your face is the only one I can see. Second, I want to talk to you."

Havanna's eyes flit from my face to my hands in hesitation—a battle in her own heart. A debate is better than sheer hatred.

"I can lead." As if that will change her mind.

She tries to hide her smile as she finally takes me up on my offer. Her strong but feminine hands sit on top of mine, her skin silky smooth as I brush my thumb over her fingers, free of her gloves. She focuses her attention to an extreme degree just below my collarbone, simply to avoid meeting my gaze.

"You can look at me, you know," I console her.

Her throat bobs. "Every time I do, it hurts."

"Tell me what to do to make it better."

She shakes her head, tearing her gaze to the oasis. "I'm having a hard time forgiving you. Not just for what happened to the Dormant King, but for pushing me away. You told him things you wouldn't tell me." Therein lies the real issue. "I've been trying to get to know you," she adds. "Your backstory. What makes you *you.*"

Warning signs of entering dangerous territory flash before me. I can't bring myself to broach that topic yet. "What about getting to know Anara? Or Ender?"

She shoots me an incredulous look. "You know what I mean. Besides, you and I both know how Anara is. And Ender is . . . surface level. You were the first friend I ever made when I left Ketra." Her sobered expression reaches her feet.

I sigh deeply, trying to find a way to explain my side of things without revealing my innermost feelings. "I suppose it was easier to tell a stranger than it was to a close friend. With a stranger, you can tell your story and never see them again, and never care about what they think of you. With a friend, whatever you tell them can change their view of you in an instant."

"This was the *Dormant King*. Our *enemy*."

"I know, but . . ." I stare at the oasis to give myself time to choose my words with caution. "I suppose that's what made me cave. The fact that I didn't care what he thought."

Havanna subtly shakes her head. "I don't get it."

I motion between us. "This . . . us . . . can change once you see all of me that's broken. I don't want to risk that. Not with you."

Her eyes brighten and her eyebrows knit, inquiring for more. "What makes me so special?"

I know she already knows the answer. Confirming her suspicion means going deeper: a relationship. The kind of relationship I can't give her. "You were the first friend I made when I left my village too. You changed my life and gave it purpose. You made me feel validated for the first time in my life."

We continue to sway to the sweet, romantic melody playing around us. "So I'm just a friend? I can never be anything else?"

She is special, more than she knows. More than just friendship. But I'm stalling. I'm not going to walk through the door she's opening for me.

"You mean a lot to me, Zappy." I brush a strand of hair behind her ear. "You really do. I can't bear the thought of losing that." My breath turns shaky. "I *can't*."

With lips downturned, her eyes well up with tears. Tears that I caused. The look of sorrow, heartbreak, and frustration sit in those beautiful eyes. "I suppose that's that, then."

Gently, affectionately, she brings a palm to my face, stroking my cheek with a softness that makes my knees buckle. I've never been shown this kind of care, love, and intimacy, yet she shoves her pain aside and gives it to me.

"Good night, Quill," she whispers just as she steps back into the crowd, away from me, dragging my heart with her.

CHAPTER 12

ANARA

Ender is a disgusting pig.

He's a living sponge soaking up the attention from all those women. Yesterday, he said that these women were mean, yet tonight, he's happily dancing with them. It doesn't make any sense.

Whatever. He's stupid.

I spare a glance at his flushed, sweaty form just as his eyes meet mine. His lips turn from the devilishly handsome grin he's been donning all night to a frown in an instant. He leaves his groupies without a second glance and forces himself through dancing bodies toward me.

"Compa! Why you no dance?"

The flames within my glare are strong enough to melt the Paluso Mountains. "Do you really have to enjoy being pawed at so much?" I snarl.

"Is been too long since I see compas with big bombas!" He motions to his chest excitedly. "Come dance!" His expression turns sultry when he adds, "I let you touch chest if you want."

My annoyance simmers to a boil and I roll my eyes. I have no desire to be just another desperate woman fawning over the same man. He missed me, which I'm realizing now is probably meant on a friendly level. Which means I've been a fool.

"You miss out," he says with a shrug, then turns back to the dancing crowd. The women close in on him, a school of fish hunting for the same pellet. I can hear him faintly when he asks them coyly, "You miss me?"

He did indeed only miss me as a friend.

A man approaches me. He has a bare chest that may as well have been carved from marble and a white-toothed smile to complement his perfection. I have every reason to accept his advances, but all I feel is utter disgust toward men as a whole.

"Buzz off," I snap before he opens his mouth. He shrinks back, his lips curling into a scoff as he walks away without another word.

Quill saunters over, downtrodden as he rubs his eyes with the heels of his hands, and plops next to me on the edge of the box garden. He follows my gaze to where it's still aimed at Ender and he must immediately sense the source of my sullen mood.

"Listen," he begins by way of consolation, "Ender is a man. Being surrounded by those women doesn't mean he wants anything with any of them other than a fun time."

"But doesn't that send the wrong message to those women?"

Quill braces his forearms on his knees. "Well, he seems to have gotten the impression that nothing will ever happen between you two. In his mind, he's doing nothing wrong."

The notion punches me in the gut. Not because it hurts, but because it's true. "I just didn't think he would enjoy this so much."

He turns to me, resting a hand on his knee. The corner of his mouth lifts and his eyebrows snap together. "You're a complicated individual."

I have been called many things. Most of which include how rude, uncaring, or insensitive I am. Mostly insults that go back to my childhood in Macaphin Village. "Complicated" was never one of them.

"Excuse me?" I bark out. "How am *I* the complicated one?"

Quill's eyebrows raise to his hairline. "Don't play dumb, Anara. You wanted nothing to do with him when he started flirting with you. Now, you look at him like he's the one thing missing in your world. The stars practically bulge from your eyes. Then you act like you want nothing more than friendship."

I laugh bitterly. "That's rich, coming from you."

His silence alone speaks volumes. He knows I'm right, and he knows exactly what I'm talking about. "I have my reasons."

"And I don't?"

Quill purses his lips, resigned to the impasse we've slammed into. He ignores the silence between us by wordlessly turning back to the party.

Much to my chagrin, he's right. I'm in the empty space between friendship and romance, and I have no idea which side to take. One way is comfortable, the other makes me vulnerable. I spent years trying *not* to be vulnerable as I dealt with the bullies in my village. Breaking that down because of a heart's desire seems ridiculous. Denying something factual as equally ridiculous.

"I don't know what happened." I release a defeated, deep sigh. "He seemed so . . . fake when we met. It was excruciating. But when he saved me from those Dormants, without a single thought for himself, everything changed. He became . . . a *person*. A person with a gentle heart. He taught me how I need to treat others better, show more compassion, and encouraged me when I didn't feel strong enough. When I didn't fully deserve it." I pick at my nails with Quill's eyes boring into me. "He's the only true friend I've ever had."

Quill stays silent for a moment while I wallow at the fact that I laid out my innermost feelings to someone I trust for the first time. "Perhaps you should tell him that."

Being vulnerable with someone that exudes strength in every angle destroys that idea. A woman in the crowd, who I've noticed has danced with the same man the whole time, takes off her mask for him. She trusts him enough to be vulnerable and shows him what hides underneath that piece of cloth. Yet, I can't bring myself to remove my own.

"I'm not that kind of woman," I remark with a low voice.

Quill scoffs and continues to stare off in the distance. The music encourages energetic dancing, people hopping from one foot to the other, their movements bouncy and seamless all at once.

"Why are you not in the crowd, King Charming?" I tease lightly, pointing to the party. "Don't you want to join Ender with the endless parade of women?"

He shakes his head. "I'm not that kind of man."

Because he has his heart set on one person, and one person only. But she's keeping him at arm's length. Just as he's been doing to her.

The whole thing between them is so stupid, it's almost funny. Quill has his reasons—whatever that means—and Havanna still thinks he possesses an inkling of traitorous behavior. Whatever the Dormant King said ran deep enough for Quill to relate to and his refusal to explain it to Havanna only creates a wedge between them.

"You're both idiots," I say.

He leans back and has the nerve to be offended. He spoke the truth to me; he can take it right back.

Without further conversation, I get up and head to Queen Calista's house, leaving him to ruminate over my words. This conversation, along with seeing Ender become a ladies' man, only creates an itch to leave and isolate myself.

The party rages on even after I've changed out of the Sabbian clothes into bedtime attire. I can spot Ender from here, being the only enormous person in town. A woman is grinding her hips on him as if she's trying to glue themselves together. I can smell her desperation all the way up here; she wants to make sure Ender will choose her.

The idea brings an unwanted punch to my heart.

I don't want him with anyone else. I want him with me. By my side only. Keeping me safe, telling me I'm his compa. His friend. Having him out there for others to feast their eyes on only answers the denials I've had about my desires.

The sting gets worse, squeezing the life out of my heart. I don't know how I lived this long without him. I was lost until we all found each other.

I slip under the covers of the most comfortable bed I've ever slept in. Wave, in his frog form, jumps on the nightstand. He touches his nose with mine, a gentle way of consoling me.

With his sweet gesture combined with my aching heart, I will the tears not to fall.

CHAPTER 13

HAVANNA

The town must have finished their party, because it's dead silent now. Which means it's the early hours of the morning. And here I am, unable to fall back asleep. I miss my Twinkle Fireflies now more than ever.

I blame Anara for suggesting that I dance with another man to make Quill jealous. It was petty.

I was all for being petty.

The man I danced with was as beautiful and as sculpted as Quill. It worked, after all. He was fully entranced with the dance moves I remember learning in Ketra, then Quill found that moment appropriate to interrupt.

Then he said everything I wanted to hear while simultaneously reducing me to unbearable longing.

You changed my life and gave it purpose.

The whole relationship can change once you see all of me that's broken. I don't want to risk that. Not with you.

You mean a lot to me.

The echoes of his sexy, deep voice tug at my heart and repeat in my mind. I mean something to him. He has feelings for me, but he refuses to express them, simply because he worries about what I will think once I get to know him. What he doesn't allow me to tell him is that nothing would ever make me look at him differently. My own background is ugly. He knows all about it, yet his view of me has never changed.

From the tidbits he told the Dormant King, he didn't have a happy childhood. That alone breaks my heart. He had me captivated with his calloused, strong hands on my waist. I was at a loss for words.

My touching his cheek was an impulse move. I had never done something so intimate with anyone, but I trusted that he would welcome it. The way he spoke to me, the way he looked at me, was full of the pain of carrying so many burdens for so long. All I wanted to do was to soothe those wounds. I wanted him to know that I felt for him. No words. Just an affectionate touch.

These thoughts are doing little to help me sleep. I step out of bed. The sound of my ruffling sheets does nothing to wake Bolt out of his sleep, his beak curled within his wing.

The last time I was in the living room, adjacent to the bar with nothing but silence, was the day I left for Killios. The moment I knew I had a place to go if I needed it. A home outside of home.

Calista sits on a bench by the window closest to the bar, fully at peace as she stares at the colors of sunrise, her favorite thing to do. She turns to face me, a warm smile dancing on her lips.

"I can't sleep," I say.

"I was surprised you could sleep at all," she remarks with amusement. "The party was loud, and your Ender was the loudest of them all."

"He's good at that." I sit next to her on the cushioned bench.

This moment brings me back in time once again. Calista taught me to see the true beauty of a sunrise in the desert. It was a sight to behold then, and it still is, with the colors layered on top of each other from bright to dark.

"Let me guess," Calista muses, "sleep eludes you because of the young man you came with yesterday."

"How did you know?"

She barks out a laugh. "He paid more attention to you than any other woman in town. And you in no way shied away from him. It doesn't take a genius to figure it out."

Heat blooms on my cheeks. I thought I was hiding it well enough that no one would suspect a thing.

"Nothing to be ashamed of, child. He is a beautiful man."

I chuckle. "He really is."

She shares a laugh. I want to dismiss it as nothing, but he was the most beautiful man I'd ever seen when I first laid eyes on him. That day on Luna Island, he made me feel safe. That everything would be all right as long as we stuck together.

I need a mother's advice, the perspective of a married woman.

"He won't open up to me," I begin when the laughter falters. "But he told the Dormant King the basics of his past while we were on Luna Island. He was telling us what life was like with the Ancestors, and Quill told him he understood. That was all the bait the Dormant King needed to sway him. He didn't turn against us, but he was close enough. All because of a background he won't tell me about, yet he wanted our *enemy* to know." Calista simply nods attentively, letting me vent in a way I've never been able to with anyone before. I motion to myself. "If anyone understands, it's me. But he worries it will change my view of him."

"The fact that he allows such worries to hold him back is indicative enough about how he feels about you," she replies with a bashful smile. "Such cares would not plague his mind if you were anything less than a potential romantic partner."

As much as that should bring me relief, it doesn't diminish the thoughts that trouble me. "I want him to know that my feelings would never change."

"Did you tell him this?"

I release a regretful sigh and shake my head. "No."

"Why not?"

Now comes the ugly truth. A truth that I'm done denying myself. "I like him. A lot. But I don't want to like him. I don't want to feel *anything*. I don't want romance."

"Romance is perfectly acceptable, child. Wonderful, even. Why deny yourself that luxury?"

"Because the last time I had feelings for someone, he was a Backer that almost got me killed. Romance just leads to disaster. If he *does* feel something, then he must not want to feel anything either. The problem is that nothing I say will matter. It's a dead end."

Calista says nothing for so long it makes me squirm. Her gaze locks on nothing in particular as she dips her head with a sorrowful, empathetic look.

"The problem is, child—" She leans to my side with a tilted smile. "—that the Dormant King deceived him and you took it personally. His response had absolutely nothing to do with you." She lays a hand on my knee. "Let it go. Forgive him."

Something about the softness of her delivery makes the blow easier to take. I held it against him, when the responsibility truly fell on the Dormant King.

I've been an absolute fool.

Calista jabs a finger into my thigh when she says, "And you also need to stop lying to yourself. You have feelings for Quill." She emphasizes with clenched fists. "Embrace it. *Feel* it. It's what makes life beautiful. When those feelings are reciprocated, it delivers a euphoria you'll never know elsewhere. Let things blossom in their own time. You will be glad you did, I promise you."

Our refusal to break down our barriers and pride only halts the progression of this relationship. Though neither one of us wants to make the first move.

I rub my eyes. "I don't know what to do. I've never felt this way, and at the same time, I'm still scared that he has the potential to be a traitor."

"He made a mistake, as you have many times over," she reminds me. "You have to decide if you can accept everything that makes him perfect *and* what makes him broken. Because, in the end, that's what true love entails."

In other words, everyone is broken in some way. I know I am.

I didn't think of myself as expecting perfection out of anyone, but I did expect it of myself. An unfair projection I placed on him.

"In the desert, a sandstorm can cause much distress," Calista says, delving into a story-time tone, "much more so if you find yourself caught in it. It blinds you, scares you, makes you feel lost and alone. Yet, it never lasts forever. Eventually, it disappears." She turns to me with a smirk. "And you find that the most beautiful things were hidden in that storm. You see it so clearly, you wonder how you missed it."

In just a few words, Calista manages to describe life in the most relatable way. Under the storm that is Quill's insecurities and flaws lies the beautiful, caring person that always guided who he is. Within the sandstorm of my own life, I wonder at how much I missed this woman who became my mother figure when I needed one most. The one I have more gratitude for than anyone else I've met. The one who tells me not what I *want* to hear, but what I *need* to hear.

I lean my head on her shoulder and watch the rest of the sunrise in satisfied silence.

CHAPTER 14

ENDER

I am officially a desirable, wanted man.

I was drawing in all the ladies like I was their prey. I wasn't there for the purpose the seeking party was intended for. I had no intention of finding a mate. I'm only seventeen.

As happy as I was to see my compos were alive and well, I was specifically happy to see Anara. I missed her companionship. I missed fighting side by side with her. I thought she was going to reciprocate when I told her I missed her. When she froze, I knew it was a mistake and I tried to hide my sinking stomach and bruised emotions. I thought she was finally warming up to me, only to take two colossal steps back.

Everyone is quiet this morning. The scraping of silverware is the only noise taking up space. Havanna and Anara frown at their breakfasts at the bar, Quill is shrinking into himself on the sofa. The tension is making me cringe.

I stretch my arms over my head, the muscles in my biceps flexing as I trot into the living room. I make a show of flashing my trademark smile that no doubt brought the ladies to their knees. "Seeking party fun," I announce. The girls pout with their lips in a hard line and Quill keeps his expression unreadable. "Women like me. I dance, they dance and touch body. I no like the masks. But I show them good time."

Anara growls obnoxiously. "All right, we get it, you had fun with a ton of women, you attract women, women think you're attractive, we've heard enough already!"

Her typical response is laced with something I've never heard from her: hurt. Quill shoots a dirty look toward her and shakes his head—a warning message that only she seems to understand. Havanna pretends none of us exist as she lazily continues eating.

Malik and Calista enter the room, dressed and ready for the journey to Arythica. "Everyone ready?" he asks with an energy that fails to be contagious. "As long as we do things according to the plan we put in place, it will go just fine."

"I can ride with Havanna on Bolt," Calista offers.

I rest my hands on my hips and shine a bright, seductive smile that I know will annoy her. "You no ride with me, compa?"

"No," she says flatly. "We need a break."

Havanna snorts a laugh as she finishes her meal.

Once we're crossing through town, Keeley sees us as she makes her rounds and bows to Malik and Calista. "May you have a safe mission, Our King and Queen."

"Thank you, Keeley," Calista responds. "I trust that you will keep everyone safe, and you have protocols in place if danger appears."

"Yes, Our Queen. Everyone is in safe hands."

"Excellent. We will be back soon."

We make our way out the entrance, the two guards standing there waving us off. We put much distance between us and the town walls to spare them from the oncoming sandstorm formed by Bennaru wingbeats.

"King Malik, Kane will carry you," Quill says as he mounts Koa's back.

"A ride on a Bennaru," Malik says to himself in disbelief. "Never thought I would experience that in this lifetime."

"We special," I supply with a wink, gaining an eye roll from both Calista and Anara as they mount their respective companions. It baffles me how short-tempered the compas are today.

Anara is the first to launch in the air. Something about her takeoff is hurried and impatient, seemingly wanting nothing to do with us anymore. Once the sand settles, Havanna and Calista meet with Anara in the sky, followed by Malik, Quill, then myself.

Flame's vulture wings beat faster through the air and glide toward Wave at my command. Even as I'm flying beside Anara, she refuses to acknowledge my presence, and it's not because she's focused on the flight.

"You dance with anyone, compa?" I ask, a weak effort to break the awkward silence.

"No."

"Why?"

"Didn't feel like it."

"Why?"

"No one asked."

Behind us, Quill overhears this conversation and flies closer. "Because you sat there looking like you ate some sour meat."

I laugh because it's true. Her countenance was less than approachable. "You could have asked me. I dance with you."

"I would have, but all those women were taking up space, and you enjoyed it all too much."

I paste on a smug smile. "Yes, I did."

Anara turns back to the empty sky in silence, terminating the conversation. Rubbing it in her face infuriates her, but I want her to tell me the reason why. After all, I'm just her friend, right?

Quill's amusement disappears as he gazes longingly at Havanna's frown with Calista sitting behind her. Now that I observe a little closer, Havanna has the same hurt expression as Anara.

She really should stop with the negative feelings she has toward him. There's nothing to be angry about; he never became a traitor. He needs to just fess up and accept how he feels about her. Their communication is deplorable. I made my intentions with Anara perfectly clear; we don't hide anything from each other.

At least, that's how it used to be.

I peer down over Flame's wing at how much smaller Petros is now as we soar over it. What used to be a large expanse of endless desert is now a plot of land as we cross over Stoneland Hills. A land completely unfamiliar to me. Even when we fly over a large forest full of lush trees, it feels like we've entered a different world. A basic part of life that we as Descendants were denied.

Staying in Vulca Mountain was satisfactory enough. I had the whole mountain to myself, not to mention the whole area where we Mulhutna reside, and the various mining areas we worked in. Having the Tyranodrake at the base of the mountain ensured that. I had plenty of space to wander around, the other Mulhutna did deliveries to other cities, and I was well cared for. I lacked nothing. Life outside being a tribal chief was nonexistent, aside from the times I enjoyed the company of other compos after a physically tiring day, ate piles of meat, and slept. I accepted my life the way it was.

Now I wonder how I lived this long never knowing who my true compos were.

It's likely the Dormants have reached this area. Quill and Koa dive a little lower, just below the other Bennarus. *We should be on the lookout in case we see anything out of place. Easier to see if we fly lower. Be prepared to attack.*

Everyone seems to follow his line of thinking as we dip lower to get closer to him. He points to the forest below, acres of green sheets of foliage.

This is where I'm from, Quill says, pointing to the forest. *Arbol Village.*

I take in the lush greenery and the wide river that weaves in and around the trees, a vein in the body of the forest. The open space in an oval shape out in the distance signifies the village's location, spotted with log huts. For a moment, I think about what Quill's life was like compared to mine, living around nothing but trees and animals.

Smoke rises from a small dot among the green, gray and pulsing like a beating heart. Then the all too familiar appearance of red, yellow, and orange flickers.

"Compo!" I bellow through the rushing air blowing over us. "Look! Fire!"

That is, I see figures skittering through the trees below me, heading straight for his old home. A fire has already started within the village while the ground is covered in broken pieces of wood and other rubble.

It's not long before screams reach up to our height. Quill dips down without warning, diving straight toward the center of disaster.

Arbol Village is under attack, he transmits. *We need to do some damage control. Let none of them get past you.*

We dive through the tops of the trees and into the forest. I get my axe ready with my flames while being careful not to touch the trees with it. Havanna electrifies her sword and uses Gridlock on the Dormants heading to the village. Anara stays above the trees and heads to the fire engulfing the forest in smoke. Soon, water is gushing down everywhere into the forest, and the torrent moves in time with Wave's flight as it puts out the fires in the village. With the Dormants held by Gridlock, Havanna hops off Bolt, aiming the tip of her blade down, then lands on the monsters. The electricity splits in all different directions that shocks the onslaught of Dormants heading toward us. Calista and Malik rush in to finish them off.

Upon closer inspection, there are scattered pillars of ice in between trees. Looking closely inside, I see a person encased in it. Someone that was attempting to flee and was frozen on the spot.

The victims may already be dead, but I take a chance when I blow fire from my hands straight onto the frozen pillar. It succumbs to my power as steam erupts, water pools into the grass, and the layers of cold shrink in size. Within a couple minutes, the ice is gone and the villager collapses to the ground, frozen and soaking wet. He turns to me, his dark hair plastered to his head and clothes drenched.

"Thank you," he whispers shakily.

"Go, find shelter!" is all I have time to say. I run with wide strides between trees toward more frozen villagers. The next group I find appears to be children who were playing on the bank of the Arbol River who attempted to run to safety. Dormants have no mercy. A crack forms in my heart and I have fire surging on all five children. I pray that they still have a chance to live, that I can save them in time.

It's a domino effect when one child after another is freed from the frozen confines. I help them all get back to their feet and encourage them to run. They do so without question, but they struggle to move speedily with cold limbs.

Pounding feet nearby catches my attention. Quill, Havanna, Malik, and Calista are all fighting off Dormants, but there are five more ready to take them down.

Havanna's going to be the first one.

I run toward them, hoping to kill them before they reach Havanna as she's fighting off the ones around her.

Quill slides on his knees in front of her out of nowhere, Pineapple Shell arrows at the ready. He lets the arrows fly, a direct hit with three small explosions that blend into one large impact. Havanna raises her hand to reach the patch of exposed sky above us, but Quill beats her to it when he nocks more arrows and fires them. They explode on impact and dust floats in front of us. The loud boom reverberates and lingers for a few seconds, and all seems calm. The only sounds we can hear are the footsteps and small voices of fleeing villagers.

The chaos has died down, but our hyper alertness is still working overtime as we frantically search our surroundings. Our rapid breaths blend together and bounce off each other, all of us expecting and ready for surprise appearances. When none appear, all that surrounds us is smoke and charred earth.

We know the worst of it is over.

Calista releases a loud exhale and turns to Quill. "Do you know if any of them made it to Arbol Village?"

He shakes his head. "Even if they did, the villagers have a spot in the forest to escape to." He points a finger upward. "Treehouses were built high enough above ground that they're not easily spotted by enemies."

Malik starts, "Perhaps you should check on them—"

"No," Quill cuts him off sharply. "I mean . . ." He clears his throat and replies softly, "No. They will be fine."

Malik dips his head in acknowledgment. "Very well."

Quill does little to hide his inner torture, eyes squeezed shut and a fingerless-gloved hand smoothing over his shoulder-length dark hair. I spare a glimpse at Havanna, the one who holds mixed emotions. Bitter yet compassionate. Something bigger than the Dormant King's tactics lies between the two of them.

We exit the forest on foot to be sure that the vicinity is clear of all monsters, then we resume flying to Arythica.

CHAPTER 15

About an hour passes before we reach Arythica's border.

The Bennarus shrink just before we reach the front gates and we enter the city that sparkles. The civilians look at us with marked disgust, eyeing us head to toe in our battle-worn gear. I hold nothing back when I scowl in return at the Arythican people, one that says they can go screw themselves. They probably haven't fought a single battle in their lives.

Then I realize, those looks are targeted at us Descendants in particular. Malik and Calista fit right in. The very epitome of royalty, albeit wearing hints of minor battle wounds.

We follow Malik's lead as he takes us around the giant, iron-wrought fence bordering the castle that gives us a full angle of the immaculately spread courtyard. Box gardens line the inside of the fence, trimmed and blooming to perfection in petaled waves of purple, white, yellow, red, and blue. Guards stroll through the courtyard in a unified march, switching positions every few seconds. A red velvet rug extends from the stairs leading to the castle all the way through the brick pathway that touches the gate. Unending wealth shines within it, so clean, bright, and manicured.

Once we reach the main entrance, it's near impossible to see past the towering shrubs that block the view of the rest of the castle. Two guards in glinting armor stand on either side of the gate, as immovable as statues. I flinch slightly as one of them actually moves, taking two steps toward us. He scans us head to toe, just as the civilians did. This time, he seems perplexed as to why we Descendants appear dirty while the royalty that stands in front of us is the image of perfection.

"How can we help you?" he asks flatly.

"I am King Malik of Sabbia, prior citizen of Arythica. We are here to speak with King Aldous."

The guard is unfazed. "And what might this be regarding?"

Calista comes forward. "We need to inquire about—"

"That is classified and quite an urgent matter," Malik interrupts, "so it would be much appreciated if you let us in immediately. We've been in communication and he is expecting our arrival."

Calista glares at him for interrupting—a lover's quarrel that will indeed be next. The guard seems dubious, but relents. "Per Arythica regulations, we must escort you into the castle."

Two guards unlock and push open the iron gates, displaying the gleaming property. Calista's glare at Malik remains as he explains, "I don't wish to give them full reason for our visit. If they know it involves heavy risk on their end, they may reject us before we have a chance to explain."

She nods and her expression softens. "That was likely a wise move."

We accompany the guards inside and are instantly flanked by four more. It's a silent walk as we follow the path of the red carpet. I quickly eye the side of the fence where the iron-clad gate is framed by a cinder-block wall, the bustling city on the other side.

Just weeks ago, Havanna and I were on the other side looking in, debating whether we would have the option to implore the king and queen for help. I thought she was crazy to even think that was a feasible option. Now, here we are.

The guards lead us up the steps to the humongous double doors that introduce us to the splendor of royals. The hallways are lined with the same velvety rug, not a wrinkle, lump, or speck of dirt in sight. Glass windows tinted subtly with pink and blue have an ethereal vibe to them as the sunlight beams onto the rugs. An eternity of unlit torches lines the walls of the hallway.

We pass a winding staircase at a corner where the hallway curves to the left, and stop in front of double doors just as huge as the ones in front of the castle. Wooden, solid, and heavy enough to require an army to open.

My heart thumps harder against my chest with each step, my palms sweaty as we get closer to our destination. Malik's warnings from the other day have my senses on high alert. Malik and Calista are eerily calm for the potential death trap we're about to encounter.

"Wait here," one of the guards commands, and all six of them slip through the doors that are as big as the Mulhutna trolls.

The castle is dead silent as we wait there for further instruction. No one talks, tension thick, and nothing to cut it with.

"So. This is fun," I say with feigned excitement. I catch Havanna rolling her eyes.

"Oh, before I forget." Malik's head perks up as he turns to face us. "We must present our weapons in front of us as we bow, so he doesn't have reason to suspect any attempts of assassination."

Weapons clang together as we all take them off our backs. "Asinine," Havanna grumbles. "First, we have to choose our words carefully so as to not get killed, then we have to be careful to not get accused of planning to kill the king. Wonderful."

"Unfortunately, it's for good reason," Calista clarifies as she collapses her spear with the press of a button, making us all jump back in surprise. "It's not the first time an assassination attempt has been made on royalty."

Havanna and I turn to each other, sharing an expression of worry. Assassination attempts on the king means they've done something that enraged their subjects, therefore deeming him worthy of death. This combined with everything else we've been told about King Aldous has my heart beating harder.

The doors to the throne room open slowly, showing us a dais and two thrones. Each seat is framed in smooth, shining gold and red velvet cushions. The floor, in yellowish, textured brick, is empty and wide enough to allow for a large group to convene.

There, in those chairs, the king and queen await our arrival. A ruby-lined golden crown sits on the king's brown hair, sharp onyx eyes cutting into each of us, and his thick, brown beard covering half of his face. The queen is a beauty even I envy, her golden-blonde hair braided over her shoulder and down to her waist. Her bright blue eyes portray the innocence of a little girl, but her scowl portrays the cold, uncompassionate heart of a tyrannical ruler. A crown of diamonds rests on her head, encased in silver rather than gold.

I have no clue where I should be, so I allow Malik and Calista to pick their positions first before the throne. Havanna lowers to one knee next to Calista on the far-left side of the room, and I kneel behind Malik on the far right. To my left is Quill, then Ender beside him. Two guards stand in position in the back, while two guards flank both sides of the dais, and two are against the wall on both sides of the room, staring at us with our weapons in our hands.

King Aldous's hands grip the armrests of his chair and takes his time studying us, one at a time. No one speaks. The quiet is near suffocating by the time the king decides to talk.

"Which one is Malik of Sabbia?" His resonant voice rumbles in the walls, frightening and dripping with power.

"This one, Your Majesty." A guard points to Malik, positioned right in front of the king.

King Aldous eyes Malik and gives him a curt nod. "You may speak."

Malik stands, hands locked in front of him. My bare knee on this stone floor is already starting to hurt. "Your Majesty, I want to con-firm that you received my correspondence regarding the situation of the kingdom."

"I have not." He says nothing more. A brush-off if there ever was one. So nonchalant, as if we were here simply to plan a party. He must be lying.

Malik dips his head. "Because of the urgency of the situation at hand, we stand before you. I have with me the Descendants of Petros. Ender, Fire Descendant; Anara, Water Descendant; Quill, Land Descendant; and Havanna, Lightning Descendant."

King Aldous and Queen Avela express their astonishment as they lean forward in their thrones. At last, a change in dynamic. "Descendants? As in Descendants of the Ancestors? Out of hiding?" Aldous exclaims.

"Yes, Your Majesty."

"How can this be?" Avela breathes heavily, her astonishment so fake I could throw up. "The Descendants haven't been seen in centuries."

"Blame Havanna," I mumble.

The sound of purposeful steps pound from behind. I'm suddenly yanked to my feet by the arm, no gentleness whatsoever as I grip my trident with my other hand. "Do not speak until you have permission, *Descendant*," the guard hisses into my ear.

The nerve of this man. Accusing me of breaking the rules *and* touching me without my permission.

I show him not to screw with me when I flip the trident over and slam the butt of it on his foot. He immediately loosens his grip and yelps in pain. Serves him right. "Do not touch me, *guard*."

"Enough!" Aldous's booming voice is intimidating enough to make one shudder. "One warning is sufficient, Sir Caldyn."

I slowly lower to my knee, holding up my trident and burning the guard alive with my stare. I suppose it's safer to say nothing for the rest of this meeting and keep all thoughts to myself. Apparently voicing them, even to myself, is inappropriate.

"I have always been intrigued by the Descendants," Aldous says thoughtfully, casually brushing off everything that happened just seconds ago. "Your powers are such that they can withstand anything that comes our way."

That man is one talented liar.

"What brings you to our throne, then?" Avela asks.

Malik, still standing, says, "If I may request my wife, Calista, and my friend, Havanna, to also stand, Your Majesty. Havanna will inform you of recent events first."

Aldous eyes Havanna, then Calista, and gives them both a curt nod. "You, who is named Havanna, speak."

CHAPTER 16

HAVANNA

I already know this is going to be very, very bad.

I knew—I *knew*—Anara would be the first to stir up trouble, although not on purpose. Her comment was a thought said out loud. It was the simple fact that she spoke at all without the king's or queen's permission.

The power in this palace is borderline arrogant. They think so much of themselves that these rules have to be set. Something as simple as talking considered inappropriate or rude.

No wonder there have been assassination attempts on him.

Confidence is key here, despite the anxiety coursing through me. I stand with my back ramrod straight, chin up. They simply wait for me to speak, bored and indifferent. That alone takes a hit at my confidence. Why bother talking if they clearly won't listen?

You need to try, I can hear Jael whispering behind me.

I clear my throat. "The Dormant King is at large," I begin shyly, then raise my volume. "He has released Dormants big and strong enough to overtake cities. Arbol Village was under attack during our journey here. Parts of Vulca Mountain are in ruins. They've even reached the desert."

King Aldous rests his chin on his fist, wearing an expression that is blank and unreadable.

"The four of us are not enough to stop him. With the sheer number of monsters we're up against, we're here to request your assistance in forming an army."

The king straightens in his seat, my declaration delivering a blow he doesn't expect as he blinks in surprise. The queen follows suit, her eyes wide yet demeaning when she asks, "Are you honestly suggesting we go to war?"

I swallow and my words come out strained. "Yes, Your Majesty."

Silence.

The tension in the room builds as the seconds tick by. The king and queen seem to consider this as they look at each other briefly, shifting in their seats. Then—

He laughs.

King Aldous *laughs.*

And Avela joins him.

Not just an amused chuckle. These laughs are boisterous enough to take the air out of their lungs. The guards in the throne room join in, although it's nervous and shaky, done simply out of duty. They're nothing but slaves that have to mirror the king's reactions in every way, and it's pathetic.

The utter disrespect and blatant mocking pisses me off. My friends and I glance at each other, shaking our heads in disbelief or shrugging, at a loss for words.

"What a preposterous suggestion!" King Aldous wheezes as he composes himself. "There is no need for war!"

He is surely out of his mind. I find it preposterous that I can't punch his pompous, beet-red face.

"There is a less disastrous solution to this." He regards Anara once he gets the giggles out. "Water Descendant. You have an ability that opens portals to other locations, is that correct?"

"Yes," she drawls with a questioning tone, wondering how this applies to anything. He stares at her, waiting for her to finish that sentence that didn't need an ending until she adds, "Your Majesty."

Satisfied, he replies, "Then it would stand to reason that you can simply use that ability to send the Dormants back to where they came from. There will be no need for a discussion of war if they're sent away." He extends his arms. "Everyone is safe. Problem solved."

My lips curl into a snarl with full contempt, ready to fight back with a slew of insults. The condescension, insolence, and selfishness call for it. But I have to tread lightly. *Be tactful.*

"As much sense as that makes, Your Majesty, doing that would solve nothing."

Avela leans forward, a method meant to intimidate her subjects. "How do you mean, Descendant?"

I swallow again. A test on if I can show them respect. Respect they don't deserve.

"The Dormant King has the ability to summon Dormants, whether they're in our world or not. If we send them back, he can summon them again. It's counterproductive."

Smooth, Zappy. Smooth, Quill purrs in my mind, forcing me to hide my grin. Ever since he slid in front of me to kill the Dormants that were heading straight for me, just a thread of my heart started to tug toward him again.

I don't run headfirst into a horde of monsters to save just anyone, he had whispered to me. *You're going to get me killed someday, Zappy.*

Once we were in the air, his words became a rotating wheel in my mind. I felt myself crumble little by little.

King Aldous gives me a wicked smile. Nothing but devious things hide in those arrogant features. "Malik, I assume you want to add to her comment?" he says in a voice loaded with snark.

Malik dips his head. "I stand by her, Your Majesty. Our best course of action now is to have the backing of the kingdom."

"Out of the question," he bites out. "My responsibility as king is to protect all who inhabit my land. I would not be doing such if I allowed war to commence."

Queen Avela seems inclined to agree as she nods, but she turns to her husband and adds in a low voice, "If I may make a suggestion, my love?"

It takes everything I have to not roll my eyes as she sucks up to her own husband. I imagine Anara doing the same thing.

"Please."

"If our purpose is to keep people safe and to avoid the Dormant King's attacks, I suggest a full lockdown."

My stomach drops and my throat lurches with a desire to scream at her.

Please don't agree to this. Please don't.

"Perhaps if everyone in the kingdom stays in the confinement of their homes, the Dormants will have nothing to go after."

She can't be serious, Quill drones. *That's not how Dormants work.*

Speak up, then. I don't trust Anara or Ender to not get us killed.

"Ah, excellent idea! We will do that."

No no no no no.

I cannot live in confinement. Not again.

Aldous addresses Malik. "You see, to live in Arythica is to live in comfort. Luxury. War disturbs such contentment."

Contentment that won't last long if the Dormants invade your city, I so badly want to scream at him.

My hands begin to shake. Sweat breaks out all over my body, my breaths shallow. A panicked response to what is to come.

"Your Majesty—"

I whip my head over my shoulder to find Quill with his head raised, but still genuflecting.

A guard marches toward him. My feet are about to move of their own accord to stop him from getting attacked, even if it means I get punished—

"Halt!" the king shouts with a palm facing the guard. Then gestures to Quill. "Rise and speak, Land Descendant."

I heave out a breath of relief. I don't need anyone facing punishment on my behalf.

"With all due respect, Your Majesty, a lockdown is just going backward—"

The guard lunges for him again, a sign that he believes Quill is speaking out of turn. Again, the king holds up his hand. "Continue."

"We have spent our entire lives in hiding. So did our Ancestors. A lockdown will only send us back to the life we tried so hard to escape from. From a personal perspective, there is nothing I want less than to be locked up somewhere when I can be of service. *We* can be of service. We would be failing at our duties as Descendants otherwise."

I find myself grinning proudly at him for holding his own and speaking up for us. His friends. Seeing him now, as a man, loyal and true . . . it's becoming harder and harder for me to keep hating him.

You have to decide if you can accept everything that makes him perfect and what makes him broken.

Calista's words ring in my mind. A reminder to shift my perspective.

"You misunderstand. You Descendants will be fighting the Dormants. Everyone else will remain in lockdown." He gives us a wicked grin I want to slap right off his face. "Then you will not be failing in your duties as Descendants."

Anara says she wishes to stab him in the foot.

I scoff as quietly as possible. *I would gladly let her.*

"My wife wishes to speak, Your Majesty," Malik interrupts my thoughts as he gazes at his kneeling wife.

"Go on," the king says, bored and done with this meeting.

Calista stands, spear held upright. "I have to agree with Quill, Your Majesty. This will simply allow the Dormant King to get what he wants while we stand by and watch as he destroys homes and attacks and kills innocent people. The very people *you* want to protect."

Thank you.

"You may very well not agree with the choice we've made," the king replies with greatly restrained anger, "but this is our land, and Avela and I make decisions for said land. You and Malik are in charge of Sabbia's well-being, hence you make whatever decisions you so choose for your people." His cold, domineering eyes glaze over all of us. "You may find it in your best interests to keep your opinions to yourself in this matter. In the meantime, Descendants, it will be up to you to live up to your duty." His wicked grin widens. "We're counting on you."

This man is my least favorite person, Quill says.

Everything in my body and spirit deflates. The hope I had that we could count on Arythica's aid was all for nothing. The one chance we had at winning this war, and it's been snatched away. Ketra will never know how hard I tried to save them.

We're going to die. All of us are. The four of us are not enough, and the king of Petros couldn't care less.

"Very well," Malik replies, just as deflated as I am. "Thank you for your time, Your Majesty."

Before we have a chance to leave in unison, Malik storms out of the throne room, rage emanating from him in every step. The king calls for the guards to escort us out, and Calista rushes to my side before she can catch up with Malik.

"We will meet again, I promise," she whispers.

My heart drops even more. I haven't had enough time with her, and it's already come to an end.

She reaches into the waistband of her skirt and pulls out a palm-sized, ragged piece of sandstone. A piece of her home. "If you ever need me, write where you are on it, and have your Bennaru deliver this to me. I will find you." Her hand clasps over mine as I take the stone. "Everything will work out the way it's meant to, child."

I start wondering if that sentiment has more than one meaning. "Thank you," I whisper.

A sense of comfort washes over me. My parents are afraid to step up, but Calista has proven time and time again how brave she is in the face of danger.

She kisses me on the cheek and rushes out of the throne room.

"You shall stay until my queen and I have written the decree," the king summons us as he stands from his throne, holding out a hand for his wife. "Once finished, you will be tasked to deliver it throughout the city. Guards, show the Descendants to their rooms for the night. This task may take a while."

CHAPTER 17

QUILL

Funny. The only kernel of kindness King Aldous managed to express was having his guards show us to the bedrooms he wanted us to stay in until he was finished with the decrees. Then telling us that we would be the ones delivering this decree scrapped that kindness immediately.

We have a lot of time on our hands with no idea how long this will take. We all go our separate ways as we explore different parts of the castle. I take in the surroundings of my room and examine its lavish style. The bed alone is large enough to hold three people, covered with a cotton-soft red velvet blanket that feels light on my fingertips. Each corner of the mattress is held by an erected bedpost with intricately carved designs all over them and gemstones weaved into the gaps. A floor-to-ceiling oval-shaped window gives me a view of the courtyard and the most manicured garden I've ever seen. The dresser across from the bed has crystal knobs and a large mirror set on top encrusted in diamonds. This may as well have been made for a spoiled princess.

The castle is a massive work of art with vaulted ceilings that reach the sky. Each gray cinder block hallway carries its own history, especially the one with paintings of Aldous's ancestors. Makes me wonder if any of these men came from the Dormant King. The family history covers both sides of one hallway, a lit torch in between every wall hanging. Each painting has a man with either a frown or a bowl-shaped haircut. I involuntarily raise a hand to my own hair every time I glance at a new portrait.

I'm so glad I'm attractive.

I follow a path to the back of the castle, the bright sunshine leading me to the open arch and then outside.

I gape at the view. A whole other courtyard lies before me, leading to a cliff that hangs over the ocean. The windows along the castle have planters that add extra color to the overall bland shade of the rest of the building. A large expanse of neatly landscaped grass, cinder block pathways, and rock pillars are scattered throughout, the ragged edges and abrupt cuts within them holding their own history. A large wall stands before me on the edge of the cliff, the background for a variety of targets that have taken a beating.

Then I see a downcast Havanna strolling around the courtyard, each step a soft kick through the grass. Her hair moves with the breeze and covers one side of her face in a beautiful sheet of brown. I watch her a little longer as I think of things to say to her. I come up empty, and I debate with myself whether I should leave her alone or talk to her anyway.

This is the ideal time to keep trying to win her over. No one standing between us. Just her and me.

She doesn't bother acknowledging me as I move to stand next to her, dangerously close to the cliff, staring at the ocean in wonderment.

"The king may be a living carcass, but I appreciate the opportunity to enjoy the view he likely takes for granted."

I chuckle. "He also has no clue that he's housing a group of people that hate his guts. Kind of ironic."

"We may as well plan our own assassination attempt."

I smirk at her. "Wow. Giving the king a taste of revenge? You play dirty, Zappy."

She returns the gesture, this time facing me. "Only way to play now."

Silence fills the space between us and the view steals our attentions. She hasn't said anything insulting to me yet, and she's willingly talking to me. I feel myself getting closer to attaining her forgiveness.

I look over to the training area with racks of arrows and everything imaginable with a blade. I need to do something—anything—with my mind to avoid thinking about quirky things to say to her. She seems content just watching the water, something I know she wishes she could enjoy without it being life-threatening.

Then an idea flashes before me.

"Want to practice archery with me?"

She finally meets my gaze, incredulous. "You know I'm not good at archery."

Time to bring on the charm. "Do you remember when I said I would teach you?" I step away from her, motioning for her to follow me. "Well, today's the day. Besides, you need to learn all the tactics you can to bring the Dormant King down. The more you know, the better your chances are at winning."

She perks up slightly when I mention our archnemesis. Something brightens her eyes: a realization. If I truly were a traitor, I wouldn't mention winning this war, let alone offering to help someone do it. I offer her my hand and put on my sexiest smile that I know she can't resist.

She hides one of her own while she deliberates. "All right. If you insist."

I didn't. Which means she's warming back up to me.

Havanna follows me to the target area where I take another bow to use. I unhitch mine from my back and present it to her with both hands. She flinches in surprise, staring at it as if it will break under her touch. "You want me to use your bow? Your *brother's* bow?"

I wink. "You should feel special." I follow that with a shrug. "Plus, it's a lot easier to learn with than most bows."

She lets a shuddered sigh escape her lips as she carefully puts her hand on my weapon. The way her fingers flex on the grip, skimming the surface from limb to limb with such gentleness and care, tells me how much she respects what this bow means to me.

I suppose that's what originally attracted me to her. Not only our banter and chemistry, but that she understood how I felt. In a way, I thought that she understood *me*. A feeling I have been denied my whole life.

Havanna grips the bow and holds it to her side. "Very well." She flashes an impish grin that is sexy as all get-out. "Teach me your ways."

I keep my victory silent as I stand by her side, handing her an arrow. "Pull straight back, keep the arrow at eye level. You don't want to hold this position for a long time because your strength can deteriorate fast with this type of bow." I nock an arrow, lift the bow, and shoot in one smooth motion. The arrow hits just outside the target, on which I blame the bow. "It's just a quick pull, aim, and fire."

She levels a gaze at me. "How do you aim then?"

"Your eyes." That garners me an eye roll and a strong attempt to hide her laughter. I chuckle lightly. "When you pull back, you keep your gaze on your target and lock it in. Try it."

Havanna stares at the target, her breaths becoming heavier as her pulse picks up speed. Her hand trembles with nervous energy.

"You're thinking too hard."

Overwhelmed with pressure, she lifts the bow and fires without any indication of aiming. The arrow shoots toward the ocean and we both watch as it descends.

"Well . . . a valiant effort."

She groans and lightly stomps her foot. "You stressed me out!" she shouts, trying to sound serious, but is actually amused. "It feels so awkward to hold."

"It takes a moment to find the right way to grip it and keep it stable until you're ready to fire." I stand behind her, maneuvering her arms and shoulders to get her position right. "Let's try again."

Every arrow after that is unpredictable, but we have fun. She laughs at herself every time she has a bad shot, and that gives me an opening to tease her about where she was aiming. "Perhaps I should aim for your nether regions," she grumbles with humor. I ask her to repeat herself, but she denies saying anything at all. It is hard for me to not laugh.

Eventually, I convince her to simply shoot an arrow straight up into the air and dodge it before it hits us on its descent. Although it didn't take *much* convincing. I told her it was a game Indigo and I played growing up, and she seemed willing to help me relive the memory.

"Isn't this really dangerous?" she asks.

"Yes. That's what makes it fun."

It is the closest I've ever felt to her. To anyone, really. With the exception of my brother.

Despite being tired and hungry, it takes a moment for either of us to depart the courtyard. We each hesitate to move. Not only because we want to keep having fun, but because this is a major turning point for us. This is more than just simple friendship and she no longer has an excuse to be angry at me.

The walls are being torn down.

A knock sounds at my door. With the sun setting, the only source of light I have are a few flickering candles on the nightstand and dresser. On the other side of the wooden, creaky door is a guard, holding an envelope sealed in wax with the king's signet ring. Underneath is a few more pieces of paper.

"The decree, sir," he says flatly, handing me the envelope. "The king asks that you hang these up in the city by way of announcement."

"You can't be serious," I grumble.

"He plans to make an official announcement tomorrow morning. He requests that these are hung up tonight and the rest delivered to all villages and citizens tomorrow morning."

"Tonight?" I exclaim. "That could take all night!"

All he responds with is a shrug and then he walks away. Free stay or not, I hate this king.

I slam the door as hard as I can, the only healthy way to release my anger right now. It swings right back open with Anara, Ender, and Havanna trailing in. They sit on my bed as I read the decree aloud. My fingers curl around the page in growing fury.

"'Send good thoughts'?" Anara repeats with disgust. "Sure, that's all we need, good thoughts from the rich people! Perhaps *that's* why we haven't killed the Dormant King yet!"

"We could always kill Aldous first," Havanna suggests jokingly. "Get it out of our system."

"Careful, you might convince us to do it," I mumble.

After walking the empty city streets for fifteen minutes, we haven't placed a single copy anywhere. A testament to how much we *don't* want to do this. Aldous took the easy way out by leaving the burden on us while he gets to sit safely in his luxurious castle drinking loads of alcohol.

"Remind me, wasn't this *your* idea?" Anara snaps to Havanna, waving the papers in front of her. "Begging the king and queen of Petros to help with something that involves a tad bit of risk?"

"This issue involves everyone. They were the best resource, considering the amount of authority they have," Havanna weakly defends herself.

"Perhaps we should have prepared ourselves a little more so we knew what we were up against," I add softly.

"Malik said he's from Arythica," Anara emphasizes each word with an irritated drone. "He should have told us if this is how the king normally is."

"Perhaps he no know?" Ender offers with a shrug. "With ridiculous rules, no one talk to king about anything."

I shake my head. "I'd die a happy man never talking to him again."

Havanna stops mid-stroll and hangs her head back. "I expected this to go much differently," she groans through a sad sigh.

We walk a few paces after her, then stop when we realize she's not next to us. My mind immediately sifts through solutions to her downcast expression. Anything to make her laugh, as she did with me earlier today. I want to be sure she doesn't give up. That she doesn't lose that will to keep fighting, to get back up and try again. All the things she's known for.

I don't say or do anything. I can't. I'm glad to have her warming up to me again, but anything more will break the boundaries I've set for myself.

Havanna catches up to us, avoiding our gazes as she flips through the pages of the decree. We drag our feet a few more paces, although reluctantly. The resistance to have any part of this builds within me. To figuratively slap the king in the face. I was adamant about never going back to Arbol Forest, and I intend for it to stay that way. Not even the king of Petros will stand in the way of that.

"That's it." I toss the copies in the air, letting them flutter aimlessly behind me. "I'm not doing this. No. I'm not going back to my village, even for this."

Havanna's eyes search me with a hint of what I believe is concern and understanding.

"I no mind go back to Vulca, but decree sucks." Ender crinkles his face in disapproval. "I no want to tell tribe to isolate."

"We *have* to," Havanna reminds me. "The king won in this decision. I'm in no mood to play with death. Everything we do will be an excuse for him to off us." Her eyebrows perk up as she shakes her head. "Although, this makes me look at the king and queen very differently."

There has to be another way. I will do anything to oppose the king, even if it means breaking the law. Laws that illuminate how haughty and self-absorbed he is.

I pick up a copy of the decree I tossed and I examine it long and hard. Forcing people to be confined in their homes for an indeterminate amount of time seems more like torture, not protection. If I were in this predicament as a king and had to write a message to the people—

My head perks up, puzzle pieces of ideas snapping into place. It's the most dangerous idea I have, defying all authority. Yet, we're not left with many choices.

"I may or may not have an idea," I announce, conniving but still unsure.

"We're all relying on the sheer confidence you're showing right now," Anara replies in a bored tone.

"I think the only way to make this work in our favor is to have a different decree, correct?" They all stare at me wordlessly. "So what if we got some new paper and . . . rewrote this thing? Copy the king's handwriting and signature, but with *our* message. What *we* need to say."

Havanna gapes at me while Ender and Anara stare in disbelief. "Are you suggesting we forge this document?" Havanna shakes her head adamantly. "That's treason. There's no way to escape death if we're caught."

I shrug nonchalantly. "We have powers. He doesn't."

"Not to mention we need his signet ring to seal it, and there's no way that's happening," Anara adds.

I retrieve the envelope with the king's wax signet and pull out a small knife from a sheath on my leg. "We cut it out and glue it over the new one."

"You would have to do it perfectly. No trace of it being tampered with," Havanna argues.

I carefully flip the knife between my fingers with the smoothness of polished metal and bring it back to my palm where I grip the hilt. "You forget that my knife skills are impeccable."

Her eyes fail to hide the gleam within them in the darkness of night. Her sigh is exasperated, but her intrigue is unmistakable with the way she follows the motions of my hand with heated desire.

"Handwriting have to look same," Ender mentions. "*Exact* same. That impossible."

Anara folds her arms, narrowing her gaze at Ender. "*You* forget that I made your outfit." She turns to me. "And *you* forget I fixed your clothes after they were nearly ripped to shreds."

Ender shrugs. "So?"

Anara rolls her eyes. "Isn't my point obvious? To make something like that takes an intricate, steady hand. And who of us has that?" She twirls her body to face us, motioning to herself. "Oh yes, that's me."

I watch Havanna shift her weight and find deep interest in the ground. No one says anything for a tense few seconds as we simultaneously process these unnerving thoughts and possibilities of taking action.

Havanna is the first to speak, hiding the twist in her lips. "I have to admit, it's a brilliant idea." The toe of her boot slides against the brick on the ground. "But this is extremely dangerous. We could very well be killed."

"Our lives have been at stake from the beginning," I remind her. "Forging the king's document is just a gentle push toward the cliff of death."

"You called me a walking death trap when we first met."

"And that still stands."

"You're not helping."

"At the very least, this could cause an uprising," Anara notes. "And by starting this war on our terms, we're going to have to practice our abilities. We need to be at our strongest."

Havanna nods slowly, conceding to the inevitable. "This is the right thing to do," she says, more to herself than us. "That's what matters most."

Silence. Each of us faces the other, waiting for someone to confirm that we are, indeed, about to commit treason.

"I'll get more paper," Anara offers. "Ender, come with me. We can sneak into one of these markets and grab some."

Havanna raises her hand. "I'll sneak into the king's quarters and take the ink and pen."

I lift my hands and give them a wry smile. "I'll sit on the fact that I'm a genius."

"Let's meet in my room." Anara rolls her shoulders back, then her neck. She turns to Havanna. "You may want to fetch some refreshments. This will take all night."

CHAPTER 18

ANARA

I've never known hand cramps like this.

Havanna and Quill help to form the right words so it sounds convincing enough to come from the king. Once I finish the first copy, it is frighteningly identical to King Aldous's handwriting. I am impressed with myself. Their part of the task over, Havanna and Quill retreat to their rooms, leaving me with just Ender; he doesn't follow after them, but I also don't ask him to stay.

My hand begins to hurt after writing the second copy of our new decree, to the point where my fingers barely flex. My eyelids are heavier after each copy, but I keep going. This needs to be done before the city wakes up in just a few hours. Pompous King Aldous will see his efforts in writing a decree was for nothing.

Then I'll have Wave do the honors for me as a macaw: post the decree on the iron-wrought fence, an area where it will be seen the most. Word will explode within seconds.

Deep, near-growling, obnoxious breaths suddenly distract me. "Holy Halivaara, you snore like a bear," I comment over my shoulder. Ender perks up with a snort. "If you're going to stay, you could at least keep me occupied."

"How?"

"I don't know. By talking, perhaps?"

"I no want distract you."

I throw a smile over my shoulder. "Your snoring already did that, but that's sweet of you to care."

"I know."

I hold back a chuckle as I keep working. My hand is clammy and a callous is forming on my middle finger, but I need to get this done. We *need* this war.

I turn around a few minutes later only to find Ender dozed off on the bed again, arms splayed out and head lolled to the side. His presence somehow makes this job feel less lonely. Serene, even.

It's taking all the brainpower I have to keep my eyes open. All I need to do is blink once and I'll be asleep in seconds.

After countless hours, deep into the night, I finally finish everything. I place my hands on the desk for support as I push myself to stand. My hand, wrist, and legs scream at me for sitting for so long, a tingling sensation running through my stiff muscles. I whine in pain with each stretch, my joints popping in response. Ender remains on my bed, oblivious to my presence as he stays asleep.

As I bend over to stretch my spine, I examine my amazing handiwork.

I, King Aldous, along with my wife, Avela, hereby decree that the entire kingdom of Petros, with the exception of Sabbia, gather for war.

We have received word that the Dormant King spoken of in legend has resurfaced, along with the Dormants. Rest assured, the De-

scendants of Fire, Water, Land, and Lightning have all been located, but their combined powers are not enough to keep everyone safe. Monster attacks are inevitable, which means that the Descendants will need the help of trained knights and soldiers to protect the kingdom. They need your help.

If you can volunteer yourself, please make your way to Arythica and await further direction from us. We wish you peace during this turbulent time, and please send good thoughts to the Descendants.

Signed,
King Aldous and Queen Avela

I'm freaking amazing. There's no doubt this will work.

"I'm done," I announce.

That perks Ender right up into a sitting position. He rubs his eyes and peers at me. "Really?" I hand him one of the papers and watch him read it. His mouth twists to the side in admiration. "Well done."

I give him a sleepy smirk. "Thanks." I take a copy and dangle it in front of Wave. "Put this one on the fence outside. If we're going to ask the kingdom for help, might as well start here." I lean down to his frog eyes and whisper, "Be discreet, all right?"

He snatches the folded paper in his mouth as Ender scoots off the bed. I toss back the corner of the covers to slip under. Blissful sleep awaits. "Good night, Anara."

I still after he says the words and find him slowly making progress for the door, where he opens it for Wave to make his exit.

I don't want Ender to leave. I like having him close to me, even if he doesn't talk. He's a comforting presence, and I'm desperate not to lose that.

My mouth can't form the words—the question I want to ask. I can't even use my vocal cords to say a simple "good night." I just stand there, arms folded across my chest with the debate arguing for first place. I hated it when he was with all those women in Sabbia. I hated admitting to myself how badly I wanted him next to me that night, telling me he wasn't going anywhere and I was important to him.

I had no reason to expect that of him. Quill was right. I've been indecisive.

The opportunity to change that is right there, and I'm hesitating. I need to stop thinking and just *jump*.

"Ender." He stills, limbs limp and tired, and silently turns his attention to me. "Will you . . . stay with me? Until I fall asleep?"

His eyes dart in all directions, caught off guard. The pause has me wary about what I just asked until he says impishly, "Why? You afraid of dark, compa?"

I scoff and feign confidence. "No."

"Then why . . ."

I have no desire to explain my reasoning. I'm not afraid of the dark, but I'm also willing to lie that I am just so I don't admit my true feelings. Being vulnerable is out of the question. The shift in mood makes me somber. "Forget it."

"No no." He backtracks and steps closer to the bed. "You ask, I stay."

I peer up at him, touched by his kindness. He has no reason to do anything I ask, but he's doing it anyway.

"Oh." I slip under the covers. "All right." I pat the spot next to me that can hold at least two Enders.

He rounds to the other side of the bed and climbs back on, settling on top of the covers. He feels miles away, but I don't push for him to be closer. Out of nowhere, he offers, "I massage hand?"

He wants to . . . massage my hand. Something so intimate and so sweet, my heart melts. "I won't say no to that," I answer with a shy smile.

Ender tenderly takes my hand and lets his strong fingers do the work. He rubs circles over my thumb muscle, the pressure so perfect and relieving I'm near tears. My eyes flutter shut, reveling in his touch.

"You have hand massage before?"

I shake my head. "No one ever offered." I roll my head to the side, letting the soft pillow contour around it. "It feels incredible."

"My tribe do this a lot," he says, sliding the pressure to a spot on my palm that I didn't realize I needed. "Our axe heavy. Mining all day take toll on hands."

"I can imagine," I reply sleepily, my lips barely moving; I'm exhausted. "Thank you."

I don't remember falling asleep.

***

It's nothing but darkness when I wake up. And I can't fall back asleep.

I turn to the space on my bed and find that Ender is fast asleep beside me. I only asked him to stay till I fell asleep, but he's still here. Perhaps he'll leave early when I've fallen back asleep. I don't want him to, though. Even having him here, just sleeping, makes me feel safe.

A piece of my tough exterior cracked when I asked him to stay. I became an entirely new person by asking that question, but only because I knew with my whole heart he wouldn't make me feel like less of one. That explains my sudden courage. Perhaps that's the secret to not being vulnerable: trusting the person well enough to know that they will still care about me.

That must be why Havanna and I get along better now. She cried on my shoulder because I told her she could. She trusted me enough to know I was being serious, no matter how out of character it was for me.

One thing we have in common, though: Our hearts tug us in directions we don't want it to.

I slip out of the covers and tiptoe to the door that creaks slightly as I open it. Ender remains asleep despite the high-pitched noise, and I sneak to the room next to mine.

Havanna's door is much quieter, but somehow, I wake her up. It's immediately evident when she grabs her sword from off the floor and holds the blade in front of her.

"Wow. You're fierce even when you're half asleep," I remark.

She sighs and drops the weapon on the bed, adjusting herself under the covers. "I wasn't asleep."

I shut the door and step closer to her. "Did you have another nightmare?"

She crosses her arms over her chest, looking out her own floor-to-ceiling window. "I don't know if I'd call this one a nightmare."

I make myself at home on the edge of the bed. "I've been curious what you dream about."

Her lips form a wry smile. "I don't want you to feel obligated to ask."

"I don't. I want to know."

Her eyes become distant and full of yearning. "Usually it's Jael appearing out of nowhere, telling me she's proud of me. To keep going." Her throat bobs. "When I first left Ketra, I had a dream that she told me to avenge her."

I shift on the edge of the bed to fully face her. I hate to admit that I'm honored that she's chosen me to open up to, thanks to Ender's advice recently about being kind.

"Tonight, it was very different."

"How?"

She switches her attention to her hands, wringing the tension within them. "We were all on Luna Island, fighting the Dormant King."

I already hate where this is going. I hate remembering how much we failed at that task.

Just be there.

Ender's words echo in my mind, right when I need them.

"We were nowhere near powerful enough to beat him, and I remember thinking, 'I don't understand. We've waited hundreds of years for this, had a lot of time to hone in our powers, and we're losing.'" She shakes her head, a bitter laugh to follow. "Quill was trying to help me—protect me. And I kept resisting him. I was on my knees, exhausted and hopeless, and Jael showed up in front of me. I couldn't see her face, but by her voice, I knew it was her. She told me—" She swallows again, speaking as if what she was told is a new concept. "—forgiveness is vital. Then she said, 'resentment will be your downfall, not the Dormant King himself, if you let it.'"

Jael said exactly what I was trying to tell her when Quill found us in the desert. She needed to let it go, and it took Jael showing up in her dream to make her see that. Although, she was already on the path to forgiveness with the way she and Quill have interacted today.

"I've been so stupid," she whispers with shame.

"I won't argue with that. But, to be fair, Quill has been too."

She shrugs, then sighs. "I need to clear the air. It's hard, though."

"It's always hard when you have to admit that you were at fault for something." I motion to myself. "You're talking to the queen of that. You're lucky, though."

Her face twists in surprise. "How?"

I brace my forearms on my knees, prepared to admit to the shame I feel for not being able to relate to the grief. "I wonder what that feels like. Having someone to miss that way, especially someone that played the role of mother and role model."

"You never had that?"

I give her a sad smile. "Not in the way you had. Not by a long shot."

"Well, perhaps you have been spared from the pain of losing someone like that." Her voice turns somber. "It's one thing to miss someone who's died. It's something else entirely to miss those who are still alive."

Just by that, I know she's referring to her parents. She told me about her encounter with them as we crossed the desert, waiting for rescue. I couldn't relate to her mixed emotions because there was a point in my life where I stopped caring about where my parents were. I may have wondered, but the fact that they dumped me in that village and never came back made it easy to assume they were dead. I stopped missing them. Hard to miss people you barely remember.

Perhaps it's the fact that she's opening herself up so much that I feel compelled to do the same. It's completely foreign to me—a language I don't speak. "I never experienced that. I never knew my parents. They left me with the chief and chieftess with no explanation. Growing up, Sharifa forced everyone to make sure I was kept safe at all times. Because I wasn't royalty or a leader of any kind, they bullied me instead. Calling me 'princess' and 'spoiled brat.'"

Havanna shifts herself to sit up straighter and folds her arms. She cocks her head, listening with her whole heart that warms mine.

"Everyone hated me. And it was allowed because we couldn't tell the truth." Memories of hiding in my cave, the snide looks the villagers gave me, the bite in my words as I fought back. Sharifa and Masina had all the power over that village, yet they were powerless against that.

"Did you tell them to just tell the truth? To spare you the misery?"

"Are you serious?" I laugh bitterly. "I asked so many times. They put my safety above all else, so it was never an option."

Havanna remains silent. It's by no means a pleasant story; I hate remembering it. In a way, I hope it helps Havanna understand me more. I wasn't ready to reveal that side of me when we first met, even when she told me her own backstory. I wasn't in the mood for pity. Yet, it's pity for each other that's drawn us closer.

Havanna swallows hard. "When I first met you, I genuinely thought you were cruel." She shakes her head in a reassuring manner. "But you're not. You just had to figure out how to navigate the cruelty thrown at you, and you built a wall."

I give her a wicked grin. "What makes you think I'm not cruel?"

She smiles. "You're in here, aren't you?"

***

Sleep overtakes me a few minutes later and I bid Havanna good night.

With a hug.

She hugs me.

This time, I let her. Because this is the start of a friendship based on understanding.

I'm practically a changed woman.

I enter my bedroom quietly and carefully shut the door. I round the wall and Ender is still sleeping on the bed.

And I find myself smiling as I slip back under the covers.

I smile even more when I turn to my side, toward the early sunlight coming in through the window.

Ender stayed the whole night.

My compo.

CHAPTER 19

ENDER

The light coming in draws me out of sleep slowly. On top of people talking wildly outside.

I'm so tired. Staying up late didn't help; although it was worth it. I had the privilege to witness Anara become an entirely different person when she asked me to stay.

Vulnerable. Afraid. Insecure.

Anara has rarely shown those parts of herself, and the times when she did, she masked it with confidence. Not very well, I might add.

Now I know something else that makes her weak: a good hand rub.

She dozed off about a minute into the massage and I just savored the quiet by watching her even breathing. So relaxed, so at peace.

I open my eyes just enough to see her smooth, creamy skin, her hair bright as the sun falling over her shoulder. She told me to leave once she fell asleep, but I couldn't get her helpless face out of my head. She seemed so lonely and in need of a compo, so I stayed.

Putting this plan in place was a lot of work, and she was the one who was making it happen. I didn't object going back to Mulhutna to see my aani and how the tribe is faring. But King Aldous's decree sucks. My objection wouldn't have helped any, though.

Everyone had a say during that meeting except me. Fear choked back any hope of speaking, out of concern of being punished. I stayed silent because I didn't want to be accountable for accidentally killing someone due to my strength.

Anara, however, wasn't afraid to fight back, and I was proud of her.

She opens her eyes to find my own examining her. Instead of grumbling in annoyance by my presence, she smiles.

For *me*.

"You stayed all night?" she mumbles into her pillow.

I tilt my head to the side. "You ask me to stay. I stay."

She blinks slowly, sending her affection across the bed that feels much too big for us. "Thank you."

The voices that woke me up turn into angry screams and protests. Anara and I perk up our heads to listen.

"I believe they got our note."

We kick ourselves out of the bed and run to the window overlooking the front courtyard. People crowd around the iron-wrought fence, angrily waving their fists.

The door bursts open with Havanna and Quill strolling in with urgency. "It's getting bad out there," Quill says when they meet us at the window. "They look like they want to kill the king."

Fists flying, pushing each other over, all fighting for the front row against the fence. The guards are setting up a pedestal, no doubt for the king to address the angry mob. The shouts topple over each other in a way that makes it difficult for us to decipher what is being said.

A few people manage to make their shouts heard, and we hear their words crystal clear.

"We haven't feared Dormants, nor do we fear them now!"

"War is not necessary!"

"Are you truly suggesting that we blindly go up against a legendary enemy?"

The reaction we were expecting.

A guard bursts into the room with a sword aimed at us, ready to strike. "Traitors!" he bellows. "You behaved in a way deserving of death!"

"Hold on." Quill holds up his hands in a silent pause, freakishly calm. "What makes you think we caused this?"

He makes a point I never considered. There were six guards in the throne room during that meeting. Any of them had a fair chance of turning against the king.

"All guards involved in that meeting were summoned for interrogation this morning," he spits, growling in fury. "Not only were we questioned, but our handwriting was examined with utmost care. None of us had the same writing as the king."

Quill's face falls. Just when he thought he tricked the guard, he hurls the proof back at us.

"All of you—" He motions to us with his sword. "— are to come with me. The king would like a word with you when he's done addressing the irate crowd."

The four of us exchange quick glances. We know what that word will be: execution.

Before any of us think of moving, Quill extends his hand, his eyes turning green.

Transmission.

The guard stops, then turns toward the door. He raises his sword to the ceiling, yelling some kind of war cry, and dashes down the hallway.

Problem solved.

"We need to leave Arythica," Havanna announces.

"And go where?" Anara shrieks. "We've exhausted all options!"

"We will figure it out. Right now, we just need to find a way out of here."

We rush out of the room, nearly crashing into each other in the door, and run down the hallway. Our hurried, combined footsteps echo through the emptiness. Not a single servant or knight roams the halls, as they're busy protecting the king from the mayhem.

Because of the decree that we spent hours working on.

The ones that we left in Anara's bedroom that are now too late to retrieve.

All that work. Burned to nothing.

We race down the spiral stairwell, run along one hallway, then find another that ends abruptly, with a door on the right that opens to the side of the courtyard covered in bushes and plants. We're facing King Aldous's back on the makeshift pedestal, steps away from freedom. His royal robes drape over his back, his golden crown gleaming in the daylight, exuding his authority and power.

We have a chance to escape without a scratch.

"Wait," Quill halts us.

"What?" Havanna whisper-shouts.

"I want to see what happens."

Havanna's face twists in unnatural ways in utter confusion. "Why? You already know he hates us."

"Exactly. He's not going to present us in the best light. So we can see how much we need to redeem ourselves."

"We're already redeeming ourselves—"

Anara shushes her with a finger pressed to her lips. "He's talking."

We peek between the gaps in the leaves and branches, crouching to see King Aldous's hands in front of him as he tries to calm the crowd. They refuse to settle down with nothing but a thirst for justice on the other side of the fence.

"At ease, my people," he consoles them with a loud, authoritative voice. "What you saw is clearly an act of terrorism, and the perpetrators have been dealt with accordingly. No war of any kind is taking place, I assure you."

"I can't believe this," Havanna whispers, shaking her head with disdain. "'An act of terrorism'? We're *terrorists* now?"

"Consider the source," Anara notes. "He's trying to paint himself in a positive light."

"Are you saying the entire decree was falsified?" a masculine voice in the crowd asks.

"Some of it is, yes," he replies, relenting to the fact that he has to defend himself. "The Dormant King of legend is at large, and I hereby decree that the whole kingdom go into lockdown immediately until all signs of danger are eliminated."

The crowd roars, shoving their arms between the bars of the fence. The protests are as earsplitting as the Mulhutna when shouting from the depths of their soul, enough to make our bones shake.

"A lockdown? That's even worse!"

"What will that accomplish?"

"This is lunacy!"

Havanna chuckles to herself. "Turns out they wouldn't have been happy with either choice."

"Either way, we committed treason," Quill points out with worry.

"Hey!" someone bellows behind us. A guard marches in our direction, a finger pointed straight ahead. "We are under the king's direct orders to have you escorted off the property immediately!"

I try not to laugh. The king is truly stupid enough to think his guards are enough to fight against us. As Quill said last night, we're the ones with the powers.

"I assure you, this decision was made with utmost care and concern for our people," the king does his best to shout over the crowd's uproar. "Please retreat to your homes and await further instructions. All businesses and trade will remain closed until further notice. Anyone who disobeys this order will be incarcerated without delay."

That gets the people moving, scurrying about as insects under a lifted rock. I suppose no one wants to be incarcerated or be at the king's mercy.

"Follow me," the guard commands, aiming a spearhead at all of us. We're escorted out of the bushes, about to touch the red carpet on the courtyard, when the king descends the pedestal. He blinks away the blazing anger burning within him.

"Well, well, well, if it isn't the traitors of Petros," King Aldous purrs as he stalks toward us, hands clasped behind his back. His stance is one of calm easiness, to the point where it makes me shudder. "You not only humiliated me and my queen, you committed treason, which is deserving of a public execution." He leans forward with a wicked, white-toothed smile. "A sight I wouldn't dare miss." I remain still, glaring at this arrogant waste of space and time. "But you are the *Descendants*," he adds mockingly, "and because of that, execution is not an option. However, from this moment on, you are all banned from Arythica. Your blatant betrayal is a disgrace to my authority and my court."

"We were trying to save you!" Anara snaps. "And the kingdom *you* are responsible for!"

"By direct disobedience? Far from it." His nose bunches as he growls at us. "No thanks to you, I have no choice but to have my commanding knight send the decree, which is exactly the kind of danger I was doing my utmost to avoid. You Descendants are the bane of my existence." He motions to the entrance. "Get out of my sight."

The guard nudges mine and Quill's shoulders, forcefully pushing us forward while he holds his spear at Anara and Havanna. We may have expected a less than favorable reaction, but not to be banned from the kingdom's capital.

We're escorted to the entrance of the city, back into the wild. Back into dangerous territory. No plan, no destination. Just us, on our own once again. Hopeless, lost, and defeated.

We drag our feet along the drawbridge that leads to the fields. Our weapons clang against our backs, the only sound drowning out our thoughts.

"We may not have our decree," Anara finally fills the silence, "but I still say we tell the kingdom we're going to war."

"But if the king's decree reaches the rest of the kingdom before we do, everyone's going to be confused," Havanna counters.

"That may have been something we should have considered before defying the king in the first place," Quill says with a sarcastic cringe.

Havanna glares at him in response. "We? *We?* Forging the decree was *your* idea, Quill!"

"In my defense, all I thought about was how pointless it was to post his decree," he argues. "Either way, we need to wait until we have a more solid plan before doing anything else. Form backup plans when things don't go the way we want."

"We left our packs in Killios," Havanna reminds us. "We can go back to retrieve them and tell Arthur what's going on. We need to see if he'll let us practice our abilities on his training grounds. And stay as long as possible until we feel ready."

None of us say anything. Questions hang in the air, ones that no one has the strength to ask. Warily, she adds, "We still want to go to war, don't we?"

"Want to? No," Anara answers. "Have to? Yes."

"The question is whether we're ultimately left with no one to rely on for help other than Sabbia," Quill says in a low voice. "And lose any chance of winning."

"We are *not* losing," Havanna scolds him. "Let's just go to Killios first."

I have a feeling this will just go the way the rest of our journey has gone.

Another destination, another dead end.

***

"Well. I can see you made a mess of yourselves," Arthur comments after listening to our update on recent events. I suppose that response is warranted.

It took us an hour to make it to Killios. Our Bennarus were in full form when we arrived, and we were allowed in without question, as if Arthur informed the whole camp about us.

145

Once we got to his house, the Bennarus shrank to be able to fit into his living space. He was elated to see that we came back from the attack on Luna Island unscathed, albeit barely. We caught him up on how that went, and relayed everything that happened between then and being banned from Arythica.

"We did what we had to do," Anara responds defensively.

"No one told you to commit treason!" Arthur says with a humorless laugh.

"Regardless," Havanna interrupts, "we need a place to practice our abilities because we need to be at our strongest when we go to war."

Arthur's eyebrows furrow. "Are you suggesting you practice your lightning and fire and water on *my* turf?"

"Yes," she drawls.

"You're all mad!" he scolds us. "You must think me a fool to want to draw Dormants to eat my crew."

The imagery combined with his words has me snickering. No one joins me, but instead, they give me dirty looks. I clear my throat and stop.

Havanna folds her arms and regards Arthur with defiance. "Then I must apologize in advance if we lose this war because of lack of preparation."

Quill cringes at Arthur. "She's got you there."

"All of us here, including our Bennarus, are fully capable of ripping Dormants to shreds," Havanna continues. "They did pretty dang good on Luna Island. We just need a safe space to get stronger."

"You shouldn't have pissed off the king then. I'm surprised he didn't have you all executed on the spot."

Havanna shrugs. "Being Descendants saved us."

"The king is a raging idiot," Anara snaps. "His head is too far up his butthole to notice it."

Quill snorts back laughter.

"She right," I say, "King Aldous need us, but he no smart. Head no belong in butthole."

Quill can't contain himself as he busts out laughing, a fist in front of his mouth. Arthur remains stone-faced, which makes Quill work to compose himself. "All right, we need to be serious here."

Arthur simply palms his face while Havanna tries her hardest to hide her smile. Anara rolls her eyes, just like the girl I know.

"Because right now, it's just the four of us against all of them," Havanna informs him with all seriousness. "If it's going to stay that way, we need to lower our chances of losing. *Please*, Arthur."

He breathes out a harsh breath, his biceps bulging as he folds his arms. "If Dormants raid my camp—"

"We will take care of it," Havanna reassures him in a soft voice.

He hesitates, his features stiff and anxious. But he relents with another sigh. "Very well. While you do that, I will work to set up reinforcements along the city walls that will alert us of an arrival. If this is what the king desires, then it shall be done." He shakes his head, a low whistle escaping his lips. "I already foresee those pests making their way here."

"To be fair, they're everywhere," Quill mentions with a shrug. "They'll make it here regardless."

Arthur wiggles a finger at him. "Fair point." He waves at us in dismissal. "Have at it, Descendants. The future rests with you."

CHAPTER 20

HAVANNA

Arthur made quick work of clearing the training area of all soldiers. In obedience to the king, he warned them to stay in their homes for the foreseeable future.

Ender and Anara practice their Fire and Water skills on each other. She erects a wall of thick ice in front of her to ward off his fire; he uses Gale to avert her ice attacks. Quill started off with staff fighting techniques with his bow, a maneuver I haven't seen since we fought on Luna Island the first time I met him.

With everything that has happened, Quill is still my friend, even if he's more than that to me. Things began to shift yesterday, and I didn't mind it.

Embrace it. Feel *it. It's what makes life beautiful.*

Even with Calista's words, I keep arguing with myself to frustration. I'm pissing myself off.

That anger proves to be good fuel for using Gridlock on objects Arthur tosses my way with a trebuchet. He started with simple things such as planks of wood, then pottery, and now a crate full of crushed metal. The crate is my breaking point as it hurtles in my direction, nearly squashing me like a bug. The wood breaks on the concrete and sends splinters in every direction.

I lean down, hands on my knees as I will the dull headache to go away. I can't stop a crate in midair. How am I going to stop the Dormant King, who is many times stronger than a full crate? We need to find out what triggers him.

His weaknesses.

Everyone, villain or not, has a weakness—a vice—that ultimately brings them to their knees. Once you pinpoint it, success is guaranteed.

My head perks up.

Arthur has been a researcher for fifteen years. That is plenty of time to study the Dormant King and solve the puzzle. What makes him tick. He figured out that he had the ability to speak into one's mind. He figured out that was how he communicated with the Backers. He may have the answer to this one.

"Arthur," I call as I approach him. He leans against the trebuchet. "I just thought of something."

He watches me with skepticism. "Yes?"

"Have you told me everything you know about the Dormant King?"

He quirks a thick, black eyebrow. "Doubt it. Why do you ask?"

"I need you to tell me what weaknesses you have found regarding the Dormant King in the fifteen years you've done research on him."

Arthur's mouth turns down as he hangs his head back. "None that I can recall." He smirks. "Do you believe having a grasp on his weakness will help you?"

"Are you saying it won't?"

"I never said that. I simply believe that you will need more at your disposal than what you can use against him, whether it's psychological, physical, or emotional."

I wait for him to say more. When he doesn't, I glare at him hard enough to shoot daggers. "You're withholding information."

Arthur hangs his head and sighs. "I'm not withholding anything. I learned my lesson the first time I made that mistake." He stands up straighter and crosses his thick arms. "Just because I did my best to find what I could, it doesn't mean I got all of my questions answered." He shrugs. "Remember, he was in another dimension for centuries. It's difficult to find someone's weakness when you cannot locate them or observe them up close."

He makes a valid point, as much as I want to deny it. I thought out of all people, he might have an idea based on his findings alone. "So you have no idea what brings him to his knees or what can cripple him?"

He wears a deep frown and shakes his head. "None. My apologies."

I nod and turn to see what my friends are doing. When my eyes lock onto Quill, I can't look away.

Using Transform, he turns the weapons rack into a walking mechanism that throws the weapons at targets. It takes everything not to marvel at how beautiful he is. He's even more so when he uses his powers.

No matter how much I want to hang on to that hate, that denial for a desire for romance, my heart wins the war.

I'm done denying it.

I have feelings for Quill.

Embrace it. Feel *it.*

When I have the chance, I know what I need to do.

"You know, I was thinking," Anara says as she approaches me and Arthur, Ender and Quill trailing behind her. "I think we need to be more creative with our abilities."

"What you mean?" Ender asks.

Anara holds a hand out, a water droplet suspended just above her palm. "Like, what if I can do more than just form a shield with ice?" She motions to Ender. "What if his fire is capable of being shaped in different ways? Or Quill can do more with the objects around him?"

Arthur lays a hand on his chin as he considers her line of thought. "Unfortunately, I have no way of training you in those ways. I have no way of relating to any of you as far as your abilities are concerned." He sighs as he takes a good look at us one at a time. "What I can do, however, is help you consider what you can already do, and build on that. For instance—" He regards Anara, his teaching mode in full bloom. "—if you can create a shield from ice alone, perhaps you can form other weapons with that element." He then turns to Ender. "Or, if you can blast fire from your hands, can you move it in other directions to better serve your purpose? Perhaps you can try forming a shield of fire, as Anara can with Upsurge."

Ender nods thoughtfully and Anara looks off to the distance pensively. Arthur then takes a couple steps closer to Quill, studying him intently. "You can force inanimate objects to move to your will. Can you control things of the land that are smaller than what you've grown accustomed to?" He points to the broken crate on the concrete. "Those pieces, for example."

I watch everyone carefully. They glance at each other, new hope beaming in all of them. Arthur gives them unique ideas and more ways to use their abilities. Ways in which they likely never considered.

Then there's me. My abilities are limited. I can only use Gridlock to freeze things. I can only use Strike when I can connect with the sky. I can form electricity with my hands and throw it. Unfortunately, I cannot wield Strike indoors.

Or . . . perhaps I haven't figured out how.

Arthur gazes at me in deep thought. "You can only strike lightning outdoors, correct?"

"Yes." I fight off the ache I get every time I remind myself of that.

"If you can build electricity with just your hands, then you may be able to channel that to the rest of your body." He taps his chin with a finger. "And if you can throw the electricity from your hand, then you must be able to project it from yourself once it's channeled through your whole body."

His train of thought makes sense. The problem is getting my mind to believe that his theory is possible.

Arthur steps away from us, as far as he can to the edge of the training grounds. He folds his arms with a confident smile. "I look forward to watching your efforts."

"Why? So you can make fun of us?" Anara quips.

Arthur shakes his head. "Nonsense. I want to be the first to witness what all of you are capable of and realize how powerful you really are." He motions forward with his hand. "Proceed."

Quill steps up to the broken pieces of crate that lie scattered in a thin layer on the ground. His hand stretches out toward it, his luscious brown eyes turning green as grass. The sawdust and splinters gather into a pile, as if blown by a gust of wind. I watch in mesmerization as he walks along the mess that submits to the command of his power. Soon, the dust is rising from the ground in a ball, followed by the larger wooden planks that lie just feet in front of him. His creation doesn't turn into a weapon. It doesn't walk or attack at his command. It just rotates in a circular motion in the air. All the pieces are licked clean from the ground and moving slowly in beautiful unison. Then it's spinning, faster and faster until it becomes a blur. He chances a quick glance at me, a blink of an eye.

Admiring my backside, Zappy?

I blush. I don't want him to notice how much I'm admiring his abilities and how incredible he looks using them; his backside is just a perk of viewing the whole package.

No. You and your ego can admire it by yourself.

I do. It's a glorious part of my morning routine.

The formation stops dead while I'm still reeling from Quill's purrs in my mind. Then the debris disintegrates and falls into a pile back on the ground. He did just what Arthur recommended, and it worked. It was amazing.

He is amazing. Nothing he can say would change my mind on that.

Ender steps forward. "Here, compo."

With his hands, he builds a globe of fire. His eyes turn an intimidating shade of deep red, the fire growing and emanating its intense heat. He puts his wrists together like he's going to be arrested, but keeps his palms apart, the fire burning between them. When he claps, the fire blasts toward Quill faster than an arrow. My heart lurches for a moment, until Quill beautifully averts the fire in a way I haven't seen him do.

A small rock formation shoots up from the ground with a lift of his hand. He forms the rock around the fire to contain it in a large, stone ball that suspends in the air just in front of him. He throws it back to Ender, where it explodes at his feet.

As soon as the fire erupts, Ender contains it. Slowly, he lifts one of his hands, the fire roaring and following his lead when it rises. It becomes a fiery wall before him—a shield—large enough to protect him entirely. I stare in awe as he proves his true mastery over the flames, living up to his name from the ages-old poem. Arthur was right once again.

Ender and Quill laugh with glee and high-five each other, shouting compliments and exclamations that all blend together into a clamor of loud voices. Anara steps forward, water ready and flooding in her palm.

"You can do it, compa," Ender encourages her.

I can read it in her face. *If I can make a shield, I can make anything.*

The water in her hand grows into a peak, straight from where it takes root in her palm. It extends longer and longer, converting to ice as it goes. The tip turns lethally sharp once it's as long as her arm. She grips her newly formed weapon at the root and swings it around as I do with my sword. We manage to jump out of the way before she can slice any of us open.

Anara swings the icicle on the ground and it shatters like glass, breaking free from her hand. Then, she holds her right hand by her left shoulder. A new weapon forms; this time, it shoots out at an alarming speed, as fast as Quill was able to contain Ender's fire with rock. She thrusts it to her side, ready to fight with it again.

"That would be effective if you somehow lose your trident," Quill points out.

Anara shrugs. "I wish I knew about this when I used Gateway for the first time and that Dormant knocked my trident out of my hand."

"What important is you know now," Ender tells her. Anara's eyes soften at his words and she nods silently.

This is the time to find out if I can strike lightning without access to the sky.

I force the electricity to my hands. The sparks snap outside of my skin. I cross my arms over my chest to force it down my arms and along my shoulders. My skin hums and vibrates, growing warmer with each passing second. The snaps and crackles are deafening as the electricity reaches my shoulders. I crouch and bring my legs to my torso to make it connect to my limbs, and it spreads. Soon, my whole body is buzzing and zapping.

I should have thought this through. I don't know if I need to throw my hands down as I always have or if I have to use a different maneuver.

"We should get out of the way," Anara warns the others. "This could cause a lot of damage."

By instinct to their reaction, I unfurl myself. Nothing happens until I stretch my arms out.

A yellow dome expands from my body. The rim covers a large vicinity of the training grounds, then stops. With nothing left to do, I instinctively throw down my hands. Bolts rain down in all directions with a buzzing sound, followed by a *boom*, some hitting the foundation of one house and the steps leading to Arthur's. Metal objects fall over and wooden barrels explode into splinters.

That answers my question. And apparently, does a lot of damage. So much so that my friends had to find higher ground to avoid getting struck.

"Holy . . ." Arthur gasps.

"Dang, Doofus, you're dangerous!" Anara exclaims off to the side.

I gaze at her, flanked by Quill and Ender. Quill wears a playful smile, one that says he knew I could do it. Ender is still processing his shock.

"That was fun," I say through a giggle, thinking about what else I could do with this new skill. Simply stretching out my arms does the trick, and the electricity went in all directions. What if I want it to go to just one place?

"I need to do that again."

"Why?" Ender asks.

"I just need to check something."

I repeat the steps in my head, folding my body so the electricity flows all over. I turn toward a target, dangerously close to where Arthur is standing. He rushes to get out of the way as soon as I thrust my arms forward. The hole that burns into the target is evidence enough that my suspicions are correct: My power will go wherever I direct it. I can cover a large area or hit just one spot.

"Stop destroying my stuff!" Arthur shouts.

I laugh softly. "You should have prepared better, I suppose."

He scoffs. "I believe that's enough practice for one day. How about supper?"

"Actually, I was going to ask her if she wanted to take up the bow again."

Quill's voice has become my new favorite sound as he appears beside me. My heart leaps every time he shines that wickedly gorgeous smile. Seeing him used to send an aching sense of longing through me. It still does. This time, though, that longing is for a whole different reason.

"Very well." He points to Anara and Ender. "If you two are finished, perhaps you can help me clean this place up."

Ender whines obnoxiously. "I no want to clean."

"Too bad," Anara snaps and pushes him forward. "Let's go, you lazy troll." She spares a quick glance in my direction, and I swear I see her flash a knowing wink at me. Excited nerves flutter through me as I turn back to Quill. Alone once again.

"I was awful at archery," I say. I cringe at the memory, but I still manage to laugh. It was fun when he was training me at King Aldous's castle. His woodsy scent, his hands shifting my hips, his lips so close to the shell of my ear flooded all my senses, the blood pounding in my ears. Hating him proved impossible, no matter how hard I tried. His gentle touch, kind words, and patience warmed the coldness I forced around my heart.

"You weren't that bad," he responds in a reassuring tone. "And you will get better. You're learning from the master, after all."

There it is. The playfulness that sucks me in every time.

Quill holds out his hand for me to take and I happily accept as he leads me to the targets lined along the building wall decimated with holes. He plops the bow into my hands, once more placing his heart and trust with me. At the castle, I felt honored to hold something so dear to him. My feelings about him were complicated, but I was still determined to be safe with it.

My shooting is better than last time. I allow my hands to get a feel for the equipment, how smooth the pull is, the fletching between my fingers as I hold the arrow still. My shots are getting closer to the target, but I'm still not quite there.

"You're thinking too hard," Quill says, just as he did in Arythica. "In the heat of battle, you won't have time for that much thinking."

"In the heat of battle, if you handed this to me, I would be dead."

Quill's lips quirk up a bit. "Give yourself some credit. Try one more time, and I'll let you throw one of my knives."

Intrigued by his offer, I get back into position. Feet planted and target locked. I nock the arrow, not taking my eyes off the target, watching it like an enemy. A Backer. I lift the bow and pull back at the same time—

"Stop thinking!"

Quill's shout makes me jump. It breaks my aim and the arrow goes nowhere near where I wanted it. It stabs a rack close by, causing it to fall over and spill the weapons all over the ground among the mess of the practice boxes.

"I just fixed that!" Arthur complains in a high-pitched voice.

I gape at Quill. "What was that for?"

"If you think too hard, you're a dead target for an enemy to pounce, and you'll lose your aim." He points at the evidence.

I shove at him, containing my laughter. "You're mean, Forest Dweller."

He chuckles softly. "You haven't called me that in a while," he says in a despondent voice that pains me even more.

I focus on the colorful fletching that I roll between my fingers. A question wants to leap off my tongue, but I hold back. He might be wary and think of me as hasty. However, it's one that can come across as making conversation.

"Quill." I swallow hard, my mouth suddenly going dry. "What are you going to do once this war is over?"

His face turns solemn as he breaks eye contact and stares off into the distance, as if the answer is out there but he can't see it. "I'm not sure yet."

My eyebrows reach my hairline. "You're not sure?"

He shrugs, a soft chuckle blowing through his lips, a host of confessions dancing in his eyes, and a debate to share them. "I didn't have everything thought out when I left Arbol Village. I just wanted to leave and see where life took me." He shrugs. "I was being spontaneous for the first time in my life."

An uncertain plan that most likely doesn't involve me. "Do you still think you can be spontaneous?"

"I'd like to be. I've started to like having unlimited options on what to do with my freedom."

"And you plan on being spontaneous . . . alone?"

He shifts uncomfortably. His prolonged silence has me shifting on my feet too. I practically feel him hiding from me again. Unspoken truths stand in the middle that neither of us are telling each other. It's all so ridiculous that I'm on the verge of screaming.

"I never want to be alone again," he admits quietly, "if that answers your question."

It's not a blunt response, but one where I can read between the lines. Whether he plans to spend his days with me or someone else, I wish to know. For now, I have to be satisfied with his answer. We find the concrete interesting as our feet shuffle over it, waiting for the other to speak, but nothing happens.

"What about you?" he asks, seemingly scared of my answer.

Over the years, I thought a lot about winning this war. Killing the Dormant King. Being free. What I didn't always consider was what I wanted to do after all is said and done.

"I'd like to find a place to settle down," I answer, which is the honest truth. "I just don't know where yet."

"Not Ketra?"

I shrug. "Only because of my best friend and the chief having resentment toward me. Other than that, perhaps Sabbia."

He raises an incredulous eyebrow. "You want to live in the desert?"

I scoff. "Ideally, no." I put on a distant expression, looking ahead of us at nothing. "But only because I want to be with Calista."

Quill nods, lips in a tight line. "Makes sense."

Through another pause, I wait for him to ask me if I plan to do this alone also, but he doesn't. I'd love for Quill to be with me. But I have to entertain the possibility that all of us will go our separate ways, and it breaks my heart.

I nod toward the target. "I think I'll stop here for now."

Quill clears his throat and nods. "All right. You did good. Getting better." He purses his lips and steps around me. The world shrinks to just the two of us. Not a single sound or thought to distract me.

"Well, good night, Zappy." He gives me a smile that holds nothing but sorrow.

I watch him retreat back to the house. The farther he walks away from me, the more the yearning deepens in my chest. I don't want him to leave. I don't want this to end. I want things to go back to the way they were with the banter I love so much. The teasing and laughter that makes it that much easier to get through the day.

I want it all back.

"Quill."

He stops and turns around, his eyes heavy with sadness. The same kind I've been feeling for far too long. The kind that aches with the heart's denial.

I see it change in an instant when I wrap my arms around him and bury my face in his chest. He stiffens to my touch, frozen solid. I give it a few seconds before I tighten my hold. His scent, his solid muscles, the way he feels in my arms, I let it encompass every fiber of my being as his arms hang limply at his sides. I want to remember how this feels, just to carry with me if something were to happen to either of us.

I'm done with the denial game, and he should be too.

"I never should have doubted you. You're the kindest person I know."

My words of solace and comfort melt the ice holding his arms captive. My heart goes in flames as his arms slide around my neck.

He slowly molds himself against me, his whole body loosening and letting go. Suddenly, he buries his nose into my neck and holds me like I'm his only lifeline. The only thing that matters to him.

Neither of us dares to move. This is new territory. Neither of us realized how badly we needed this to happen. A pivotal moment. He does little to hide his emotion when his sniffs move my hair and the soft exhale of his breath flutters against my neck. I absorb it all and allow it to become a part of me.

I loosen my grip, and he hesitates for a split second before he lets go of me. I feel a crack in my heart as his eyes brim in red, speaking more than any words ever could. I hold his face in my hands and give him a reassuring smile before I head back to the house.

"Good night, Forest Dweller."

CHAPTER 21

ANARA

I don't even have to ask.

Once I'm ready for bed, Ender settles beside me. He is a respectable gentleman when he gets situated on top of the covers and keeps his distance. I know he wants to join the clamor of soldiers dining in the hall across the camp, drinking and saying stupid crap to each other, but he stays with me instead. Training together today brought us even closer in a way I never imagined. I worried that I annoyed him, yet he *asked* me if I needed him to stay with me again. I couldn't say no.

With him next to me, his face so peaceful in deep sleep, I feel safe, just as I did the first time. I fall asleep faster now. All I need to help my sleepless nights is to have a safe presence. A presence that accepts me, one that I trust with my life.

The last time we were in this cramped bedroom, we were en route to Luna Island, and Havanna was crying in the bed next to me. She cried on my lap until we both fell asleep. The beginning of a new friendship, thanks to the compo beside me.

Then my peace completely vanishes.

Screeching noises, explosions, and shouting commands have me sitting straight up. I can feel Ender launching off the bed with enough momentum that my body reaches midair before slamming back down on the mattress. Wave licks my face and paws at my arms to get me moving.

Arthur bursts in as everyone else is leaving. "We're under attack! Dormants are crossing the city walls! Hurry up!"

I scramble for my trident, bumping into corners of mattresses and the walls before I finally find it among the dark, and race outside. Arthur is nowhere to be seen now and everything is in utter chaos.

Houses are on fire. Lightning bolts strike in all directions. Quill is on the other side of the training grounds firing Pineapple Shell arrows everywhere and Ender is forming his wall of fire and burning Dormants alive with it. I fail to see where I can be of use until I see the shadows of Dormants dancing among the flames growing bigger as they hurtle toward me. I race down the steps from the front of the house with my hand getting colder and colder, and I think about training yesterday. We figured out what else we could do with our abilities, and it was more than we ever imagined. I have that chance now when I come up with an idea to keep the Dormants from getting closer.

I palm the concrete with my ice-covered hand. A sheet of ice expands at the speed of a crashing wave that spreads straight toward the Dormants. The slippery texture has them losing their balance. As they struggle to regain footing, I step onto the ice and use my trident to propel me forward, sliding along on my boots. Using my trident to go for the kill is a no-brainer, but something occurs to me: If I can force water *into* something, surely, I can force it out.

An evil grin plays on my lips as I extend my hand. Water appears on their skin that starts off as beads, then progresses to trickles until it becomes rivers of liquid spilling to their feet from every orifice. Upsurge dehydrates them from the inside out, their bodies gaunt and dry as sand. My trident delivers the final blow that mixes the dust with the water. With Ender's fire in such close proximity, the ice melts quickly. Screams of soldiers are followed by the roars of Dormants that get louder as I close the distance on the east wall bordering the city. Smoke permeates all senses, the cries of the injured and the roars of Dormants stuck in my head enough to ignite nightmares. The incoming trauma that crawls through me sends bile to the back of my throat. I force it down with a hard swallow and focus on even breathing as I run. I have no room for vulnerability now.

I round a wooden building to find a soldier writhing against a Dormant's grip, his leg a mangled mess. His screams of agony pierce my ears as the condition of his leg gets worse. Two more show up with flashing teeth. All I have time for is to create enough water in my palm to take out all three of them. I lift two of them off the ground with the water, then turn it into a skewer that rips through them like cotton. The prongs of my trident perforate the other Dormant and I rip it out of its body. They all flop over, then burst into dust.

Quill's voice encircles my mind. *Go to every corner of the camp and make sure we've cleared everything.*

The soldier remains immobile and gravely injured. I can't find it in me to leave him, bleeding and wailing.

Ender wouldn't.

I summon more water to my palm, then shower it over the victim's leg to clean the wound. I do my best to block out his incessant screams that dare break my focus, the water running clearer the more I pour. The second I stop, the bleeding continues. The wound is too deep. He'll bleed to death before dawn breaks. His eyes sear into mine, wordlessly pleading me to help him.

I may not have anything to go home to, but he might.

Behind me is a door to a small, two-story home. I loop my arms under the soldier's armpits, drag him backward to the door, and gently lay him down. After a few vigorous kicks on the door, I resume bringing him to safety.

I'm immediately met with a kitchen, fully stocked with a wood stove, fireplace, a wash basin, and stacks of cloth on the space next to the burners of the stove. A staircase spirals to the second floor, which naturally creates a dark, safe crawl space underneath to store old chairs and furniture. I shut the door behind us and set the back of a chair under the knob to lock it.

"I'm finding something to wrap your leg with, stay with me," I explain to him, to which he responds with a nod. "Stay still, don't move. I'll have to leave once I'm done, but stay in here and recover. If you go out there and die trying to fight, I'm not responsible. Understand?"

His face is wrinkled in excruciating pain, but he nods again. Like he's going to be much use in his state.

I snatch the handful of towels from the wood stove and kneel next to him. I tie the ends of four together to create a long band of cloth and tightly wrap it around his leg that has him hissing and bucking with the contact. I keep wrapping until I can tuck in a corner into the cloth. Once I'm sure the wound isn't bleeding through, I loop my arms under his pits again and drag him to the space under the stairs. I rearrange boxes and furniture around to shield him in.

"Now listen to me." My gaze connects with his. "Stay here, and *do not move*. If anything makes its way in here, don't make a sound and stay completely still. You will have less of a chance of being detected that way. Understand?"

He nods, his body tense in reaction to the pain. "Thank you," he strains to say.

I head back to the door and leave him there, hoping he will survive the night.

The sounds outside seem to have quieted. All I can detect is crackling wood and the strong, thick scent of smoke. The smell of loss and desolation. Smoke reaches my throat and burns, filling up my lungs and shortening my breath.

I can only see a few feet in front of me. Even then, I can barely open my eyes from the sting of smoke. The smell invades my skin, my hair, my clothes. I run through it, hoping it will be clear in a different part of the camp. With the chaos dying down, I don't know how to find my friends. Panic races through my veins, unsure and lost.

This scenario brings me back to the other dimension. Dead silence. The purple mist clouding my surroundings with all the Dormant King's creations lurking among it. I'm right back in that place now, especially when a dark shadow blocks my path. Then another.

With a thrust of my hand, a long, knife-sharp icicle shoots out of my palm. The newly discovered backup weapon I have at my disposal.

I cut through the smoke with it until I hit a Dormant, and finish it off with a stab in the chest. Then kill the other one with a twist and swipe of my hand across its face. Victory surges through me when the red dissipates from their eyes and dust billows around me. A tentacle shoots at me as I start to emerge into clearer air and wraps around my neck.

Its mouth comes into full view while the other tentacle has an icicle ready. The icicle in my hand doesn't make for a good angle to let me loose. Despair sinks to my stomach. Death by Dormant was absolutely not how I want to leave this world.

The Dormant's body unexpectedly splits in half. The grip on my neck immediately loosens and I'm surrounded with plumes of dust. Ender stands before me.

With a Dormant creeping up behind him.

I open my mouth to sound my warning, only for him to turn and swing his axe. It makes a pathetic cry as the blades sink into its head.

Ender turns back to me, displaying a stunningly handsome side smile when he holds his hand out for me to take. "Quill and Havanna on other side. Bennarus searching rest of camp. Come."

I fist his shirt, clinging to his chest for dear life as he lifts me back to my feet.

"Thank you," I wheeze out.

By some miracle, we escape the smoke and come to a clear neighborhood. The dirty brick streets are swarmed with frantic soldiers, men, and women. Holes are the new style of most of the houses that are not consumed by fire. I begin to think it's because of the random Dormant attack . . .

Until I hear the caw and shrieks above us that grab everyone's attention.

A group of four Dormants soar above us.

CHAPTER 22

QUILL

All battles we fight together seem effortless. Havanna and I take one side together, and Ender manages to find Anara and fight with her in another area.

Havanna asks the people if they're hurt. Arthur is yelling for everyone to hide in the underground shelter at the training grounds. People start to head in that direction when Ender and Anara find us.

"We no done," Ender says, pointing to the sky at four Dormants hovering over us. Havanna groans while Anara curses under her breath. Havanna wastes no time in summoning Strike again, her hand glowing bright as a lantern in the night. Her preparation is interrupted when a Dormant rains fire from its mouth, barely singeing us as we move out of the way. The next Dormant flicks icicles, one by one, stabbing the brick streets like knives.

Anara summons a sheet of ice big enough to shield the four of us as one assault after another attempts to slay us. With the constant fire, her shield rapidly melts onto our bodies.

"I can't hold them!" she shouts, straining with the effort.

Ender becomes a walking blowtorch as he darts out of the shelter of the shield and sends gusts of fire at the monsters. Anara's sheet cracks in the middle. Havanna prepares to use Strike again. We turn to the army in the air and I take out my bow to fire.

"Quill!" Havanna screams, but she's too late to warn me.

A Dormant swoops down from behind and snatches my bow.

"Hey!" I yell as it flies off with the only thing I have left of my brother. It crosses the walls of the camp and heads off into the expansive land. Without my bow, I'm nothing. Even my powers are useless. My stomach plummets with hopelessness as I attempt to run after it to see where it's going.

"Bolt!" Havanna calls behind me.

Pounding feet round the house close by. Bolt's muscular gorilla form plows toward his owner at full speed, kicking up dust in his wake. Havanna sheathes her sword and runs toward her Bennaru. "We need to chase that Dormant! Eagle, now!"

My hopelessness dissolves. Bolt shifts into an eagle and Havanna jumps onto his back. They take off for the skies, dragging my utter disbelief with them.

She's going after that Dormant. Just to retrieve my bow.

"If I didn't know you owned her heart, that was a telltale sign right there," Anara mentions, pointing at Havanna and Bolt.

There may be truth to that. Yesterday, Havanna hugged me. Told me things that erased the doubts I always had about myself. Told me I was kind. Words that were a balm to my wounds.

The only person I could rely on for affirmation or any kind of affection was Indigo, and even that wasn't always consistent. Being unloved my whole life, that one hug from her filled a void that made years of longing and emotion tighten my throat. I forgot how good affection felt. How good it felt just to be hugged. I owe her for breathing life back into me. I owe her my protection.

I've been an idiot.

I whistle for Koa. *Let's get my bow. Follow Bolt.*

Only a few seconds pass before I hear the flaps of heavily beating wings.

"Wave! Let's go!" Anara calls.

"We come with you," Ender announces. "And get head out of butthole!"

Anara scoffs and rolls her eyes when Wave catches up to her as a jaguar and makes quick work of shifting into a macaw. Talons clasp around the hand I reach overhead, and we're in the air. I grip chunks of feathers on his neck with anxiety and urgency. Koa feels it too and flaps his wings stronger and harder. We make steady progress toward Havanna, although not fast enough.

The sky presents a change in colors to signal sunrise's beginning, the cloud cover blocking its true radiance and making it more difficult to see where the Dormant is headed. Havanna and Bolt are currently the size of my thumb. Too far for me to gain on.

Down below, Petros is in grave danger. Moving dots indicate fleeing civilians and villagers. The darker, larger dots that follow them are the Dormants. Some stop moving as they collapse and completely still. Plumes of smoke pump upward and blend with the clouds. The grass that used to be a full, healthy green is now burnt to a crisp. A few flashes of white pop in succession. The fleeing spots freeze in place, staying encased in the white substance.

Ice. The Dormants are freezing people to death. This has gone from a bad situation to a dire one.

Faster, I urge Koa, patting him on the neck to encourage him. He creates a few more large flaps that push us forward and gain us a view of a civilization ahead.

Havanna and Bolt slowly descend, led by the Dormant. I twist around and find Anara and Ender following us on their Bennarus, bent forward and eager. All helping me retrieve my bow.

The friends I never knew I needed.

We land in front of the entrance to a city, our Bennarus turning into their smaller forms and nestling on our shoulders. The pathways are muddy, dirty, and scattered with paper, broken wooden boxes, and crates. All the buildings lack sufficient light, dark and depressing. The smell is a rancid combination of body odor and human waste, strong enough to make my nose crinkle and bile to rise.

We were led to Siro. What I don't understand is why we're here of all places.

The answer stands before us the deeper we venture inside. A large group of people dressed in rags, covered in dirt and grime, sit in a line along the wall of a stone building. Blindfolded with a single cloth and whimpering in fear for their lives. The Dormant flies over the enemies holding them hostage and lands on the roof, my bow in its mouth.

The Dormant King stands with the remaining Backers before the hostages. His black clothes billow with the subtle breeze that chills us to the bone, and the crown of thorns rests on his grayish-pale skin. He turns and gives us a wicked snarl that says he's done playing games.

The Bennarus inflate into their fighting forms as they sense the danger before us, growling on approaching their enemy. The Dormant King is too quick when, with a swipe of his hand, traps them against a nearby wall.

"My my, you Descendants managed to find each other," he croons, then scowls at Anara. "You, Water Descendant, surprise me the most. You have more smarts than I give you credit for, being able to make it out of my home."

"You put me in an area that was full of water," Anara says in her notoriously snarky tone. "I'd say you're the one with no smarts."

"On the contrary. My lovely friend brought you here, didn't it?" He peers at the Dormant in question, still perched on the roof of the wall above the hostages. "You fell right into my trap." He winks at us with nothing but arrogance. The Dormant King's eyes blaze with a determination that makes itself at home in his bones. "I will stop at nothing to bring Petros to its knees." He holds a hand out to a Backer, a hard stare aimed at the people against the wall. The Backer carefully lays a glowing blade on his palm. He aims it at a man's throat. "I will start with the people with no smarts whatsoever. Try and stop me."

Portals open behind us, reminding us of the power he copied from Anara.

No. Not this again.

My feet slide backward in the mud and gravitate to the open hole behind me. I fall to my knees as I attempt to claw myself away from it. Mud covers my hands, clothes, under my fingernails that split and bleed from my efforts.

A gust of wind pushes against me, against the hole. Behind me, Ender uses Gale to reverse the air pulling us toward the portals, pushing us away from them.

"Hmm, this presents a challenge," the Dormant King hums. "Good thing I'm the most powerful king this land has ever seen!"

Water builds between his hands. Each drop turns into a stream, into a river, until a torrent develops and he sends it at us. The heavy rush has the potential to take us all down.

Anara uses Upsurge and diverts the torrent down an alley before it can touch us. Dormants appear from alleyways and buildings, prowling for their next mission.

"Quill, compo," Ender whispers. "Tell Dormants to come here. I have plan."

I aim my hand toward the Dormants surrounding their owner. *You want us? Come get us.*

Their heads perk up, eyes locked on us. Then they charge in a thunderous rhythm.

Ender steps up beside me, coated in mud. He claps once and spreads his hands apart, a wall of fire forming with the growing gap of his palms that serves as a protective barrier between us and the Dormants, then he shoves it forward. It plows through them, burning them all at once. I can't help but grin at the Dormant King's grim expression.

We're strong, and he knows it.

"Let's finish this," Havanna growls.

We don't wait for another forceful attack. It goes from a steady walk to a full-on sprint toward the Dormant King and his Backers.

CHAPTER 23

HAVANNA

The Dormant on the roof drops the bow into the Backer's hands and the battle begins. He and six other Backers split up and run through different alleyways. A wise method of diversion, making this mission complicated. Quill palms a knife on his thigh and makes for the Backer holding his bow.

"I'll go help Quill. I'll be back," I tell Anara and Ender, and take off without waiting for their responses. I don't know what mysterious power possesses me to chase that Dormant for Quill's bow. All I know is, the idea of losing something that means the world to you by an evil source is enough to make me lose my own mind. The armband from Jael is a part of me and my very being. For Quill's bow, it's different. It's his means of living. Of fighting back. Of protecting.

I head down the path Quill went and attempt to follow the footprints. Muddy water and possibly waste spatters all up my boots, pants, and my bare arms. Each step, each spatter, is a test of self-control to hold back from vomiting from the smell. The slippery surface makes speed near impossible until I reach compact ground toward the back of the city. I turn to the right to a dirty path that runs between the city barrier and another run-down building.

A Backer cuts my path short and swings his blade at me. I manage to duck just in time as it nearly misses my torso, then grab my sword and strike back.

"You dare destroy our fortress and our companions?" The Backer inches closer to me as I move backward, upper lip curled, the tips of our blades aimed at each other. With one hand behind my back, I get Strike ready.

"You dare kill Jael?"

Before he can respond, I connect my hand to the sky and throw it down with a bolt that kills him in an instant.

"And I dare destroy you," I murmur.

I veer to the left and beg mentally for Quill to tell me where he is. I wind through cottages on the verge of collapse while screaming at my own senses to ignore the awful stench of this place.

A pained screech leads me to the direction I need to go. I pray it isn't Quill when I run between two cottages located close to each other and come up to another muddy pathway. I run straight in the middle of Quill and the Backer, who has a knife embedded in his back and lying face down in the mud. Quill catches his breath with a satisfied smile, partially hunched over. I smile back at him when I go to retrieve the bow that the Backer dropped.

I pick up the weapon, shake off the excess mud, and toss it to him. His satisfied smile grows.

"Thank you."

A loud whooshing of flapping wings gives us no time to celebrate this small victory. I turn, believing that my Bennaru has come to retrieve me—

"Havanna!"

A Dormant's talons open and dive straight for my arms, then I'm airborne.

Siro becomes smaller and smaller the higher we go. Nothing below me to land on safely, nothing to secure me in place, and not knowing whether the Dormant is going to let me go or not has my screams tearing my throat to shreds. I kick my feet and grab at the talons digging into my bare skin. My weight dragging down makes the talon embed itself into my skin and draw blood.

Arrows flit by, a sign of Quill coming to my rescue again. One narrowly misses my leg and zips past us. As long as the Dormant is zigzagging in the sky, he isn't going to make a good shot.

The bow is slippery and that freaking Dormant won't stop moving. But I'm coming for you, Zappy.

Hope rekindles within me, albeit short-lived. The Dormant turns and flies back to Siro just as we were crossing over grassy land. I see a hint of the gray of Quill's shirt, his arm aimed at us as he uses Transmission to lure the Dormant back. The battle is lost when it turns around to head back to its original destination. The Dormant King wins this time. Using Gridlock on it will send us both plummeting to the earth, so here I remain trapped. It roars into the wind, unrestrained and triumphant.

My body sways with the momentum as it dives, then soars back upward. I don't recognize the pain as I attempt to tear my arm out of its grasp, creating a deep, red gash in place of my olive branch tattoo and the inside of my left forearm. The beats of my heart increase in speed, panic and outrage constrict in my chest as I try to find a way to breathe.

Koa releases a war cry in the form of a shrill caw and plunges forward to gain in on us. They're still not close enough to grab me or get a good aim on the Dormant. Below me is nothing but grass and spots of trees. Just ahead is what I recognize as Douma Lake, where we camped a couple weeks ago. If the Dormant drops me, I'm done for.

Its claws still have a hold on my hand, giving me no room to slip from its grasp. Even with my body swinging in unnatural ways, I pull my hand down as hard as I can possibly muster. Anything to give me a sliver of hope of breaking free, despite the blood trickling down my arms.

By some miracle, I manage to free my left hand. Its foot reaches back to grab it, but I wave it about to avoid its clutches and grab for the sword still strapped to my back. In one movement, I unsheathe it and slice its underbelly. It screams loud enough to shake the kingdom and releases me.

Leaving me to free fall straight toward Douma Lake.

I scream my heart out, despair and tears following closely behind. Death will consume me within minutes and nothing can help me. The water I've begged to experience my whole life will be my end. Ketra will never know how hard I tried to save them. Petros will never know how hard I tried.

When I can turn my body enough to face upward, I see Quill. No Bennaru to guide him. No Dormant. Executing a perfect downward dive as he free falls toward me.

He will be too late.

CHAPTER 24

ENDER

Just as Anara and I prepare our abilities and gain on the Dormant King, he pulls a fast one on us.

A hole opens behind him and he steps into it, bringing two Backers with him. The hole closes and the place where he was holds no trace of him.

Anara and I skid to a stop, frantically searching the area.

"Did they just use Gateway to escape?" Anara shouts.

I don't respond. I'm too occupied being on the lookout. From what I understand about Gateway, he could use it to reappear anywhere he wants. He could show up behind me and kill me when I least expect it.

"I can't believe this," she mutters, cursing under her breath. "Freaking Havanna just had to drop us to help her boy toy."

I have a different view on the matter. It's not just the Dormant King we have to fight; it's the rest of his Backers. The four of us are not enough to do it all. The need for an army is an emergency situation now.

A *whoosh* gives away his resurgence when a black hole opens up within fifteen feet of us, but without the Backers. I use Blaze as soon as I spot him. Anara charges forward with her trident as he takes the nearby mud with Upsurge and causes it to move in circular motions. The spinning wheel of mud makes a perfect shield for my attacks. Anara, using Upsurge herself, moves his mud wheel back to the ground. He gets hit with my fire and falls onto his back, burn marks appearing on his skin immediately. He leans up to use Manipulation to block it from coming any farther and throws it back to me. I simply absorb it into my body through my hands, then channel it to my arm as I reach for my axe.

The Dormant King somehow forgets that Anara is right behind him, trident ready to stab him in the back. My axe becomes engulfed in flames and I give her a subtle nod: She gets him from behind and I'll attack him in front.

That nod gives me away. He twists behind him and throws Anara against a wall with Manipulation faster than I can get a single word out of my mouth. The impact is hard enough that her body thuds face-first on the ground. She doesn't move to recover. Hurt enough to let my anger fuel the fire in my axe.

Nobody hurts my compa.

I swing the axe over my head and slam it down, covering the ground with my fire and forcing it toward him as fast as Havanna's lightning. He turns in time to use Manipulation to hold it back. A sheen of sweat glistens on his forehead, the effort depleting his energy. It only motivates me to push my fire toward him more. This game of pushing against each other only becomes an unavoidable impasse. He won't back down, and neither will I.

"You Descendants are so stupid," he shouts with a strained voice. He gives my fire one final, powerful shove and it reverses its course. I let the ground absorb the remaining flames when I push down with my hand.

Suddenly, I'm hovering about ten feet in the air. My cape whips about behind me, then wraps around my neck. My hands reach for it by instinct to tear at it, but it only tightens. Blood rushes to my face and head. I kick at nothing, pulling and clawing at the cloth as it slowly cuts off my air supply. The cape only reflects my effort with a few measly shreds. Death by my own clothing is not how I want to go, but I'm powerless against it. The Dormant King's Manipulation is too strong for my own muscles.

Anara is still face down in the mud.

Get up compa. Get up. You're stronger than this.

"When will you see that I cannot be defeated?" he shouts with triumph. He loosens it off my neck just enough to create a simple noose, hanging the loose material in the air above me, and releases my body from suspension. He's nearly successful in trying to hang me, but I pull the cloth from my neck just enough that I can still hold myself up. The noose tightens even more.

I'm completely unable to breathe now. I will be dead within seconds.

I put all the energy I have into my hands, then use Blaze on the cape. The material is made with Fire Stones, which may take longer to burn this off, but I have to try. Anara hasn't recovered. I need to stay alive to save her.

The fire permeates the cape, only reaching the first layer on the noose. I cry out with a roar that could take down a Dormant as I force the fire farther, deeper, until I feel it against my skin. My eyes shut tightly as I throw my all into saving myself.

Just as I'm tumbling to the edge of death, everything is released and I fall with a *thud*. I lightly massage my throat, red and tender with burns. I work to refill my lungs with as heavy of breaths as I can muster that only come out in wheezes.

The next moment I can lift my head, the Dormant King's dirty boots stop within inches of me. His hand grips my neck and tightens.

"Thanks to you, I'm much closer to my destiny."

Purple tendrils run along his hand, wrist, and arm. I have nothing in me to stop him. I'm rapidly declining in strength and power, leaving me limp and useless. His hand does nothing to suffocate me, but the fire within me dies off, as if put out with water. I let him have it. All I have the strength for is finding my breath again.

He lets go of me and shoves me over like a broken toy no longer useful for playing. Lifeless in the mud, I hear an odd *thud*. I shift my eyes just enough to see the Dormant King fall face down.

With a trident stuck in his back.

Covered in mud, Anara stands just feet behind him with clenched fists and an angry glare. Relief floods my veins to see her alive and standing. I need to get over my near-lifeless state and get up. I push myself to my knees and tear off my cape with a vengeance.

The relief is rapidly replaced with dread when the Dormant King moves. Then he uses an elbow to push himself forward, then the other in an army crawl toward me.

"A flimsy trident is not enough to stop me," he grunts out. "I will crush you all with the might of a thousand kingdoms."

He doesn't have a chance to prove himself when Anara collects enough water and mud in her hands to form a rope. It zips in a stream toward the Dormant King and wraps around his ankle to pull him away from me. He turns over onto his side and turns the liquid to icicles at a concerningly fast rate and fires them at her. A motion of her hand shatters the ice at her will.

The trident ends up in his hands, ripped clean from his back. He throws it at me before I can move.

Straight to my chest.

I stumble back from the force. Somehow, I don't feel much of anything. Anara's mouth is wide open in a bloodcurdling scream that I can't hear. My fingers reach for the trident and I yank it out. Three holes take up space under my ribs, the middle being the deepest, and two smaller ones on either side making just a divot into my skin. Blood trickles from all of them, heavy, flowing creeks along my torso, and drips onto the mud beneath me. It's then that I feel an excruciating stinging and overwhelming throbbing.

"I told you, I am not one to be defeated," the Dormant King growls hoarsely, the holes on his back closing up and healing. Anara forms another attack with Upsurge and runs forward just as the Dormant King creates a portal that he jumps into with ease. The hole closes before she can reach him, causing her to skid to a stop.

Anger seeps into her expression and there are dribbling tears on her cheeks to show for it. Tears I want to wipe away from her beautiful face while I tell her I'm going to be all right. Even if I'm hollow and empty.

That was my plan before everything went black.

CHAPTER 25

QUILL

I've done aerial shooting before. I've jumped off trees that reached the sky. I've experienced falling long distances with only a branch to stop my descent.

Never in my life have I jumped off my Bennaru without thinking to save a girl.

The moment the Dormant dropped her, I commanded Koa to finish it off, and I jumped. I have never fallen this far with nothing to land on or hold me, and it's scaring the daylights out of me. I do my share of screaming, overwhelmed with adrenaline, as I tumble in the air. I adjust to the amount of air pushing against me and the gravity shoving me down. I contort my body to find the right position, straightening out when I'm finally diving headfirst.

And all I see is her.

Havanna's hair blows from behind her as she falls, framing her perfect, gorgeous face that holds a resolved dread. She knows this is her end if I don't reach her.

I extend my hand toward her, increasing my speed. She likely has less than a minute before she lands in the water. I shove that thought aside, putting it with the other thoughts and fears I will address later. I have to think of something else. *Now.*

Koa, I need you to hurry and catch us. Bolt, you need to get here. No questions.

Koa wastes no time in finding me, based on the sound of his beating wings. From the corner of my eye, he's also diving headfirst, but not toward Havanna. He reaches to grab me with his talons to save me. His owner. The one that has priority above anyone else. My life is the least of my priorities.

"No! Let me go!" I swat at his talons and I'm tumbling again. "Catch her! She's going to die in the water if you don't make it in time!"

Koa caws in protest, but he finally listens to me and dives for her at an alarming rate. He swoops underneath Havanna's falling body just in time to catch her, mere feet above the water's surface. I have half a second to realize that Koa hasn't flown away yet. He's hovering, waiting for me.

When I land on his back with such force, Koa becomes off-balance and Havanna and I topple off and land in the water.

Cold seeps into my bones. The movement of water rushes into my ears, even more so when I wave my hands, about to level myself. Each motion is met with the resistance from my clothes. I open my eyes and it stings like nothing else, but I shove that in the box of my mind as I look for Havanna.

A form darker than the water shakes and trembles with bubbles trailing upward. I curse to myself and launch in her direction. The water is killing her right in front of me. I reach for her hand and yank her body toward me, holding her close to my chest as I kick with all my might.

Only seconds pass when I recognize Koa's shadow, his beating wings forming ripples that move my hair in all directions. His claws scrape against my forearms, then tighten around my wrist, tugging me with all his might out of the water. In his other talon is Havanna, hanging limply as he holds onto her ankle. Our combined weight for Koa to carry causes us to scratch the surface of the lake until we reach the shore. He gently sets us on the grass, where I immediately scramble blindly for anything that might feel like Havanna.

A figure in black lays limply beside me and I claw through the grass to get to her.

"Havanna!" I grip her shoulders and shake her limp body. A lack of response sends me into a deep hysteria. My throat tightens, my breaths constricting as I shake her again. Her body still convulses beneath my grasp. Cold, low energy and sheer dread send trembles spreading to every limb. "Havanna!"

Water shows its signs of working against her electricity. Blisters form on her arms. Her skin turns from a tinge of red to a deep blood red.

This is exactly how I felt when Indigo was dying in my arms. I was too late and I was hopeless and helpless to save him. I fear I'm too late for her too.

Not again not again not again not again.

The sound of flapping wings thunders next to me and Bolt lands feet away and shifts into a gorilla. His urgent steps rumble the earth as he races to Havanna to nudge her with his furry hand, accompanied by scared whines and huffs.

"Bolt, stop." I pat him on the head. The tremble in my body reveals itself in my voice. "Stop for a minute."

I lay my ear on her heart. It's beating.

I place a finger under her nostrils to feel for the heat of her breath. I watch for the rise and fall of her chest, and nothing happens.

She needs to be dry. There's only one way to do that, even if she's humiliated later. Any fighting chance is worth taking.

"Koa . . ." I turn to my Bennaru, now in wolf form. "Help me get her clothes off. You too, Bolt."

I avert my eyes the best I can as Bolt changes to a gorilla form and lifts her shirt over her head with his ape fingers. I unbutton her pants and shove them down her hips, making sure not to peer at what's underneath. Koa tugs one of the pant legs down her ankles and I grasp the other and pull them off. This is not how I imagined seeing her for the first time, but I'm desperate. I even lift her head up to gather her hair and lay it on the grass so it doesn't touch her neck.

"Dry her off with your fur," I command both Bennarus.

Koa slumps his body along her bare torso as Bolt uses the hair on his arms to work on her legs. The blisters dissipate ever so slightly, but she's still not breathing.

"Come on, Zappy," I beg her. "I need you to heal. *Heal!*"

That single word flashes a memory before my eyes and I freeze.

The Dormant King healed my arm wound with Transform. He healed his own wounds when I threw a knife at him. With the way he moves around now, no one would guess that he had been stabbed.

Transform can *heal.*

"I don't know if this will work," I say, "but I'm going to try."

I hold a hand over her bare torso, barely catching a glimpse of her leather underwear, a thread tying it together at her hips. I immediately look away and focus on letting Transform work through my body. Nothing seems to happen at first, with the exception of the redness of her skin turning to a shade of pink. The blisters melt into her skin. I picture the muscles in her body, her stomach, her lungs, all full of water, and command it upward toward her throat to come out her mouth. I continue to let my mind imagine the water working through the intestines, between her ribs, away from her heart.

Two minutes pass. Nothing happens. She stays unconscious, limp on the grass. My head begins to ache as the seconds tick by, her skin begins to go back to its tan complexion, but she still doesn't wake up. The exertion has me grunting out in frustration, in rage, in fear.

"Come on, WAKE UP!" I grind out through my clenched teeth, the pressure building behind my eyes. "Listen to me. I never meant to hurt you, in any way, shape, or form. I'm sorry. I'm so sorry." I swallow deeply with what I'm going to say next. Words I have never said out loud to anyone. I continue in a shaky, near whisper. "I care so much about you, and not only as just a friend. If nothing else, you have to know that. You've saved me and been there for me more than anyone I've known. You've shown me affection and love in a way no one in my life ever has. It's impossible not to fall for you even more."

I feel the need to tell her more. I don't know if I can claim that I love her. Rather, I don't know if I *should*.

I intensify Transform, my headache a near–blinding pulse in my temples. "You need to live," I whisper. "I need you to live so I can make things right. I will never push you away. I will never hurt you again. I will go wherever you go when this is all over. I promise. *Please*, Havanna."

Her body lurches. I turn completely rigid when water dribbles out of her mouth. Her head rolls to the side and she coughs out more.

I'm not dreaming. She's alive.

I start to laugh in relief.

"That's good, isn't it?" I ask Bolt in desperation, to which he responds with a huff. Havanna coughs a few more times and her eyes finally open to slits. I blow out breaths of relief that turn into soft laughter. I forget that I even have a headache.

I take her face in my hands and plant a kiss on her forehead. Something else I have never done with anyone. I gaze into her eyes that widen a little more, dazed, but awake nonetheless. That's all I can hope for.

Her eyebrows bunch together as she studies me, as if trying to remember who I am. I pray that her injuries haven't ruined her memory.

"Quill," she says softly.

"Hey." I brush a hair out of her face.

"Did you . . . did you save me?"

The headache comes back with a vengeance, a reminder of how hard I worked to save her. "If my splitting headache is any indication, then yes."

Her eyes roam down to her body. "Um, what happened to my clothes?"

"I was trying to get you as dry as I could," I desperately explain. "I didn't see anything, I swear."

She smiles weakly. "Thank you."

I continue to examine her, remembering how scared I was of losing her minutes ago. How I jumped and dove for her without a second thought. The dance of relief, terror, panic, and adrenaline fighting each other in my mind and body. The exertion I put into Transform that nearly killed me.

The relief of seeing her alive seems to have given me a moment to react to the aftershock of extreme anxiety. Suddenly, I'm taken over by a cold sweat and something working its way from my stomach to my throat.

I hold up a finger. "Hold that thought."

I get up and run to the water's edge and make it just in time to hunch over and empty the contents of my stomach onto the sand. My belly contracts a couple more times before I finally stop, the last of my strength staring back at me in a disgusting puddle.

A couple steps back toward Havanna is all it takes for me to collapse onto the grass.

CHAPTER 26

ANARA

I have never seen Ender get hurt in battle. I assumed nothing was capable of bringing him down. Now he's dying by the Dormant King's hand, lying in the mud while holding his bleeding torso. The blood seeps between his fingers with no signs of stopping. This wouldn't have happened if Havanna didn't ditch us for the forest boy.

My feet don't move fast enough as I rush to him and skid to his side. The agony is evident in his shallow breathing and the way his face contorts. I have never seen him this way, and it's breaking my heart.

"Here, lift your hand." I guide him as I move his bloodstained fingers to the side. "I'm going to try to clean it up."

I hover my palm over his wounds. Barely a splash emits from my skin. No matter how hard I try to force more, I don't have enough water in my body to help him. I grunt with my impatience and reach for a bottle attached to my hip. I rip the cap off and chug the water. The pressure of drinking it so forcefully pokes at my throat, but I push it away. I force the water to my palm again; this time, a consistent stream spills onto his chest and I work to rinse off the blood. The tinged water pours off his side, spattering the mud onto my face and hair. He grunts again at the sting, his breaths labored and quick.

"Please don't die," I whisper more to myself than him, just to encourage my power to keep going.

My words are more audible than I realize, though, and my best friend's hand entangles with mine with a gentleness that is so contrary to his huge, bulky frame.

"I no die," he says hoarsely.

I scale my hands up and down his arms, around his torso. "He copied your powers, didn't he?"

He nods weakly, eyebrows bunched together in worry. "Is all right, though. This nothing. I strong."

I shake my head, doing my utmost to keep my tears at bay. "It's not nothing to me." My hand tightens around his. "You're my closest friend. And I . . ." I choke through a sob. "I don't want to lose you. I *can't.*"

His thumb draws circles over my palm. "I no go anywhere. I be all right."

I bring his hand to my mouth, placing a tender kiss and letting my tears fall on it. I pray to anything and anyone that he pulls through and heals. I refuse to lose the one and only friend I've ever had.

Kane, Wave, and Flame race back to the scene, covered in mud and dust. They surround us with their noses in our faces, assessing the situation. Flame leans down to Ender's blood-encrusted hand and proceeds to lick. I pat Flame's tiger head in thanks for being the perfect guardian.

The flap of bird wings signals Quill's and Havanna's arrival. His clothes are drenched, sticking tightly to his muscled figure. Her overly red skin catches my attention. Not the kind of red one experiences being exposed to cold weather, but a much deeper shade, like

Ender's skin. Something happened to them, but I have no room in my head to inquire, or care. They *left* us to fend for ourselves.

"Where were you guys?" I don't conceal the anger coursing through me. "We could've used you over here!"

"There's a valid explanation," Quill states plainly while he dismounts Koa. He rushes to Ender's aid. "What happened? Are you all right?"

Ender waves in weak dismissal. "I fine."

Quill holds his hand over Ender's wounds, his palm glowing a bright green.

"What are you hoping to accomplish by doing that?" I snap.

"The Dormant King taught me that Transform can heal. I'm going to see if it will work."

"I'm going to let these people go," Havanna mumbles, slumped over as she slowly makes her way to the people still blindfolded against the wall.

The urge to repeat the question of what happened with him and Havanna hangs at the tip of my tongue as he holds a hand over Ender's ribs. It quakes, a sheen of sweat beading his brow and forehead. His labored breaths turn into quiet grunts, the strain of this draining him much too easily.

He deflates with a harsh exhale. "I can't." His head hangs limply with an arm draped against Ender's chest. He leans up and hurriedly removes the weapons off his back, then peels off his wet shirt. The muscles of his biceps and his tight abs contract as he bundles the shirt in his hands.

"What are you doing?"

"We need to stop the bleeding." He places the wet cloth on the wounds and presses down. Ender blinks heavily, his face crinkling in pain at the eyes and mouth. All I can manage to do is observe his struggle and hold onto his hand like our lives depend on it.

Distant clamor gradually fills the air as the people are freed from the confines of blindfolds and bound wrists. Havanna drags her feet coming back to us, collapsing in on herself and exhausted.

"Where's the Dormant King?" she asks weakly. Her eyes seem distant, glazed over, and not fully present.

"He used Gateway to escape."

Quill perks up and stills. *"What?"*

"That's right." I flap my arms in anger and exasperation, then stand as my voice raises in volume. "He can use Gateway to evade our attacks. He can escape and come back as he pleases. And I'm guessing that he took the rest of the Backers with him too. Which you both would have seen if you didn't ditch us for a *bow!*" My blazing glare aims at Havanna. "He didn't request your help!" Next, I regard Quill. "And *you* could have fought without your bow. You *both* should have stayed and helped us!"

Havanna's jaw ticks, her own anger coloring her cheeks. "Well, someone had to get the Backers!" she snaps.

"You should not have ditched us," I reply with a tightened jaw. "Quill would have been fine without your help! Two of us fighting the Dormant King isn't enough. You of all people know that!"

"How was I supposed to help you if I didn't have my bow?" Quill retorts.

I shake my head and swat their replies away. I don't have time to address those arguments, nor do I care to. "The point is, we are officially screwed!" She shoves her fingers into her hair. "There's no way to beat him if he can use that against us. We have no way of predicting his next moves! On top of it all, he copied Ender's powers, and he's even more powerful than he was before." I laugh with absolutely no humor, just pure insanity. "Congratulations, guys! We're done for!"

Quill palms his face and sighs, words escaping him, and looks off to the distance. Ender remains silent, his head rolled away from me. I observe carefully how he breathes to catch anything out of the ordinary. He tries to take in even breaths, but his stomach contracts with each labored intake of air.

Havanna collapses to her knees, then falls back on her butt in the mud. "Crap."

Quill turns to his shirt pressed against Ender. "We need to get him help before we do anything else," he suggests. "We'll be worse off without him."

"What we do?" Ender asks softly. "Quill need shirt. My chest hurt."

Havanna curses silently to herself, her hands gripping both sides of her head and elbows leaned on her bent knees. She stares at her feet, unblinking. "There's only one place that's remotely close to here that can help him."

"Where?" I ask out of desperation.

She blows out a long, heavy sigh. "Ketra."

CHAPTER 27

HAVANNA

I was on the brink of death today. Lying in the grass, fighting for my life. I opened my eyes and there he was, kissing me on the head and flashing me that gorgeous smile.

After he vomited and passed out, I managed to crawl over to him to see if he was all right. He woke up after a few seconds, but his headache was raging. As he laid his cheek on the grass, I ran my fingers through his hair, behind his ear, away from his face. He leaned into my touch and relaxed, almost to the point of falling asleep. I took the time to examine him while reeling from the sacrifices he made to save me, at greater risk to himself. A testament to his kind heart and loyalty that only confirms one thing.

I'm in love with him. It's the only thing I know without a doubt.

He gave all of himself—even falling through the sky—to save me. He took the time to teach me archery. He let me use his bow—the most important thing to him. He interrupted my dance with another man just to have a chance to talk with me.

He doesn't have to say it. Jumping off his Bennaru just to have a chance of saving me was all I needed to affirm his feelings for me.

Calista was right. I need to embrace it.

With the four of us on our Bennarus, Ender limply strapped to Flame as we soar over Alberi Jungle, I have to put my romantic emotions aside. Ender is gravely injured, the Dormant King can escape any dangerous situation he finds himself in with Gateway, and Ketra is the closest place that can help. We're so screwed if that's the tool the Dormant King is using to his advantage. An army is probably not going to be of any benefit now. On top of the stack of problems in my mind, I'm returning to Ketra for the first time since I left, and I'm dreading it.

Aria. Thaeus. Vincent. I have missed all of them dearly. Whether they have forgiven me or not is still unknown. With each second that passes, more knots tie tighter in my stomach.

Their forgiveness will mean everything if they can help heal Ender.

Once I start preparing for landing just on the border of my village, the Descendants follow suit. With the sun barely changing the colors of the sky, the guards may not notice our arrival.

We slowly descend, my heart dropping to my stomach. All the sounds and sights of home rush through me: the twinkle of torches all through the village, the faint sound of Ketra Falls, and the beach close by. It's nostalgic and bittersweet, and makes my eyes sting with tears.

I'm back home to a village that may welcome me with unopened arms.

We land just outside the vine-covered entrance that borders Ketra and the Dark Woods, just when the voices of the guards take up more space in the air. As they approach us, the Bennarus shift to their smaller forms, we assist Ender to his feet and help him stay upright, and I take the few seconds we have to see how far the village has come.

It was a disaster when I left. It's been cleaned up now, so much so that it doesn't appear that damage took place at all. Huts have been rebuilt and polished to a shine I've never seen before, with perfectly carved wood planks and shaved tree branches. Such a small detail makes my heart sink even more. My departure was all they needed to make different decisions on what wood to use for their huts. It's so stupid to feel this way.

"Intruder!" one of the guards bellows from the depths of his diaphragm. They aim their spears and swords directly at our chests. The gleaming metal in the moonlight, clear as glass, is absolutely the work of none other than Thaeus. "Intruder in our midst!"

I hold my palms out to calm them down. "It's all right. All is well. I'm from here."

They examine me a little more closely with their heads tilted to the side. One of them holds up a lantern and steps closer to observe my face. I recognize him; he's been a guard for the village since I was young. When Jael was the chief.

His face brightens in recognition. "Havanna?"

"Yes, it's me."

Quill and Anara are struggling to keep Ender on his feet, the wounds on his abs drying while his head hangs down limply. He tries to hide it, but Quill shivers from being cold without a shirt, which is now covered in blood.

"We need help." I turn to assess Ender's weakened state. "He's been injured. I need Thaeus to get Healing Salve."

The guards come right to Ender's aid, taking him off Quill's and Anara's hands. They struggle under his weight as they lift with their legs to keep his feet from dragging. One guard commands the other to retrieve Thaeus and my heart lurches. He hasn't forgiven me for leaving Ketra or causing its destruction, I'm sure. He won't come.

The eatery sits off to the right, just outside the vine entrance, where it always was. I push away the memories that are connected to the sight and come up with an idea. "Lay him down on the tables in there."

They don't ask questions. We follow the group of guards and Ender up the steps into the eatery. Flame follows beside them to make sure they handle him with care. The clamor of sweeping kitchen equipment off surfaces and the *thump* of the guards laying him down on a table thunders the quiet air. The urgency of the situation is evident with the commands the guards shout at each other. Quill's and Anara's faces are blank, void and empty of all emotion. Exhaustion paints the undersides of their eyes.

Ender's features contort in pain, the blood dried and crusted on his clothes that Flame makes quick work of licking again. Quill does his best when he gives him his bloodied shirt to cover his open wounds. Anara sits beside Ender's left and holds his hand while I hold the other for comfort. He barely grasps mine in return, his eyelids getting heavy.

"Where is Thaeus?" I shout with urgency.

Just as I thought. He's not coming.

Powerful, urgent footsteps surge up the stairs to the entrance of the eatery. The huge shadow takes up the space in the doorframe, flanked by a guard. I know it's him.

Thaeus.

The chief of Ketra.

My friend.

"Massy." He breathes out heavily. "It really is you."

Massy.

He called me that all the time when I was growing up. I forgot how much I missed it.

Everything that's happened, seeing Thaeus, and remembering my whole childhood—the emotions are overwhelming. Sobs rack my body and I lose the strength to stand. He crosses the dining area in a few steps and pulls me into his arms. Even now, that gentle interior of his hasn't changed. All of the emotions circling around the memories and the love I have for the people here have me sobbing into his ratty shirt. The worn clothes he wore as a blacksmith haven't changed since his new status of becoming chief. It feels like home for the first time in months. His bulging arms tighten around me, so fatherly as he lays a kiss on the crown of my head.

With his intimidating shape and a voice that comes from the depths of his soul, almost as big as Ender's, I expected to be met with hostility and anger. His height alone intimidated me when I first arrived in Ketra, when he stood to leave Jael's hut. As I got older, he turned out to be the gentlest giant I have ever known.

"What are you doing here?" he asks worriedly. "Are you all right? Did you find the Dormant King?"

I turn to Ender, lying with his back flat on two wooden tables made into a makeshift stretcher, his breathing still shallow. His chest barely lifts with each breath. Anara stays abnormally quiet as she keeps a careful eye on him. Quill's shirtless state tests my self-control greatly as I examine his beautifully carved pecs, biceps, and abs that shiver in the cold. I muster up enough focus to avert my gaze. "That's a whole other story. We need Healing Salve. And a shirt."

Thaeus addresses the guard flanking him. "Have Vincent retrieve a shirt. I'll get the Salve."

"I'll go with you."

He doesn't argue with me as we leave the eatery. Just across the way is the apothecary, just as it always was. I always went there for Battle Elixir and Sleeper's Brew, both of which I used extensively. Tetia had a successful business here with her specialty potions and recipes.

We stop right in front of the door to the apothecary and our eyes meet. "I'm glad you're alive, Massy." He examines me, and I forget that I have deep gashes on my arm from the Dormant's grip. "With the exception of that, you look very well."

I examine him too. Vibrant, healthy, and happy. In the dimness of sunrise's beginning, I still see the soot on his worn clothes, burn marks and scabbed gashes on his hands, the epitome of a blacksmith who never stopped.

"You look exactly the same," I reply with a smirk that disappears the moment I think of asking the question that's been in the forefront of my mind. "How is everyone?"

Thaeus fumbles with the keys in his trousers. "Very well. Ketra is almost the way it was before, one day at a time." He lets himself into the apothecary to look for the medicine. "I believe she keeps the Salve over here."

I step in after him and take it all in. Herbal, floral, and perfumed scents blend into a thick aroma. Potion bottles lining the far wall on a tiered shelf glow as bright as my Fireflies, giving us just enough light to see our way around. Along the back of the shop are a few large cast-iron pots set on top of unlit burners. Everything is just as I remember. I used to browse in here for hours with Jael, mesmerized with the intended purpose of each bottle. I was tempted on more than one occasion to spend my week's earnings on just elixirs, potions, and remedies. Tetia never shared her recipes, but I managed to replicate some in my own time.

Along the far wall is a window that gives a direct view of the training area. That section of low-cut grass was my first home, besides the eatery and my own hut. I flash back to the day I knelt in the grass and cried because I missed when Papa trained me with the sword. That was the same day I found the sword that I now carry on my back. Jael told me it was hers when she became a warrior and let me keep it. That was the place where I showed up Darius as he was trying to prove how amazing he was.

There, in that training area, is where I became the fighter I am now.

"Found it." Thaeus comes back with four large containers of the pink-hued Salve that I remember so well and used myself on more than one occasion. He shifts the medicine in his grip. "This should be enough. What do you think? Your friend is about as large as I am, and I use about the same amount."

I manage a nod as I reach my hand out to help him carry the medicine. I don't make for the door right away. I still have things I want to ask.

As if reading my mind, he says, "She misses you, you know."

The idea of Aria missing me has played in my mind more than once, but I always shrugged it off because I didn't believe there was a chance she was thinking of me. Thaeus may be telling the truth, or this is some tactic to get us to reconcile. "Does she?"

He nods. "She tries to hide it, but she's been worried about you. She especially misses working with you at the eatery." He lays a strong hand on my shoulder. "She would be glad to see you're still alive. Perhaps you should find her."

I cringe at the thought of waking her up this early. The last time I did, I was leaving Ketra for good, and the conversation didn't go the way I had hoped. "Perhaps when the sun rises and Ender is taken care of."

He motions to my arm again. "What about you?"

I chuckle bitterly. "I've been through worse. I'm fine."

"Havanna?" a loud whisper sounds outside.

I turn to leave the apothecary, Thaeus following close behind, only to run into the two people who were angrier with me than everyone else.

Vincent.

And Aria.

I barely notice Vincent as I take in my best friend. Her black hair is a ratted mess of tight curls with eyes that were half open one second and wide as an owl's the next. Her eyes are a hard stare accompanying a rigid posture, unforgotten grudges in her features. Her golden, tanned skin is clear, vibrant, and beautiful. Not a single change since our last encounter.

Except for the ring on her left ring finger. A textured band with a single circular diamond. The sign of a milestone I missed. My heart cracks wide open.

That hard stare crumbles in seconds. She succumbs to tears, a hand placed over her mouth. Not angry tears, but ones that confirm exactly what Thaeus said. Exactly how I have felt the last couple months.

I close the distance between us and wrap my arms around her neck. She doesn't hesitate to hug me back. Her body trembles with sobs in my arms, holding on for dear life, and I can't help but cry for the second time since I've arrived. Tears that we both needed to shed for so long, now out in the open, soaking into each other's clothes.

"I'm sorry," she finally says into my hair. The first thing she says, and it shatters me.

The remaining tears of joy fall on her shoulder. "Me too."

CHAPTER 28

QUILL

"King Aldous has decreed a lockdown, has he?" Thaeus grumbles in displeasure. "And you massies want to go to war instead. That is . . . quite the debacle."

The tension is stretched taut. An enemy in our midst and an injured warrior puts everyone in the wringer. We managed to get Ender out of his clothes and spread the Healing Salve over his wounds. We made a makeshift bed on the floor to lay him down in a more comfortable position since we didn't want to risk moving him a long distance and hurting him more. He's half asleep now, although breathing unevenly. Anara hasn't left his side for a moment, and neither has Flame. Kane, on the other hand, has chosen to befriend Havanna's best friend, Aria. All it took was for her to scratch his shrew chin, and he climbed onto her shoulder.

The corner of the eatery is crowded with us Descendants, Thaeus, Aria, and a guy named Vincent who loaned me a dark-blue, long-sleeved shirt. When we all came together, Vincent simply gave a side smile to Havanna and a short hug. "Glad you're safe," he had said softly into her hair. Someone she must have had a fight with before she left.

"We tried to talk him out of it, but he wouldn't budge," Havanna fills him in. "We need an army. Plain and simple."

"I was told yesterday that fires were started in Alberi Jungle," Vincent adds. "They could be closing in as we speak. There's no time to gather an army."

"An army may not even be a solution anymore," Anara says in a low, tired voice, never breaking her gaze from Ender. "The Dormant King has Gateway. He's practically indestructible."

"Which leaves no pattern for you to follow," Thaeus says thoughtfully.

"What would you suggest?" Havanna asks.

Thaeus spreads his arms in exasperation. "I'm a tribal chief, not an army officer."

"Petros hasn't had a war in five hundred years," Vincent notes. "This isn't exactly an area of expertise for any of us."

"My father told me that everyone has a weakness that brings them to their knees," Havanna says. "I can't find one for the Dormant King."

Patterns. Army. Weakness. Gateway. The words go in circles in my mind, hitting against each other in order to form sentences or ideas that are plausible.

Nothing. I have nothing.

"His thirst for power isn't already a weakness?" I challenge.

"And *being* powerful is not," Anara counters.

"When Halivaara spoke to me, it said 'greed is poison to the heart,'" Havanna reminds her. "There's something to those words we're not seeing."

"You met Halivaara?" Thaeus questions breathlessly. He leans back in his chair. "The *entity* Halivaara?"

Havanna nods. "It didn't seem real, but it spoke to me. It knew who I was."

"Can you go back and speak to it?" Aria asks. "You're a Descendant. What if it gives you the answers you need?"

"It gave me answers, but they're not clear. If I go back, it may not help. I asked how to defeat the Dormant King, and that's what it said. Then said something about limits, and when he reaches his, it will be his downfall."

A limit being someone's downfall. That's equivalent to someone reaching their limit of alcohol consumption and dying of alcohol poisoning. The Dormant King has all of our abilities, except for Havanna's. None of the Descendants have ever had more than two abilities. For the Dormant King, it's an overload.

"So reaching a certain level of power will be what kills him," I say out loud. "Once he's an expert in using all of the abilities he's claimed, it will just kill him. As an Ancestor, he may only be able to handle so much power. Yes?"

"That makes sense," Thaeus acknowledges.

Havanna dismisses the notion with a shake of her head. "That seems too easy. Wouldn't copying Ender's powers have killed him instantly?"

"Perhaps that's why he escaped," Anara notes. "He may have been at a weak point and knew he needed to run." She scoffs. "Coward."

"What about written records?" Aria pipes in again.

Havanna sighs heavily. "My mother told me the Ancestors probably paid careful attention to not leave a paper trail so as to not be found. If anything about the Dormant King was written, it was never passed down, or found." She shrugs sadly. "What we know is all we have to go on."

"I believe what must be done is simple, yet unpleasant," Vincent speaks up and turns to Havanna. "You got an answer from Hali-vaara itself. It very well may be the only answer we will receive. It's up to us to decipher it with the knowledge we have. And perhaps your only solution for the time being is forming an army." He wants to add more. Much to our disadvantage, we already know what he's leaving unsaid.

"Sounds like we lose then," Anara says, defeated. "Will we even have time?"

"Yes," Havanna punches out adamantly. "We just need to find a way to get it done quickly."

I promised myself the day I left to have nothing to do with Arbol Village again, but I debated with myself to have Koa send a note specifically to Nyx. No one else I can think of will help, and it seems inconsiderate to ask her for help when I didn't even say goodbye when I left. It may be best to leave her alone.

Havanna rises to her feet. "While we all think, I can make us some Bakki."

"Bakki?" Anara asks with her nose crinkled in distaste.

"Oh yes," Thaeus says to Havanna's retreating back. "Massy here made a mean Bakki when she owned the eatery."

"She also made Winterbulb Wine," Vincent adds. "It was scrumptious."

She turns to face us once he mentions it and regards me with heightened eyebrows and a lopsided grin to confirm his statement. There's a hint of mischief in that smile that makes my heart skip a beat. I'm not a wine person, but I will try anything she gives me. Even if she made pig slop, I'd still try it.

"I'd like to try some."

She and Aria start for the kitchen. The conversation turns to idle talk, and I sit back and watch Havanna in adoration. Anara stays at Ender's side, lying beside him in his makeshift cot and resting with her head on his shoulder.

When Havanna laughs—the special one that I have the privilege to hear when I make dumb quips—it only adds to her beauty. The pink shade of dawn from the window tells us we've been awake for far too long. My mind is so worn down I can't think. My muscles ache and cry out every time I do something as small as moving my leg.

Havanna carries two dark-green glass bottles by the neck in one hand and two round glasses in the other, a scene I remember all too well in Arbol Village that indicated lots of drinking and impending fighting. She pours me a glass of the deep, near-black liquid that comes out thick as molasses. Those tired, sleep-deprived eyes glimmer with anticipation as she slides it to me. She pours a glass of a light wood-colored liquid and slides it to Thaeus. Corn Whiskey. A strong alcoholic drink I usually prefer.

I take a sip of the Winterbulb Wine and let it sit in my mouth. The consistency of oil and sugar sits on my tongue and stains the roof of my mouth and the back of my throat with its flavor. Once I swallow, I finally taste how incredibly tart it is. Dry as the skin of a grape. My face twists as the sourness attacks the inside of my cheeks and makes them water.

I hum in approval, just to appease her with some reaction. "Wow."

Havanna crosses her arms, a smile teasing her lips that can see right through my pretense. "You don't like it."

I shrug as I swirl the wine in the glass, unsure of the right words. "It's . . . all right."

"Just a tip, massy," Thaeus cuts in, slapping a hand on my shoulder. "You don't want to call a lady's cooking or recipes 'all right.'"

Havanna chuckles and shakes her head. "You're not exactly good at hiding your distaste for it."

"Allow me to rephrase." I swallow the rest of the glass, the leftover residue stuck to the inside like jam. My face twists again in its biting aftertaste. "It's tasty." She rolls her eyes, Anara snorts, and I emphasize with my hands. "I'm just used to the strength of Corn Whiskey."

"We have loads of that too!" Thaeus announces, taking the bottle and pouring me some over the leftover wine. Whether this will impact the taste, I don't know, but we're drinking, and I don't care.

Ender stirs, grunting to get himself in a comfortable position. Anara watches him, extremely focused, but shocked as if she's witnessing him waking from the dead. I'm also surprised, since he's been asleep for hours now.

"We drink alcohol?" he rasps.

I smile with pride that he feels well enough to be humorous. I clench my lips together and scoot over to clap him on the shoulder softly. "Yes, we do, compo."

Havanna drops to her knees and wraps her arms around Ender's neck. "So glad you're all right," she whispers. "How are you feeling?"

Ender brings a hand to his injuries that are covered in Healing Salve and carefully feels around them. "Still hurts. I sore."

"Havanna, perhaps you should bring out another glass," Thaeus suggests. Once she comes back, she brings a few more glasses. Everyone, including Aria, begins enjoying the spread.

"Sometimes inebriations make injuries hurt less. A valid reason for drinking," Thaeus says in a low voice to Ender, then raises his Corn Whiskey. "Drink up, massies!"

CHAPTER 29

ENDER

T haeus was right. Alcohol helped numb the pain in my chest.

I'm sure I downed an entire bottle of Corn Whiskey. I've never had alcohol, but everyone else is drinking. I simply want to join the crowd and make the aching stop.

We drink. A lot.

And I enjoy it.

I feel happier. I laugh. I am unable to move. My vision is impaired and my head starts feeling woozy after a whole bottle, then I decide I should go to sleep. It is very early morning by the time everyone finally decides to get some rest. Aria closes the eatery so I can have the space to myself.

The first sight upon opening my eyes is my compa, lying right next to me and deep asleep on the hard, uneven floor of the eatery.

The status of our relationship has changed drastically in the last few days. She's the first compa I have ever shared a bed with. I sleep next to her because it makes her feel better. At least, I thought that was the only reason she wanted me there with her the first time. All the nights after that, though, I stayed with her because I knew she wanted to feel safe. She didn't fight it when I laid next to her, nor did she touch me. I respected her space, but I still questioned what exactly I was doing. I questioned if this was a one-sided arrangement.

Seeing her beside me now, though, answers the question. She'll be there for me when I need her. Whether this is simply a treasured friendship for her or it's more—as it always has been for me—I still don't know.

Daylight intensifies its shine as it pours into the front windows. Anara groans and flips onto her back. She rolls her head toward me and lights up upon seeing me awake. "How are you feeling?" she asks through her deep morning voice.

I attempt to lift myself upright only to feel major cramping instead of incessant stinging. "Better. May need more Salve. I no go anywhere till I better."

Anara shifts herself to lean against the wall. "I can get you some more Salve. We're going to have to get moving soon, though, whether you're completely better or not. I don't want to sound insensitive, but we can't afford to sit around and not take action."

I scoff. "I be fine in two days."

She shakes her head. "No, Ender. For you, we're talking weeks. Maybe months. We don't have that kind of time. The Dormant King will have all of Petros under his rule by then." She takes my fingers into her hand, staring at each one as if they have individual stories to tell. "We can't fight without you. Compo."

Compo. She called me compo.

She really cares about me.

The panic in her voice incites a need in me to make things better for her. We're in a predicament beyond our control with little time for a solution. I have to convince her I will be well enough to fight before the Dormant King can act again. I will fight with my compos, whether I'm ready to or not.

"Trust me. I be fine in couple days. I need Salve, though."

She doesn't respond. Her gaze stays glued to my hand. "I just feel like we're stalling. Like we're making one bad decision after another."

"We went in blind, compa. More than once. We still blind. But we get there." I put a fist over my heart. "Mulhutna promise."

She flashes me a proud smile, her ocean-blue eyes swimming in the daylight. Her hand reaches for my cheek and strokes it with a gentleness that is so unlike her, but makes her all the more beautiful. "You surprise me sometimes."

"Why? I too lazy to come up with plan?"

"You're definitely lazy." I don't bother denying that observation as I chuckle under the skin of her palm. "But you're the most dedicated, loyal person I've ever known, even when you're badly hurt. We need that in order to do this together."

"Just because I hurt no mean I change."

"Good. Otherwise I'd have to punch you."

Havanna mentioned that we need an army, and we may have to look at things from a different angle. It rang in my mind for a while, even before I went back to sleep. For once, I *might* have something that can help us. I mentally slap myself for not having thought of it before now.

Before I can tell Anara, I have no time to react when she lunges at me and lays a chaste, loving kiss on my cheek. "I'll get you more Salve." Her skin grows pink the moment she turns away from me and she rises to her feet.

"Compa." She stops and turns, an amused glare aimed only at me. "Can you get Quill? I need him."

Her expression shifts to one of curiosity, but she shrugs and leaves. I shift again to lean against the wall, absorbing the quiet of the building as my idea turns in my mind. My compos are going to thank me so much for coming up with it.

It's going to change the war as we know it.

＊＊＊

"What you think? Good, yes?"

Anara summoned Quill from Thaeus's hut as I asked. Once she returned with him, I asked her to give us a moment. She rolled her eyes, made a comment about a budding romance between Quill and me, and announced that she was going to hang out at the beach. I told Quill the idea I came up with, and now he's smiling in approval. My chest swells with pride that he likes it.

"It's brilliant, compo," he says hesitantly after a few silent seconds. I begin to assume he's only telling me that to appease me. I may want to feel validated, but I also want honesty.

"You no seem sure."

"I just . . ." He lays a hand on his chin, a distant but thoughtful expression clouded over him. "When do we do this? We don't know where the Dormant King is right now."

I deliberate with a hum. "We no delay. We go tomorrow."

Quill gives me a crooked smile. "I agree." He crosses his arms. "But you need to be in much better shape before you fight with us again. On the other hand, you like having everything done for you, so this is like a vacation."

"Anara say same thing," I say through laughter. "I like fighting. I no like cleaning. Or chores. I no like chores."

"Well, no one likes chores," Quill retorts. "The only time I care about things like washing clothes is when I want to smell clean. Ladies like that." He ends his statement with a wink.

I flex my biceps. "Ladies like muscle too." I make my pecs dance and Quill howls in laughter.

We're still laughing when Anara marches inside, dragging Havanna by the hand behind her. Havanna is obviously not here by choice with the way her head hangs back in irritation.

"All right, this is ridiculous," Anara snaps. "We've been in this tiny village long enough and I'm getting impatient." She lets go of Havanna and puts her hands on her hips, authoritative and insistent. "I say we go to the cave where Havanna found Halivaara and ask it to heal Ender." She claps at us. "Now. Get packing."

Havanna turns her body to regain her patience with the request. Aria had asked the same question about Halivaara and Havanna didn't have a favorable answer. Anara, being Anara, doesn't accept unfavorable answers.

"Halivaara basically disappeared after I talked with it," she explains in a low voice. "Whether it actually lives in that cave or I just happened to stumble upon it, I don't know."

"Well, we won't know if we just stand here," Anara says, annoyed. She turns to Havanna with a burning glare. "We need to do something. *Now.*"

Havanna places her hands on her hips, squaring up to Anara. "Why are you acting like us being here is *my* fault?"

"It *is* your fault!" she exclaims.

Everyone stills. Silence buzzes between us. All Quill and I can think to do is give each other an awkward look.

"If you hadn't chased after Quill like a pathetic, romantic sap, we would've had a shot with the Dormant King! Instead, you left us outnumbered and it nearly killed Ender!"

Havanna's expression shifts to a deep red, her tongue rolling over her teeth under her lips. She turns her head away right when I catch a glimpse of her eyes glimmering with tears.

"Hold on," Quill belts out in defense, rising to his feet. "Don't blame her. There were Backers and they all spread out. It was best that we split up to take them down. I didn't have my bow and there was no chance of me doing it on my own."

Anara mulls over Quill's words, her eyes twitching. She looks to me for an answer. She's looked to me for guidance when it comes to personal relationships. I always told her what we Mulhutna do to mend things. I know for sure she remembers that my tribe regards each other as brothers and sisters. She also remembers what I told her about being a compassionate, patient friend. Both qualities that she lacks at the moment.

I give her a slight nod.

"You're right," she tells Quill, then turns back to Havanna. "I'm sorry, Doofus," she says with genuine sorrow, even with the name-calling. "This has just been stressful."

Havanna simply nods. "I know." She releases a quick sigh to regain her composure. "Which is why I've decided to send a note for those who want to join us in forming an army. I'll have the Bennarus deliver it."

Quill and I exchange a knowing glance. We have to let them know. "Quill and I go to Vulca tomorrow. We have plan."

Anara's eyes narrow at us. She crosses her arms over her chest and shifts from one foot to the other. "What plan?"

"You'll see," Quill adds with a wink. *I want to see the looks on their faces when they see,* he says. I nod.

"Why won't you tell us?" Havanna asks skeptically.

"We wait for you to see," I answer, pasting on a fake smile.

"All right, be shady," Anara draws out with a snide tone. She turns to Havanna. "But how are we doing any of this if we don't know where the Dormant King is?"

"Better to have an army ready than to be caught off guard," Havanna says. "We can update the leaders and captains once he's been spotted."

"So your solution is to drag hundreds of people around looking for the Dormant King without a single clue where he is?"

"You have a better plan?"

Anara slowly nods, staring her down for her smart remark, but says nothing. "All right. Let's do that." She sighs. "The king easily could have done things that way."

"He has head up butthole, remember?" I quip, and Quill busts out in laughter. The girls attempt—and fail—to hide their smiles, and they end up laughing right along with us. The tension just moments ago melts away like a frozen lake under the sun.

We're a team. We've always been a team.

"I'm in agreement with Zappy's plan," Quill says, winking at Havanna in his usual charming way.

Anara and Havanna find a table close to us and sit. "Good. Back to writing letters we go."

CHAPTER 30

HAVANNA

"How have things been since I've been gone?" I finally have a chance to ask Aria.

Each Bennaru, including Kane, was given a copy of the note that calls for action, then sent on their way with clear instructions. I'm saving the items given to me from my parents and Calista when I know for sure where the Dormant King is. If things go as planned, the Bennarus will be back in Ketra within a few hours.

Aria and I have been walking in circles around the village for an hour, and everyone has expressed how glad they are to see me alive and well, some more excited than others. Even the family I'd given leftover food to hugged me. The reception has been better than I anticipated, even if the reactions aren't exactly enthusiastic.

"It's been making good progress. I run the eatery fine enough." She eyes me with what seems like yearning. "It's not the same without you."

"Well, clearly you've done well for yourself," I note, pointing to the ring on her finger.

Aria examines the silver band lined with diamonds, mindlessly turning it. A smile shines on her face with all the happiness in her heart. "Being with him has been amazing," she says with such reminisce. "The way he proposed was perfect." She motions to the beach as we head in that direction. "He got down on one knee, held the ring in his hand, told me how much he loved me, and told me he would choose no other to be his wife." Her eyes glow with love and affection. "It was simple, but it was perfect. Just the way I wanted it."

We reach the sand of the beach, stopping just before the ocean's edge, and sit. "I hate that I missed it."

"Me too. I wasted too much time being angry when I should have been understanding and compassionate." She worms an arm around my shoulder. "I really missed you."

I stare out in the ocean and sigh in content. The waves come and go, the burden of our strained relationship pulling back into the ocean. From the moment I left the village, I worried she would never forgive me. I wondered if she was even thinking of me. To know that she was means more than she realizes.

"Perhaps when things settle down, you can come to the wedding," she suggests, then nudges me playfully. "You can bring Quill with you."

I explained my and Quill's entire history, even divulging the mo-ment I realized I was in love with him. She assured me that the time will come when he will open up his heart to me, and foresees it happening soon. We agreed that being in love is the most wonderful feeling. For her it is; she knows very well how Claeron feels about her. For me, it's wonderful yet torturous to not know for sure about Quill.

"Possibly," I answer through a sigh.

"I earnestly hope neither one of you lingers too long in the un-known," she advises. "If it were me, I would be angry at myself if I lost Claeron and I never had the chance to tell him how I feel."

I realized how I felt about Quill when I woke from consciousness. At my lowest, I desperately wanted to tell him. In case I lost him. Or if I did actually lose my life. Since then, there has been no opportunity for a private conversation.

Here, in the safety and quiet of Ketra, the opportunity is open, yet I'm stalling. I don't know how or when to tell him.

"Would you consider returning to Ketra?" Aria asks. I sense the hope in her tone.

All I can see when I revisit the village is traces of Jael. The underground compound. The training area. The apothecary. They all remind me of the times she was by my side. Even beyond the grave, she's here with me. Every single night. When I have to relive the grief all over again.

In other ways, I do miss it here. If everything works out with Quill, I don't know if he will come back and visit with me. I already know I will only be where he wants to be.

"I'm not sure." I straighten up from her grasp and wrap my arms around my knees. "Perhaps one day the grief won't be so strong that not everything will remind me of Jael." I shrug. "One can hope."

Aria nods. "The village misses her." She grasps my shoulder. "But don't be gone for too much longer. Contrary to what you believe, everyone wants you to be all right."

"I won't be all right till the Dormant King is dead," I mumble in a tired voice. I regard her with all sincerity, just for her to know I mean what I'm about to say. "I hope you know that I won't stop until he's dead. Until he's paid for what he took from you and the village."

Aria clenches her lips and nods, worry traced in her features. "I know. That's what scares me."

"You can always help us fight," I say casually, as if my suggestion isn't a life-or-death matter. "We need all the help we can get."

She scoffs. "I'm nowhere near as powerful as you are. I would be dead in minutes."

I swat her arm. "I would have your back, don't worry."

We stare out into the ocean, watching the setting sun darken the world around us. Each passing minute changes the color of the sky, the waves lapping at our toes to blend with the ambience.

"Remember when you first used lightning and I caught you?" Aria chuckles. "I was *enraged* that you didn't tell me."

"Believe me, I remember."

Her tone changes from reminiscent to a version of pride. "At the same time, I thought, 'she's going to be absolutely *lethal* someday.' Then you killed every single enemy with lightning during the raid. It scared me how powerful you were. But in that moment, I knew without a doubt, whatever you fought for, you would win. No contest."

I gave everything I had to use Strike during that raid. It nearly destroyed me. It was just the beginning of understanding my powers. I realize now that I've come a long way since then.

"I don't know how I'm going to win, though," I respond in a defeated tone. "I don't even know what I'm doing anymore."

"That's all right. Even the best of fighters are lost sometimes. They always find their way, though."

I turn to her, smiling proudly. She's grown since I left. Mature and wise. I may have missed that stage of her life, but we're here now as if nothing ever happened. Like we've always been the closest of friends.

We still are.

I lay my head on her shoulder and wrap my arms around her. "I missed you."

She laughs and returns the hug. We stay that way until darkness encompasses the entire sky. Silent in our reunion.

Footsteps interrupt our relaxing silence, leading from the pavement directly to the shore. I turn and see Quill approaching us, a hand wrapped around a glass of Corn Whiskey.

"There you are, Zappy."

"Forest Dweller," I welcome him playfully.

"I was hoping you were all right. I was worried you were still upset from earlier." He raises his glass. "I also hope I didn't make you feel bad that I like Corn Whiskey more than that wine."

Aria and I both giggle. "Not at all."

"Good." He takes a sip from his glass, the silence growing between us every second.

Aria takes this as a cue to leave. She stands and clears her throat. "I will let you two be." She slaps the sand off her clothes, then saunters past Quill. "I'll see you back at my hut, Havanna."

I nod toward her retreating back. Quill gives me a small, awkward smile and passes the time with another sip of Whiskey. He makes no moves to leave and no more claims that he only came to check on me. He's here for a reason.

"I meant to thank you for saving me," I say to fill the silence.

Quill stills, his glass frozen at his lips. "You did that already."

"Yes, but it deserves more gratitude. You could have died."

He shrugs. "It's not a big deal. I'd rather you just forget about it."

I flinch at this change of attitude. "Why?"

He angrily steps forward and leans close to my face. He raises his voice when he adamantly says, "Because it will just make you think that there is more to this than there is, and there isn't. There never will be."

Unbelievable. Still in denial. I still have to work to crack open that closed heart of his. Anger mixed with despair fills my veins; my breaths become harsh. I don't understand what changed between arriving in Ketra to now.

"You're *still* pretending?" I hiss.

Quill holds up his hands in defeat. "I'm not getting into this." He turns to leave. This time, I'm not letting him walk away.

I catch up to him before he reaches the pavement leading to the village and grab his shoulder to force him to look at me. "You know what? I don't believe that you feel nothing. And I know you don't believe it yourself. If that's truly how you felt, you wouldn't have jumped off your *freaking* Bennaru to save me."

"That doesn't prove anything."

"It proves *everything*." I step closer till I'm inches from his face. I'm done with this game and I'm going to fight the answers out of him. "I'm done being pushed around, Quill. I'm done trying to figure out what it is you're feeling. I need to know what's going on."

"I told you—"

"*Now*, Quill."

His breaths become harsher, his chest puffing out farther with each exhale as he stares me down. In those dark brown eyes, I see the emotional pain I've begged to draw out of him, the debate to let himself go. To reveal himself.

Each second passes and he says nothing. I'm not relenting. It's the perfect time to implement Aria's words. I don't want to linger anymore.

I grit my teeth and step back, arms spread out in exasperation. "You know we almost died the other day. Every single day we're facing death. We have no clue which moment will be our last." My throat swells with an oncoming sob. "When I woke up and saw you holding me, I was deathly afraid I would never be able to know you the way I want to if I was gone, or if something happened to you. And I realized I would be so devastated, so angry with myself if I never told you . . ." I turn my head so he doesn't see my tears. "If I never told you that I love you."

The words come out and I nearly vomit in the sand. I have never fallen in love, let alone told someone how I felt in the most intimate, romantic sense. I can't take back the words, not now.

I don't hear him breathe. I can't bear to see if he's even standing in front of me anymore. I simply swallow down the tears and wait for him to say something. Anything.

"You love me." It's a plain, blank statement. No question or sense of wonder.

I nod.

"You can't love me." He scoffs. "You don't know me. And once you do, you'll see I'm not loveable."

My jaw hangs. He's stomping on my feelings, something I didn't think someone as kind as him was capable of. "Don't you dare tell me what to feel," I reply with a heavy quake in my voice. I'm one step away from slapping him.

"All right. You love me." He swallows the rest of his Whiskey in one gulp and tosses the glass in the sand like a useless rock. "You want to know me? You want to know *everything*? Because I guarantee you will feel very different by the time I'm done."

I say nothing. I can't find the words to say anything. I simply let him talk.

"Would you still love me if I told you my parents hated me? They told me my powers were worthless, and I only existed to be my brother's bodyguard. Or how about that my brother was the only one in my family that made me feel at least a little bit valuable?" He leans closer to me. "Would you still love me if I told you a grown woman stole my first kiss and forced herself on me? Or that she ruined my reputation in the village—a place known for its *chasteness*, mind you—because I rejected her advances? And that she told everyone I was sleeping with my best friend—who's *gay*, by the way—when I actually only went to her house to sleep on the *floor* because I needed to get away from my own family?" His voice begins to shake, his eyes brimming with unshed tears as he points at himself. "How about when Indigo died in my arms when it was too late to save him?" He shakes his head and runs his fingers through his hair. "Would you still love me if you knew that I left Nyx's house at the same time I always did, but my parents caught me, and it was the first time my father actually hit me? My brother had just died and he had the nerve to backhand me. That was all it took for me to leave and never go back." The tears fall down his cheeks and my heart breaks just as his voice does. "Are you happy? Is that everything you wanted to know? Because it's a pain I carry with me every single day. What you're really seeing is a facade." He flaps his arms. "Now you know everything. Now you can decide if you still love me enough to carry that burden."

He finishes, catching his breath as if he's just returned from a run. My heart completely falls apart, collapses, and tears fall down my own cheeks. I want nothing more than to heal his pain. To be the one to make his life better. He's been through much more than I ever have, enough to make him a bitter, angry, hateful person.

Just like the Dormant King.

The Dormant King let it define him. Quill didn't. He went through it and turned it into everything he refused to be. He became the loyal, caring, loving, funny, playful person standing before me despite the lack of love he was denied. The love he never should have gone without.

The love I so badly want to give him.

I cover my mouth, a barrier for the tears running down my cheeks. I sniffle loud enough for him to notice.

"No," he snaps, wiggling a scolding finger at me. "I didn't tell you any of that so you could pity me." He repeats with clenched teeth, "I do not want your pity."

I point to my face, my voice breaking. "You think this is pity? Because it's not." I step closer to him and harden my gaze. "I'm crying because despite those horrible, *horrible* things you endured, you came out the other side to become a good person. The *best* person. The most loyal, kind, self-sacrificing person I've ever known. You may think you're putting up a facade, but I know in my heart that what I see is who you truly are." I shake my head. "You worried that this would change my view of you. It doesn't." I hold a hand to my chest. "It makes me love you more."

A choked sob escapes him, his shoulders relaxing. Tears continue to run down his face as he debates with himself, looking at me, then away, and he relents.

He takes two strides toward me, holds my face, and kisses me.

My first kiss.

My whole body goes limp to his touch. I focus on the feel of his lips stained with the salt of our tears, the roughness of his hands on my cheeks as he pours his whole heart into the gesture. My arms act of their own accord and rest on his biceps, then slide up to cup his neck. He deepens the kiss, my lips moving in perfect tandem with his, savoring each other in a desperate, hungry way. As long as I can make it last, I don't care if I ever breathe again.

He breaks the kiss and leans his forehead against mine, our breaths matching each other as he gently holds my face in his hands. "I'd hate myself if I never told you I love you too."

The words send my heart into flutters. He sees me as worthy of love. Someone who would never betray me. I grab his face and kiss him again, harder this time. With each breath, each kiss, I wait for the moment I wake up from the dream.

I owe Calista for this.

I break the kiss and lay my head on his chest. I wrap my arms around him, taking in the ridges of strong muscles on his back and the sound of his heartbeat against my ear. The sound I want to listen to forever.

"Thank you for loving me," Quill murmurs into my hair, his voice deep and sultry.

"You make it easy."

He takes me in his arms, softly rocking me side to side. "There have been so many things missing in my life. But I was too stubborn to see that you were one of them."

I lift my head to look up at him. "If you think about it, we're the perfect blend of chaos, strength, and beauty."

"No, you're the chaos and strength. I'm just beautiful." I roll my eyes and he chuckles. I shift my head so I'm looking at him again. He strokes my cheek and flashes an adoring smile he only gives to me. "I suppose you're beautiful too."

CHAPTER 31

QUILL

She loves me.

She loves *me*.

After I poured out my soul to her, after telling her everything that makes me a heavy burden, she still loves me.

I'm living a wish I've had for so long.

Even now, holding her in my arms as we cuddle in the sand of the beach, none of it seems real. She extinguished all the beliefs I had about myself that my parents instilled in me, a relief I accepted I would never have. I'm a brand-new person. An exhilarating, freeing feeling.

I went to that beach to talk to her and be near her, but never intended for the conversation to go this route. My being so scared of losing her made me want to push her away again, but that was a lame, feeble attempt. I couldn't even convince myself that's what I wanted. I loved her too much to follow through.

Neither one of us can sleep. The realization, the understanding, the happiness, all of it buzzes through us enough to keep us afloat for hours. I'm not going to get enough sleep tonight, and I'm fine with that. As we've been talking and kissing for most of the night, I don't believe she minds either.

I tell her every minute detail of my life, starting with my earliest memory and how it all built up into one ugly trap I was desperate to escape from. She listens intently, shedding more tears as a sign of her heart breaking all over again. She reassures me throughout my story that it hasn't changed her feelings for me in the slightest. Everything was on the line. All the things I was determined to hide from her, yet she became a private journal I never had.

Her head nestles against my chest, her ear directly above my racing heart. I let her use my arm as a pillow as I run my other hand from her hip to her shoulder and back down.

"Looking back, I think I fell in love with you when you were dancing with that man in Sabbia," I say, my thumb now tracing circles on her hip. "He had better abs than me and I wasn't having it."

Havanna laughs and pushes at my shoulder. "Because having abs is the deal-breaker here."

"Always." I lean in to kiss her on the nose. I rest my head on my bicep, just staring into those gorgeous eyes, her brown hair a curtain for her cheek.

"It was when I woke up after you saved me," she says, her voice hoarse from crying and talking. "I used to think nothing fazed you until I saw how scared you were." She swallows. "Then you said you were exhausted, and I realized I had never seen you so . . . drained. All because you were trying so hard to save me." She quirks her lips. "I felt like I was worth something for the first time in months."

I slide my hand from her hip to her face, combing her hair behind her ear. "You are."

"And so are you." She gives me a peck on the lips. "Although, watching you throw up wasn't so attractive."

"Good to know that bodily functions from extremely high doses of adrenaline push you over the edge."

"Oh yes. Unfortunately, I'm going to have to break up with you."

"Oh, you—" I climb over her body and pin down her arms, my nose inches from hers. "I'm not going anywhere for a long, long time."

She pretends to concede. "I suppose I have no choice but to accept it."

This banter is exactly why I can't let her go. We've become different people together in the best way. The perfect blend.

I bring my lips down to hers once again, reveling in the way they feel against mine. Tender, loving, and sweet.

Everything we are.

Everything that makes us work together.

***

It's early morning when I wake up. And there we are, still lying in the sand. Havanna is beside me, asleep. So at peace. As much as I'd love to watch her all day, I'm starving.

I lightly shake her awake, earning me a groan. She reaches her arms over her head and stretches her legs, then relaxes back on the sand, a lazy smile she saves for only me. "Did you get your beauty sleep?" she asks groggily.

I chuckle and kiss her on the head. "Oh yes. I'm gorgeous now."

She gives me an unsure expression. "That's debatable."

"My beauty is the main reason you love me."

"It's a perk."

She keeps on the lazy smile, staring into my eyes with such love. Love that I've never received from anyone. "Last night was . . ." She pauses to find the right word, but it escapes her.

She doesn't have to.

"It was." I stroke her cheek and kiss her, the warmth of her lips coursing through me. "Too bad Ender and I have to leave."

Havanna groans. "That's right."

"You can see me off, if you want."

She gives me a skeptical look, but relents to my answer. "Fine."

After stretching our aching bodies and scraping off all the sand, we leave the beach. I take her hand in mine and intertwine our fingers. Something else I have never done before.

Aria rushes to our side from her hut, then eyes our hands. "Oh, *that's* where you've been all night." She winks seductively. "Bolt and Koa were curious."

The mouse and hummingbird flutter from her shoulder and onto ours. Kane, the shrew, stays lovingly nestled in her hair.

"I would have told you if I wasn't so . . ." Havanna sneaks a mischievous glance my way. "Distracted."

Aria holds up a hand. "Say no more. I'm just glad it worked out."

Havanna swings our connected hands. "Me too."

The three of us walk together toward the other end of the village where the eatery is. Havanna and Aria exchange muttered sentences that I can't hear, but I'm too distracted to eavesdrop. I'm holding hands with the girl I love. I've kissed her more times than I can count.

Upon arriving, we find Thaeus speaking to a man at the vine entrance, where Ender waits for me with Anara by his side. The man wears a neatly pressed jacket and trousers, his hair immaculately styled and combed away from his face, perfectly immovable as if carved from wax. His wide eyes of genuine fear distract from his immaculate appearance.

"What's going on?" Aria whispers.

Thaeus hears us approaching and turns to wave us over with urgency. "You need to hear this." He runs a hand through his blond hair.

I take Havanna's hand and pull her toward Thaeus, Aria following closely behind. The polished man eyes us head to toe with hands behind his back, a sneer of derision underneath his pompous attitude at our appearance before he resumes retelling whatever horror he revealed to Thaeus.

He's probably from Arythica.

I agree, Havanna replies. *He's terrible at hiding it.*

"Arythica has been attacked," the man says.

Called it.

"A horde of these . . . *creatures* invaded our city," he says, a chill coursing through him. "Nothing I have ever seen before. They're huge and black with red eyes that pierce your soul, and these rope-like things that fling dangerous objects."

Oh no.

"They were killing people left and right," he continues in a low, horrified voice. His face becomes paler with each word. "Others have fled. I'm unaware of where they went, as I was one of few who escaped the castle of the king."

Ender stares in confused shock while Anara's eyes are distant and unfocused. I see Havanna swallow hard, her palms sweating beneath mine. *The castle . . . They probably found their way to the king and queen.*

King Aldous is likely dead by now.

"Did you see anyone with these creatures?" Anara asks. "Perhaps someone with pale skin, ragged black clothes, anyone that looked unlike those in Arythica?"

His heaving breaths become more rapid, his eyes distant as he tries to recall recent events. "All I remember are these awful monsters raiding the castle. As I was running, I saw someone holding the king and queen hostage with no hope of escape. Queen Avela seemed to be choking, but the attacker wasn't touching them. It was the work of some magic he was wielding."

Well, that answers that.

The Dormant King is trying to overthrow their authority, Havanna says.

"Are the king and queen still alive?" Thaeus asks with worry.

"I'm afraid I don't know," the man replies. "I fled to the safest and farthest place I knew of from Arythica."

I turn to Ender with a small dip of my head. He nods back. It's time to go.

Flame falls to the grass as a gecko, then springs into a vulture. Behind me, Koa has ballooned into a hawk, ready to go.

Havanna regards Aria. "I know you're scared of doing something as big as this, but if you're able, we need your help. You have to decide now, because we have to leave immediately."

Aria glances between her and Thaeus, questions and doubts racing through her mind.

Just then, horrendous screams echo in the Dark Woods. Tree branches snap and crackle; a low hum of footsteps follows. And they only get louder.

Havanna curses under her breath. "We have company. You should get everyone to the compound."

"I'll get the Calling Conch," Thaeus says, his tone laced with fear. He turns to the Arythican man. "You. Come with me."

I motion to Ender. "All right, let's go."

Havanna grabs my arm hard and pulls me back. "No, wait. Don't," she voices in a panic.

"I need to help Ender. I promise I will meet you in Arythica."

Havanna adamantly shakes her head. "Don't. Please. What if something happens to you and I don't see you again?" Her lips quiver as she holds back tears. "I don't want to lose you the way I did my parents. I can't do it again. I can't."

When Ender told me what he needed me for, I didn't think Havanna and I would become anything, so I never considered her feelings on the matter. I still told myself I wasn't worthy of her . . . until last night. With those pleading eyes brimming with tears, I want more than ever to stay. She has to see that this is going to help her achieve her goal.

I take her face in my hands and bring myself level to her. "Listen to me. I'm not leaving you. I'm *never* leaving you. I promise you I will be right at your side to fight. Ender and I will both be there. We just have to do this one thing that can change the chances we have in this war."

"We just . . ." She swallows hard. "We just started. I don't want to lose you."

"You won't." I make sure not to blink so she knows how serious I am. "I promise nothing will tear us apart. I need you to trust me." I graze my thumbs along her cheeks. "Do you trust me?"

Her hands grip my wrists, averting her gaze to the ground. "I—"

"Do you trust me?"

The question hangs in the air and becomes the most important one I can ask. It determines the status and depth of our relationship, and I need that now more than ever. We both do.

At last, she nods. "Yes. With my whole life."

I kiss her hard then, making sure to remember how she feels in my arms, how it feels to own her heart. "I love you."

She forces a smile. "I love you."

I'm about to turn away from the girl I love to go on this mission until she shouts, "Wait!" I see her frantically run to the apothecary close by, then comes out with four potion bottles in her arms. She hands me two. "Battle Elixir. You and Ender will need it."

I find a pocket for one of the bottles and kiss her on the head. "I promise I'll be fighting with you."

She nods, tears dotting her cheeks. "I believe you."

I kiss her one final time and run to our Bennarus. I hand a Battle Elixir to Ender before hopping onto Koa's back. We launch into the sky and we're on our way.

I'm relying on you to keep me alive, compo, I coach Ender. *I have a girl I need to stay alive for.*

So do I, compo. So do I.

CHAPTER 32

ANARA

I'm a massive mess of emotions.

I finally found it in me to tell Ender how worried I was about him, given that he wasn't completely healed. When he only gave me a squeeze of my hand before he took off, I knew I was too late.

Last night was a sign of further change. I laid next to him on a medical bed in a tent. It wasn't comfortable, but I didn't care. I just wanted to be near him. This time, he asked me to stay, and he wasn't so far away from me. He carefully draped an arm over my waist and splayed his hand over my stomach. He held me close to his torso, his whole body a raging fire inside to keep me warm. Yet I pushed away to avoid hurting him. "Is fine," he told me, his breath soft puffs in my ear. "No hurt as much."

"I just don't want to make it worse," I had whispered to him over my shoulder.

He nestled his head into my neck and said, "You would never."

The flurry of warm affection that flooded through me was a feeling I never wanted to forget as I fell asleep.

Now, I'm left with the Electric Doofus to fight off some Dormants. She gazes at me with terror as she grabs the hilt of her sword, and I remember the story she told me when we first met. Because of those freaking Dormants and Backers attacking her village, she lost her mother figure and the respect of the people. With more Dormants in the woods fast approaching, it appears the scenario is about to repeat itself. I grab hold of my trident and dip my chin toward the woods as a signal to head there before they reach the village. Wave erupts into a jaguar, Bolt a gorilla, and they wait by our sides for the sign to go.

The sound of a conch screeches into the air, and all chaos ensues.

Havanna and I charge through the vines and into the woods. The black bodies of Dormants blending with the darkness doesn't bode well for us. Bolt and Wave charge forward and split up, hunting between all the trees rooted closely together and blanketing us from all sunlight.

"I can't see a freaking thing!" I snap.

Something swings at me and I'm sent flying backward with a shriek. My back hits a tree branch, where I ricochet and I face-plant in the dirt. Sharp pain and stinging are all I feel when my breath is knocked out of me. Perhaps I should have kept my mouth shut.

Electricity is thrown in my direction, but stops short when it hits an object and shocks it. The Dormant convulses with the electrical impact, which gives me a chance to produce an icicle sword to finish it off.

Wave calls out ahead of me, along with the shriek of another Dormant. I follow my Bennaru's voice, weaving in between trees as fast as I can. Bark scrapes against my arms and knees. An intense stinging sensation covers my exposed skin and my back screams at me with each step deeper into the dark. My boot catches on a thick root on the ground and I fall face-first into the dirt. I yell out in pure frustration that this has happened twice in the last few minutes. I push myself up and keep running—

Only to stop dead in front of a pair of red eyes.

The eyes jump for me before I can scream. My life ends here, in an effort to save a village that isn't even mine, but found it in my heart to fight beside my friend.

I close my eyes and wait for the disaster to end, but I feel nothing. The Dormant screams, then all goes quiet. Once I open my eyes, I barely make out Wave's frame in front of me. He trots back to me with a nonchalance that doesn't look like he just killed a monster and saved my life.

"Thank you." I pat his furry back. "Lead me back with your night vision."

He plods along ahead of me. The noise of cracking branches and dead leaves leave the perfect trail for me to follow without tripping and hitting wooden obstacles.

Until a cracking branch snaps behind me.

I turn with my trident and thrust it forward without a second thought. The prongs make contact between a set of red eyes that immediately disappear. The dust coats my sweaty arms and legs, blending with the blood of my injuries. I fear other monsters lurking in the shadows so quietly that I have no idea they're there.

Insecurity makes a raging comeback. A panicking heart and rapid breaths weaken my limbs, the trident slick in my grasp.

Where is Ender when I need him? Why did he have to leave? Why why why why?

I close my eyes and breathe. In. Out. In. Out. I can do this without him. I *have* to do this without him. He's my closest friend, but he can't always be there. He's not my crutch. He's my *friend.*

No. Screw that. He's more than that to me. There's no push and pull anymore.

I bring back the emotions from last night. I never want to forget how his arm felt around my body, how his words made me feel beautiful and worthy. Warmth and strong affection flood over me, killing any trace of panic and insecurity that was there just moments ago. My breaths even out and my eyes open to the quiet facade of night.

My legs finally get enough feeling to move forward and listen for the sounds of my Bennaru to follow. Faintly, in the distance, I hear Havanna's grunts and the metallic sounds of her sword colliding with other objects. Strained screams follow each slash.

I speed up to follow the noise. "Havanna?" No response. More grunts. "Havanna!"

"Need help over here!" is her only response. "They're almost in the village!"

I speed up to a run, the sounds growing louder. Red eyes swim all around me, but the frames of individual Dormants are hard to spot. I summon Upsurge through my arms and into my hands. I aim at all the red eyes I can see and siphon all the moisture out of them. Choking sounds, high- and low-pitched, blend together as I imagine them becoming as dry as a dead leaf. The noises stop abruptly, and I can see Havanna's frame slump over within the darkness.

"Thank you," she says tiredly.

"Why didn't you use Strike on all of them?"

She scoffs. "There were too many I couldn't see."

I slowly approach her with large steps to avoid tripping on any-thing. Bolt's gorilla grunts sound behind me as he meets Havanna. "What about the technique you were learning at Arthur's?"

She responds with an uncertain mumble. "I didn't want to start a fire." A pause. "Where were you? I called for you several times."

Right in the middle of calming my panic attack. Right when I was remembering how much I love Ender and how I miss him.

"Went to save my Bennaru," I say, flustered.

"Fair enough." She turns and starts back to the vined entrance shining with daylight, the only place where light exists near here. "We should let Thaeus know that the crisis has been averted and that we're heading to Arythica."

I follow the sounds of all the footsteps. "Do you think he'll come with us?"

A hesitant, thoughtful pause, followed by a sigh. "I hope so. But we shouldn't count on it."

***

"Listen to me," Havanna talks to Bolt, holding a note in each hand. "I need you to deliver these immediately. This one goes to Calista in Sabbia, and this one goes to my parents in Paluso Mountains." She puts them in one of his talons to hold. "They'll know what it means. Meet us back in Arythica. All right?"

Bolt, now an eagle, nods. Worry fills all the lines of her face as she takes his head in her hands and leans her forehead against his.

"Be safe. I love you."

With a strong flap of his wings, he's in the air.

Wave, now a macaw, waits for us to climb onto his back. Havanna had spoken to both Vincent and Thaeus about joining us, and they agreed to meeting us there after arrangements were made for the care of the village. Aria was less agreeable, simply because of fear of not being able to make it back to her fiancé. She didn't seem to like it when my original personality reared its ugly head with the words, "If you want to help your friend, stop being scared."

I'm not one to approach for pep talks.

I relate to her when it comes to Ender, but I suppose there's a certain reassurance in knowing that he's fighting with me.

Thaeus, Vincent, and Aria watch us take to the skies toward Arythica.

With this distance between the ground and the sky, the damage is more evident than we expected. Scattered bodies. Fallen trees. Rubble turning the grass to a new color. People fleeing for shelter.

The desperation for this war to end sets in. We Descendants will finally live in peace and be allowed to explore the land we live in, without the fear of monsters attacking us in our sleep or killing others in cold blood. I may not care what happens to Macaphin Village with the exception of Sharifa and Masina, but I, in no way, want to fail in protecting everyone else and be held responsible for it. I need to be free. I need to discover the person I was meant to become. I want to do all of that with Ender.

"Do we have a plan?" I ask over my shoulder over the sound of rushing air and Wave's wings.

"I believe the only thing we can do is what Arthur told us before we went to Luna Island."

"Which is?"

"Clear the city of Dormants, then address the real problem that's holding the king and queen hostage."

I vigorously shake my head as I picture the scenarios that we will possibly deal with upon arrival. I don't want to deal with the guilt of not arriving on time to save the kingdom's royalty. "I sincerely hope they're still alive when we get there."

This may be a trap, but the exact purpose he's doing it for is beyond me. He has Quill's, Ender's, and my powers. The last of the powers he needs are Havanna's.

Perhaps that's what this trap is for. The question is, what is the plan once all the powers have been acquired? Take over the kingdom? Is that all he's really doing this for? What was the point of having Backers do his dirty work for five hundred years if that's all he wanted to accomplish?

All of it ends with an empty purpose.

On Luna Island, he lectured us on his past. He and the Ancestors didn't get along. He felt worthless. Mocked. Inferior. To the point where it consumed him, and he wanted to prove himself by claiming so much power that the Ancestors had no choice but to fall to their knees. Then he recruited Backers who adopted the same bitter attitude. He carried the burden of that hate for centuries so he could burn us alive.

I lived with hate for a long time, but not so much that whatever heart I had was shattered. Lucky for Havanna, she found me when I still had a shard of one. I never want to become the Dormant King. I never want to be tempted to travel down that road again.

I will kill him before I let that happen.

***

It takes about an hour for us to reach the vicinity of Arythica, completely devoid of life.

Wave descends upon arrival. The state of the city becomes clearer with every second we lower ourselves to land. Not one citizen roams the street. What once was a bright, vibrant city is now an empty mass of thick gloom, a mirror of the Dormant King himself. Broken windows, roofs caved in, pieces of rubble and brick covering the pathways and dimming its shining exterior. Knowing Arythica as a bustling city of wealth and glamour, the condition it's in now is very much out of the ordinary. The Dormant King made quick work in causing this place to go downhill.

We make a running landing off Wave's back and he converts to a jaguar. The drawbridge to the city is in the moat, broken in half and submerged in the water. The cheerful ambience has vanished and is replaced with despair and silence. Holes and shattered windows decorate the buildings, doors unhinged and wood scattered in the cobblestone paths.

Havanna unsheathes her sword, scanning the area around us. "This is bad."

I turn to my right and still. "No. *That's* bad."

I point to what was once a solid, iron-wrought fence that bordered the castle that now has fallen over, caved in and open to the courtyard that was a pleasure to admire. Dirt, leaves, branches, and pieces of brick garden cover the space.

Hands tightly holding my trident, we step into the courtyard, slow and deliberate. The eerie quiet makes any noise that much louder, a potential to wake up any sleeping beast in the castle. Walking up the steps to the grand entrance, I remember how clean and spotless everything was; not a speck of dust could be found anywhere. The red rug that runs through the hallways is plush under my boots, a sensation I was never accustomed to feeling. I was raised being barefoot everywhere.

Pictures that were once on the walls have collapsed and their frames broken beyond repair. Rocks and glass litter the carpeting, the open windows inviting a chilling breeze. The stairwell that took us to our rooms is completely blockaded with a fallen ceiling.

It's impossible to fake my bewilderment. I can't do anything but stare at it all with my eyebrows up to my hairline. Havanna turns to me and swallows hard, reflecting my shock. But within the mess and the silence, it's difficult to decipher where the Dormant King might be.

A groan of pain makes us rear back and ready our weapons, only to find that the sound was near a pile of rubble. An injured man lies there, eyes distant and dazed with a gash on his forehead. We run straight for him to claw off the debris pinning his legs down. His head lolls to the side, his sweat-laden hair plastered to his skin and crusted in blood. Then he lolls it to the other side, back and forth.

He's shaking his head.

A warning.

"We're not going to hurt you," I assure him. "Can you tell us what happened?"

He struggles to breathe, his speaking with pauses between words. "Your . . . Majesty . . . hostage. Monsters . . . in the city."

"Do you know where they are?" Havanna asks.

His only answer is his eyes darting down the hallway to the double doors.

The throne room.

We rise from our knees to head to the throne room until his voice stops us. "No. He's dangerous . . . impossible to . . . kill. He . . . will . . . kill you."

We've reflected his same feelings lately. As his savior, I feel I need to reassure him. "It's all right. We have an army coming to help us."

"He has monsters in the castle," he says in a rushed breath. "You . . . won't win. He's . . . too . . . strong."

Havanna and I exchange a wary glance. I do everything I can to ignore the inkling that the man is right.

Screams echo between the slightly open double doors.

"Enough!" King Aldous's voice booms down the hall. "You have incurred enough damage as it is!"

"Relinquish your throne!" *The Dormant King.*

I angle my trident to a comfortable grip to throw on a whim. Havanna keeps a hand on the hilt of her sword, preparing it with her electricity.

In the throne room, bodies are scattered everywhere. I recognize the guard that I stabbed in the foot the last time we were here. Along with the other guards who once worked for King Aldous. A Backer holds a blade to the king's neck in his throne while six more stand on either side of the chair. Queen Avela is on the floor, bruises and gashes covering her body, hair in disarray, and she freezes in place with a simple outstretch of the Dormant King's hand. She chokes under his hold, trying and failing to gasp for air.

Havanna thrusts her sword and throws a bolt of electricity at the Dormant King. He doesn't see it coming fast enough and electrocutes. Avela gasps deeply as the Dormant King loses his grip on her throat while he falls on all fours. Steam emits from his clothes and burn marks appear on his skin.

The odd part, I begin to realize, is that the Backers are assisting the Dormant King and not attacking us.

The remaining Backers step down from the dais to help their master to his feet, and King Aldous fumbles to crawl to his injured wife. She sobs into his chest as he holds her close, whispering into her ear. My mind floods with memories of Ender and his arms wrapped so lovingly around me, protecting me. Tears fill my eyes. Any thought of losing him is too much to bear.

Not here. I have to be alert of any ambush.

"Master, the Descendants are here," one of them says. "We are almost successful in gaining the kingdom's power. I believe it's time."

I don't like the sound of that. My grip on my trident tightens. "Time for what?" I ask.

Another Backer delivers a sly smile, eyeing us as fresh prey. "Time for us to receive the powers we've been promised."

CHAPTER 33

HAVANNA

This. This is the part I've longed to see, all while dreading it too.

The Dormant King promised the Backers to pass down his powers when he claimed all of them. We kept interrupting any chance he had of passing them down and securing a stronger army. Now that we're here, hell-bent on destroying their master, this is the moment to make it happen.

"Under different circumstances, I would agree." The Dormant King walks around his Backers, hands held behind him. He aims a burning gaze at the king and queen, helplessly sprawled on the floor. "But I haven't yet secured the throne that belonged to me centuries ago." Then, he turns that same gaze straight to me, chills trickling down my spine. "And I have more abilities to claim."

"Master, you have a sufficient amount of power," a Backer argues. "If you give them to us now, we have a better chance of taking down our enemies. *Your* enemies."

Before they can think of making their next move, Anara chucks her trident at them. The Dormant King is quick to stop it and turn it back on her. I use Gridlock on it before it has a chance to touch her, then I'm flung off my feet into the nearest wall. The entire back of my head screams at me as I fall to the ground like a sack of rice. I have just enough strength to lift my head and see Anara charge at the Dormant King, just to have him zip away with Gateway and reappear in a split second to toss her to the nearest wall, her trident landing with a *clang* just feet away from her. He holds us in our positions, standing board straight and emanating arrogance.

"Perhaps you're right," he plainly says to the Backers. "This has been easy enough, but having you all at my side, multitudes more powerful, we will no doubt secure the throne."

"Over my dead body!"

King Aldous is brave enough to stand, puffing out his chest in defiance. His haughty, superior attitude will do nothing against the Dormant King's power.

He eyes Aldous with admiration. "You have guts, Your Majesty," he croons. "Alas, your defiance will be all for naught."

Aldous is soon lifted off his feet, a limp doll in the air. Avela watches in horror, helpless to do anything about what the Dormant King will do next. She attempts to reach for his ankle to pull him down, but she's shoved away from him. Aldous, straining to breathe under the grip, floats closer to the Dormant King and hovers a body length above him.

"I shall take the reins of Petros and turn this kingdom the way it was meant to be."

Everything inside me clenches and seizes, but I work to grab my sword and send electricity through it. I don't like the king as a person, but I can't stand watching Avela look on as her husband is slowly tortured.

The Dormant King leans forward in an intimidating manner, evil humor and darkness dancing all around him. "And I will do it over your dead body."

One crack of the neck and Aldous is dead.

Avela releases a bloodcurdling scream, tears falling down her face as her husband's limp body hangs midair.

"Now that's done," he says with nonchalance, tossing the body to the floor like an empty sack. Avela wails loudly, grabbing and pulling her hair in overwhelming grief. I didn't like either one of them, but I never wished this kind of pain on them. I swallow down the contents of my stomach that beg to rise, trying to erase the way Aldous's head twists in an unnatural angle. The sound alone will haunt my dreams for a lifetime.

Anara, on the other side of the room, summons Upsurge into her hand. The ball of water grows each second, concentration and fury fueling her power more and more.

"You, on the other hand, are just a nuisance," he comments toward her, using Manipulation to stop her, then opens a portal behind her. "How about you buy us some time?"

"No!" I scream at the top of my lungs, using all the strength in my arms and legs to return to my feet. I use Gridlock to freeze her, then swipe my hand to the side so she flies away from the portal. The hole closes up.

"I'm getting *really* fed up with being thrown around!" Anara screams in pure rage as she pushes herself back up.

"Get used to it," the Dormant King snaps. "I dealt with it for years before I was banished."

With Manipulation, he takes away my sword and her trident and lays them on the dais. Then takes a wailing Avela and glues her to her throne. "You all have too much of an advantage." He turns to his Backers. "Come. I'll sit on my new throne, and I'll do the honor of sharing my powers."

I stretch out my hand to use Gridlock on him, but he acts quicker. He brings me closer to Anara and pins us to the wall. "Now what fun will this be if you cannot watch me claim what's mine?" he purrs, then forcefully grabs a Backer. "Give me your hand."

This is the moment the Dormant King's entire purpose comes to life, and we're powerless to stop it. My goal in redeeming my people, the ones I love, has all been for nothing. The Dormant King and his Backers will have the advantage and Anara and I will be eliminated.

The Dormant King keeps his grasp on the Backer's wrist, eyes shut tightly in concentration. We all wait for something incredible to happen: colors transferring into the Backer's arm or the Backer suddenly able to manipulate water and air.

A few seconds. A minute. Nothing happens. They just hold hands within the awkward tension.

"What are you doing?" the Backer snaps. "Why is this taking so long?"

"Shut up!" he snaps back.

Sweat beads his forehead. His breaths turn harsh. And still, nothing happens.

The other Backers turn to each other in confusion. "What's going on?"

Anara and I exchange an astonished look. He formed his army with a simple promise. They lived and died for that promise. Without the Dormant King holding up his end of the bargain, the last five hundred years of looking for us Descendants was a waste.

"I don't understand it," the Dormant King mumbles, staring in terror at the disgrace he's bringing upon himself and his army. His concentration on us falters, leaving Anara and me free of confinement. We're too stunned with the scene before us to make any moves.

The Dormant King rips the Backer's arm away from him and grabs another, trying the same technique on him. Only to be met with more failure.

"I don't believe this," Anara says, barely audible.

"You fake!" a Backer shouts loud enough to spit, drawing his blade. "You liar!"

"You deceitful cockroach!" another shouts, also drawing his weapon.

The Dormant King rises from the throne, rearing back with the onslaught of threats.

"Are you suggesting that you have promised us your powers for centuries and you are unable to give them?"

"We spent centuries doing *your* hunting, *your* killing, and you give us *nothing!*"

The Dormant King refuses to show even a hint of regret. "You accepted the assignment without proof of my ability to share my power. I refuse to accept the blame for your ignorance!"

The rest of the Backers surround him with their blades aimed at his chest and throat, growling at their targeted prey. "It's time you pay for your lies and deceit!"

"We would much rather fight you beside the Descendants than spend another second in your inferiority!"

I scoff. It's much too late for the Backers to redeem themselves in any capacity. They're too far deep in errors.

"Ha!" He creates ice on his fingers that twirl and grow in thickness along his arms. "That is a battle you will lose."

The Backers launch at him with their weapons that he blocks with his iced arms, then escapes with Gateway as soon as the portal opens. He reappears behind them, his hands turning red as he gets ready to use Blaze. They charge at him as he tries to force the fire out of his palms, but it fails. Instead, embers burst from his skin, an extinguished fire in his palm. I glance at Anara, then turn back to the fight in front of us. Not once have I seen the Dormant King unable to use any of the abilities he's acquired. This changes everything.

He's unable to use Blaze. But why?

I shake the question out of my head. We need the Dormant King dead before he officially replaces Aldous as the king of Petros.

I recall my new skill during training and curl so all my limbs are touching. The desire to strike lightning in this castle, grouped with anger toward the mess the Dormant King has created for centuries, and everything he's done to my friends all surges through me. Buzzing and vibrating sensations take over the surface of my skin, as if something inside me has taken all my muscles and gently shaken them. The feeling increases until sparks pop and zap around me until my whole body is covered with it, hot to the touch.

"I'll keep them distracted," Anara says. I barely register what she says as she scurries away and I focus heavily on my ability.

Anara heads to Avela, who's still frozen in grief and not at all registering what's going on around her. She opens Gateway and pushes the queen through the portal, sending her to safety. It takes eight seconds for everything to fall apart, one after the other.

One. The Dormant King notices Anara.

Two. I push my hands forward and send an electric dome to my targets.

Three. A portal opens behind the Dormant King.

Four. I throw my hands down.

Five. Lightning rains.

Six. The Dormant King disappears.

Seven. The Backers take the impact of my attack and are killed.

Eight. The Dormant King reappears behind Anara and causes rubble to rise in a circle at his command.

I run up to the dais to retrieve our weapons as rocks pelt into the shield Anara crafted from Upsurge. She's brought to her knees as she continuously adds ice to it, but the attacks don't cease.

"Anara!"

She turns to me just as I toss her her trident and I force electricity into my sword. The Dormant King aims a hand in my direction and everything in me seizes. Invisible hands clasp around my mind.

Kneel.

My knees buckle, but I fight back. My entire being—my very means of survival—centers on one objective: rejecting his control. Even my breathing stops as I'm shutting my eyes and grunting in extreme effort.

Kill the Water Descendant.

"No!" I scream, falling to my knees and pulling my hair away from my scalp. My arm shakes as I resist it reaching for my sword. A desire to kill Anara pushes for space against my conscience that doesn't want to do it.

Kill her.

"STOP IT!"

Anara's shield crumbles and she thrusts the prongs of her trident at the Dormant King. Upon instinct, he raises his palm to block her attack, only for the middle and longest prong to penetrate his hand. The room erupts in a high-pitched cry and the invisible hands release their hold on my mind. I fall forward, my limbs free of all strength.

I find it in me to lift my head just enough to see Anara rip the trident out of his hand, then flip it to hit him in his chest with all her might. He stumbles off the dais and rolls to the floor, joining the king he murdered.

Familiar roars and shrieks flow from the hallway to the throne room. Pounding feet rumble the stone floor beneath us, a dreadful sign of what's coming for us. Wave's roar blends in, and based on the increased volume in high-pitched shrieks, he's trying to buy us time. Only, he will not be enough to do it on his own.

We're at a disadvantage. No army beside us, only Anara and me fighting the most powerful enemy in the kingdom, and a horde of his monsters that can tear us apart fighting their way past Wave.

I send electricity to my sword. One more feeble attempt to show him that he cannot win. At the same time, Anara is summoning Upsurge as the Dormant King stumbles to get back to his feet.

Just as Quill and I finally find each other, it ends this way. I'll never be able to tell him I love him one more time. The Dormant King will show everyone that I'm the fool who believed she could bring him down. Everyone will believe my determination was laughable and never respect how hard I tried.

He stretches out his hand—

Havanna. Anara.

Quill. Quill is alive.

Incoming.

The window in the throne room shatters, glass shards spilling all over the floor. Three large creatures fly in, cawing a war cry.

Koa.

Flame.

Then Bolt.

Koa heads straight for the Dormant King and digs his talons in his shoulders. He yelps in pain as Koa lifts him up and carries him back through the broken window.

Bolt flies to me and extends his talons, his humongous wings flapping to keep him afloat, waiting impatiently for me to reach up and grab hold.

"Perfect timing."

When I finally muster enough strength to lift my arm, he hurriedly grasps my wrist and also flies back out the window.

Suspended in midair as I summon the strength to keep fighting, the only thought that floods my mind is relief that Quill is alive.

He kept his promise.

Bolt soars over the cliff where the castle rests, then banks left to take us to the wide-open field of green outside the city. It's then that I have to blink twice to make sure I'm not dreaming at what I see.

An entire army of hundreds closing in on Arythica. I see what our support consists of, and I smile so wide it hurts.

Thaeus.

Aria.

The Mulhutna.

Calista. Malik. And the rest of Sabbia.

Ender.

And Quill, perched on the head of the Tyranodrake.

Koa drops the Dormant King like a dead rodent on the opposite side of us where he beholds the scene in front of him. Bolt and Flame bring me and Anara to the ground in front of the army. I turn and come face-to-face with Calista.

Somehow, seeing her invigorates me, being the epitome of strength and fearlessness as she holds her spear upright. Then, I remember what I'm doing this for. *Who* I'm doing this for. She, among hundreds of others, have my back, very well knowing the risks that are to come. That never stopped them. I'm tired, but I can't let it stop me.

The smile on her face holds back her excitement and pride, and I beam at her. Malik comes to stand beside her and grasps her shoulder with a loving smile, proud to be fighting alongside his wife.

Keeley joins in on the union when she nudges me with her elbow while wearing a grin, an unspoken agreement that we're friends. Ever since I saved her and the Sabbians from the Backers and Dormants, she's never failed to show me respect and admiration. I smile back and stroke her arm.

Tena and Anca, Ender's mother and compo, appear next to him. Anca and Ender exchange a hearty bump of the fists, a mutual brotherly love. Tena hugs her son from the side, her fists aflame in a roaring fire that does nothing to singe Ender's skin. He gives her a kiss on the head, looking ahead to the enemy before us.

Thaeus and Aria appear also, ready at my sides. He grips my shoulder, leaning his forehead onto mine. My eyes close with the contact. "You ready to do this, massy?"

I breathe through my nose. "More than ever."

Aria takes my hand in hers and squeezes. I break contact with Thaeus and regard my best friend. Tears make an unexpected appearance in my eyes. Perhaps it's because of the seriousness of this battle and the desire to have everyone involved survive. "Stay alive so you can be with Claeron," I say.

Aria nods, wiping the tears out of her own eyes. "There's no other option."

As if in agreement, a shrew appears from her neck. I realize it's Kane when he leaps off her shoulder and balloons into a bull, his horns dipped low.

"He's taken a liking to me," she says sheepishly, patting Kane on the back. He snorts in approval with her touch. Wordlessly and with a subtle nod, they're ready to attack. Nothing standing between us and the Dormant King. Hundreds of us against one.

Finally, the moment I've dreamed about for years has arrived.

CHAPTER 34

ENDER

Nothing feels more liberating than marching to battle with the backing of your entire tribe *and* their guardian monster. In all the years I've been a tribal chief and we were blessed with the Tyranodrake, I have never come face-to-face with it. I know that it is our best weapon if we have any chance of beating the Dormant King. Somehow, Quill proves how powerful he really is to be able to manage a creature of that size. And doing so with such grace.

While we were at Vulca Mountain, I took the opportunity to return to my tribe and let Aani know I was alive and well. She held me and cried for a long time. She held her own, being the Mulhutna chief by herself, but it was clear she was somewhat crippled with missing me. "I'm so glad you're all right," she sobbed into my torso.

Aani was devastated when I told her that Arythica, her hometown, was destroyed by the Dormant King. That alone motivated her to get the entire tribe to follow me back down the mountain to battle. As we were heading to Arythica, hordes of support rode in on their steeds in all directions in unison. They acted in a heartbeat after receiving Havanna's note from Ketra.

The Dormant King was responsible for my aanu's death, a Mul-hutna chief my compos loved and respected. This is a chance to avenge him, and they were going to take it.

You are all delusional if you think you're enough to defeat me. I hear his voice in my head, unsure if he's addressing every single one of us closing in on him or just us Descendants. *You forget what I have at my disposal.*

It's impossible to forget when the ground rumbles and Dormants emerge in all directions. Some come pouring out of Arythica to aid their master, and it becomes the biggest army I've ever seen. Bigger than ours.

This is why we have the Tyranodrake.

"All-out assault!" Havanna screams.

I breathe in. And out. War is amidst us. It's now or never.

I raise my axe in the air. "For Petros!" I bellow from the depths of my diaphragm. The Tyranodrake roars loud enough for everyone to feel it in our chests.

We charge. The way we all move together, so fluid and seamless, voicing our own war cries, is a euphoric feeling. Calista, Malik, and Keeley charge forward with their scimitars and spear held over their heads. Anca's footsteps rumble beneath me as he runs toward the chaos with my aani by his side.

The Dormant King holds out his hand in our direction, and the Dormants charge forward. He disappears from the scene, a coward leaving his army to fight the battle on their own. Fortunately, Quill warned everyone fighting on our side that this might happen.

Remember what I told you, Quill says. *Be on the lookout in all directions. He can show up anytime, anywhere.*

I make sure to keep an eye out for anything appearing suddenly as I throw my axe down and send strings of fire skidding through the grass, burning the Dormants on the spot. Then spin in multiple circles to eliminate the ones attempting to trap me.

Intense heat comes from dozens of feet to my right. An overwhelming, unpleasant aroma of rotten flesh and sulfur fills my nostrils. Fire engulfs layers of Dormants that melt into ashy particles in seconds. The Tyranodrake sweeps its head side to side, crouched low and blowing fire at everything in its path. All I manage to do is stare in awe at this marvelous creature at work.

From the Tyranodrake's head, Quill glances at me with the same amount of awe. *Did you know it could do that?*

Nope.

In the center of battle, stone and dirt emerges from the ground. At first, it starts out as a pointy, jagged pillar. The tips curl inward to create massive boulders as big as Arythica's castle split in half until they're carved in perfectly round shapes. They drop on both Dormants and warriors, as if cut from the ropes that suspended them in the air. They roll and crush everything in their paths, aiming for the Tyranodrake. Its spiked tail is powerful enough to swing down and crumble it to large pieces as it continues to trample on Dormants and snap its jaws at everything in its path.

An idea forms in my mind. Similar to something Quill and I have done before.

I summon Gale, moving my arms in a circular motion. The air obeys the command of my hand as it spins faster and faster into the form of a tornado. The force becomes so strong that it lifts the pieces of boulder and pummels through Dormants. More emerge from the ground to replace the ones that are killed. With Transmission, Quill informs me of what he's going to do with the heavy pieces of earth so I'm not caught off guard. That's when the rocks split in four different directions and crush objects in their way.

I run to avoid the impact of the rock through the battlefield and stop to help anyone in distress. It unnerves me when I see bodies of the fallen scattered in the grass—a victory for the Dormant King. Anger at the sight fuels me to hit harder with Blaze and burn the enemies alive. Each swing of my axe leaves a trail of flames that brings down the monsters who are getting the upper hand. I hardly progress a few steps through the violence before I have to assist someone else. Most of the Dormants are twice the size of the average person. With just a handheld weapon to fight with, those ones will have difficulty facing one alone.

I save a Sabbian woman choking with a tentacle wrapped around her neck.

I save a compo captured by a flying Dormant when I throw a ball of fire toward it.

I save Quill when a Dormant crawls onto the Tyranodrake's back and makes a beeline for him.

I save someone when a Dormant's fire burns his shield to ashes. As it tries killing him with an icicle to the heart, I manage to melt it in midair before it reaches him.

Suddenly, I'm frozen in my stance. Every muscle feels as if it's being held back by a rope. I'm twisted in a full circle to face the culprit.

"So disappointing. I thought I killed you," the Dormant King says while holding me in place with Manipulation.

"No one kill me."

With his other hand, he's attempting to summon Blaze. His palm turns red, his features contorting as the fire burns his skin.

This opening is a perfect chance to attack him, but he has my limbs completely immovable.

The color dies off. Just as it did in Siro.

"Why does that ability fail me so?" he shouts in frustration. The slight distraction breaks his focus on me and I can move again. I get Blaze to work in seconds and shoot it at him. The fire engulfs his clothes and he immediately extinguishes them with water. Steam erupts from his body and I notice the fire barely touched him. The air formed by the fires surges together and lifts me high enough above the ground to make everyone below me seem tiny. A sheet of ice forms underneath me in a split second as I plummet back to the ground, a landing that will break every bone in my body. I fail to understand how he can use Upsurge and Gale, but not Blaze. Not exactly helpful to use against him as he has all our other abilities.

Except Havanna.

As soon as my stomach drops from the thought of broken bones, I stop falling. I'm frozen, suspended above the ice. Flame swoops in, a war cry belting out as he grabs me with his talons.

Thank you, Havanna.

Flame tosses me onto his vulture back, then changes to tiger form in seconds as we swoop lower. I ride with him through the sea of Dormants that continue to appear out of nowhere, swinging my axe in every direction while he uses his iron-strong jaws to clamp on and tear them apart.

A dome of yellow film expands above us and borders the Dormants. I warn Flame that we need to get out of Havanna's vicinity. He turns back into a vulture and springs in the air with smooth effort. Lightning rains down just as we make the escape. We circle back, a thick cloud of dust breezing in our direction and temporarily blinding us. It becomes so thick we can barely see five feet ahead.

Rumbling, shouting, and shrieking all blend together as a reminder that the victory is short-lived.

CHAPTER 35

QUILL

Havanna's strike did wonders to decrease the enemies we have fighting against us. It is a fleeting relief, until the Dormant King summons more Dormants. Trapped with him on Luna Island, what I saw making its way to the coast was simply scratching the surface. With the way it is now, Ender's idea of getting the Tyranodrake was a genius one, though. Without it, we would be severely outnumbered.

Looking for Havanna from this distance is difficult, being so high up from the ground and perched on the Tyranodrake's head. Dormants are springing from the ground at an alarming rate, yet I don't see the Dormant King anywhere. I tell Koa to pick me up from the Tyranodrake's head, which he obediently does when he lurches from battle. I leap onto his back and swoop down to where Dormants surround a crowd of soldiers. I pull out some Pineapple Shell arrows and get to work shooting them down, one set after the other, explosion after explosion going off on impact. I circle the scene and find obvious signs of Dormants rising and shoot them down before they make any moves. When a lump rises from the grass, I know it's one of them, and that's when I act. I'm making progress until a Dormant dive-bombs at me, snapping its jaws dangerously close to my ear. I nock an arrow and shoot it. When I reach for another, my stomach drops.

I only have one left.

My heart pounds against my chest. With only one arrow, I have to save it for a dire situation. I have no use for my bow now.

More flying Dormants dive-bomb at me and Koa, one after the other, only increasing the panic in my heart. No matter how many times Koa swoops down and back up to escape their taunts, they don't stop scraping my neck and back with their talons. I take my bow and convert it to a staff—the only way I can use it now.

I resort to Transmission. Not on them, but the Tyranodrake. *Burn them up.*

The Tyranodrake twists its long neck in my direction, then turns its body fully when it gets on its hind legs and slams its feet back down. Its mouth opens toward us and we dive just before a tunnel of fire jets at the flying Dormants, the residual heat turning my cheeks red.

We circle back to the fight to check on my friends, particularly the ones that mean the world to Havanna. I didn't save Indigo in time and she couldn't save Jael. We can't afford to lose anyone else.

A flying Dormant soaring toward us at top speed steals my attention, and its jaws latch on below Koa's neck.

"Hey!" I scream. I launch forward and use my bare hands to loosen its grip.

Koa cries in distress, twirling continuously to throw the Dormant off. The world goes upside down and rights itself repeatedly, spinning and spinning and spinning. My stomach roils and bile rises. I hang onto his feathered neck for dear life and get my bodily functions under control.

The very thought of losing Havanna in any way is painful enough to even fathom. Losing my Bennaru will rip my heart out and bleed until there's nothing left.

I need you to right yourself for a minute. I'll take care of this.

Koa obediently stops spinning, but cries as the Dormant keeps trying to drag us back down. I reach for a knife on my leg and stab the Dormant through its snout with all the force I can muster. Its jaws release, but it turns to use its talons to grab Koa's neck instead. Koa turns sideways to escape its attempted grasp and flies off. The Dormant is relentless in its pursuit, its talons ready to grab anything. When it gets close enough, I slash at its feet. It wails, but remains afloat, although it's taking more effort on its part as it flutters below us, ready to use its tentacles as weapons.

The Tyranodrake is busy eliminating the throngs of monsters, so I need to take care of this one on my own. Which will mean I have to take another risk.

I'll tell you when to catch me.

I jump off Koa's back. I ready my knife the closer I get to the Dormant, and land on its head before it can do anything else. My other hand grips a tentacle, just to hang on to something. It's soft and has elasticity, similar to squeezing a cotton ball, and stretches similar to melted cheese. I bend its head backward from the force of my pull, and we're descending quicker than I expect. I plunge the knife into its neck and let go, creating a slit down to its belly. It dissipates to dust and I'm free falling again.

Now.

The ground is getting closer and closer. A reminder of this exact scenario with Havanna. Just in time, Koa catches me.

We take to the skies again and I look over his neck. Two large, red dots are prominent in his grayish feathers.

"Oh, buddy, you're bleeding." I lay a hand on the injury, getting blood on my hands as I pour Transform into him. I will for his skin to close over it, the blood vessels to connect and operate again. I keep my hand planted there, forcing my wishes for this to work through my arm and humming through my hand. Once the holes turn to puny dots, I stop. I need to reserve my energy for more dire situations.

There's going to be a lot of those.

CHAPTER 36

Anara

As far as I know, no one from Macaphin Village is in this war. Says a lot about my so-called family. Which means I need to do everything I can to protect the ones that have become my family.

One of whom is about to be killed by the Dormant King himself.

Havanna swings her sword in all directions, never missing a beat. Dormant after Dormant is slain, dust in the wake of her sword as it covers her clothes and hair. Dirty cuts and bruises all over her skin, the sword clutched tightly in her right hand, she stands as the epitome of a warrior.

Manipulation seizes her entire body. Her sword hits the ground with a *clang* and her body bends backward. I make a run for it with my trident gripped tightly. I plan out my attack with each step and pick up the pace before he stabs her with ice. The bottle of Battle Elixir molds into my hand as I grab hold of it, toss the cork to the side, and down it in one gulp. I need all the strength I can get if I'm going to help win this war.

I drop to my knees and slide along the grass toward him, slicing my trident along the back of his legs. The Dormant King cries out in near-bloodcurdling anguish. I race to Havanna, who just dropped to the ground and is gasping in pain from the abnormal angles of her body.

"You pest!" the Dormant King spits.

I retrieve Havanna's sword from the ground and toss it to her while aiming my smirk at him. "That I am."

He aims a hand at Havanna with a pointed, sharp stream of water that rapidly lengthens as it reaches for her. I swing my trident down in time to cut it off before it holds her captive by the waist. A Dormant springs up in front of her as a distraction and the Dormant King glares at me.

"You really know how to piss me off," he snaps, baring his teeth at me. "You keep standing in my way."

"It's what I'm here for."

I thrust my trident forward, but it hits a wall. An invisible one. The Dormant King doesn't even have to raise his hand to use Manipulation on me. His irritatingly arrogant smirk is a telltale sign that this is too easy for him. He begins to maneuver around me to get to a distracted Havanna until I swipe my trident under his feet and trip him. The rage that brings foam to his mouth gives me unspoken joy. I picture that feeling growing as Upsurge builds in my hand. As long as he stays on his back, this will be an easy kill. As much as I want to siphon water out of him, his being this powerful will probably mean I will never be able to dehydrate him completely if Upsurge runs through his body constantly. One more thing to make this difficult that I don't have the courage to test out.

Upsurge is cut off before I even have a chance to make something of it. Manipulation snatches the trident from my hand.

And proceeds to warp the prongs beyond repair.

The trident I trained with.

The trident passed down to me from the parents I never met.

The trident that molded me into the warrior I am now.

Anger is a turbulent river in my veins. He's taken so much from all of us, and now he's taking my very means of protection. Upsurge can only do so much and Gateway will be useless here.

Without my trident, I have nothing.

I *am* nothing.

All my energy, all my focus, goes into forming Upsurge into my hands. Balls of liquid grow within my palms that I clap together to make a giant one. Then I pull what I now call an "Ender move."

I slam my fists on the ground with a furious scream. Two streams fire forward toward the Dormant King, liquid blades cutting divots through the grass. My power is stopped short, though, when I feel a suction behind me.

Everything goes black.

During the split second it takes for me to be transported from the Dormant King to right in the middle of the conflict, I'm pissed off that every single move I made up to this point set me at a dead end. Each time I have an idea, each time I have a feeling it would be an easy kill, the Dormant King proves me wrong.

He thinks *I've* angered him?

He's angered me an infinite amount more.

Dormants crowd around me the moment I appear. I instinctively reach for my trident behind me, only to remember that I don't have it anymore.

I suppose I have to rely on Upsurge from now on.

They're closing in quickly. I build Upsurge again, but it's going to take time to have enough water to take them all out.

Time I don't have.

My heart races with every passing second. I'm dehydrated and I can't reach for more water. The ground trembles beneath me with the arrival of my savior and I can't control the smile it brings me.

Ender slashes his axe in all directions, trailing fire behind him. He hits so hard that the Dormants either soar into the sky or they turn to dust. He sends a trail of fire weaving through any remaining ones that try to sneak up on us that effectively clear the area.

He winks. "Nice see you."

It occurs to me that I haven't seen him since we were in Ketra. I'm relieved he's all right. "Thank you."

He leans forward to help me to my feet. He yelps in pain when he pulls me up, his other hand covering his torso.

Crap. His wounds.

I move his arm to see three holes bleeding through his clothes. "Ender, you're bleeding again."

"Is fine."

He hoists the axe over his shoulder, doing nothing to hide his discomfort. He's my family now. I vowed to protect him at all costs. In his weakened state, he's an incredibly easy target. Despite his strength, he's not immune to weakness and injury.

"No. I'm getting you out of here."

I open a portal behind him with the intent of transporting him to the Tyranodrake's back. From that distance from the heart of conflict, he can pull himself together.

I take his hand and we go through the portal. We're on the creature's back within seconds, where I try to position him to sit upright against the bottom of its elongated neck away from the row of spikes that run from its head to tail. It moves at a snail's pace, one step at a time. We can barely feel the motion as it swings its tail back and forth, making it a decent spot to recoup.

"Do you have your Battle Elixir?"

He nods with an intense level of pain contorting his face when he reaches into a pocket. He pops the cork off the bottle and downs the liquid. "It no last long," he remarks. "This war last long time."

Incoming.

Quill's tone signals something bad. And it's crawling up the Tyranodrake's body.

The creature swivels its head to reach behind it as Dormants get to work climbing up its legs, making Ender topple forward. The loud snap of its jaws vibrates in our stomachs as it clamps around a group of attackers. It only makes a small dent in their progression.

It turns in a circle to reach other parts of its body, the Dormants making quick work of clawing their tentacles on the skin of its back. It roars loud enough to be heard for miles, then swiftly turns its neck to the other side and starts snapping its jaws again.

"I help," Ender announces, surging fire through his hands and blowing it at all the monsters coming his way. Ice grows into pinpricks on my fingertips, just enough that I won't completely deplete myself in helping Ender. The small shards fire off my fingers in quick succession, shooting the Dormants in the chest that Ender finishes off with Blaze.

A deep inhale groans through the Tyranodrake's elongated neck, its entire body becoming so hot that I break out in a sweat in seconds.

"It blow fire!" Ender shouts. He lunges for me, covering my entire body with his own. The heat from his skin combined with the Tyranodrake becomes nearly suffocating. The amount of sweat covering my body feels as if I just dipped into a hot spring. Fast and hot breaths dry out my mouth; my limbs turn fluid. Despite the creature's movements having us rolling along its back and ruining our balance, Ender doesn't fail to protect me from burning.

Just when I think I've reached my heat tolerance, it gets worse.

The Tyranodrake breathes more fire. Intense heat cocoons us. When its mouth moves down toward its legs to burn off the remaining invaders, it cools ever so slightly.

Ender lifts his body from mine with a pained groan, sitting back on his knees. I need to catch my breath now that I finally have ample air, but we don't have time. He helps me to my feet again, only to behold a worse scene.

Flying Dormants diving straight at us.

Dread coats my body in a cold sweat. There has to be ten of them, and I'm left to take them on myself as Ender attempts to recover his balance.

Two war cries from a pair of powerful birds echo behind me and I smirk.

Flame and Wave soar above the Tyranodrake's head as fast as a windstorm, straight for the herd of Dormants. As soon as they collide with the enemies, they turn into their feline versions and tear them apart, hopping from one to the next. Within seconds, they're dust that floats into the air.

The Tyranodrake plows through the Dormants, nothing but blades of grass in comparison to it. On all fours, it raises its spiked tail and throws it down, then drags it along the grass over the mounds that house oncoming Dormants. With the amount that seems to pour in continuously, I worry we won't have enough strength to win this fight.

"You go fight," Ender weakly calls from behind me. I turn to regard him, fall back on my butt, and hold myself up with my hands. "Petros need you. I be fine." He waves in dismissal. "I need few minutes."

The last thing I want to feel is regret for leaving my best friend behind to fight a war he should be a part of. If something happens to him and I'm not there to save him . . . I can't even imagine the possibility.

My throat is tight as I swallow. He looks at me curiously, waiting for action. To decide what to do.

I love him. I can't leave him.

"No." I crawl to his side along the creature's back, following the ridges of its spikes that line its spine. "I'll help you fight from here."

"But—"

I shush him with a finger to his lips. "It's all right. It's the least I can do."

Telling him I love him now would be poor timing. I don't want him to believe I'm saying it because death seems imminent. I want him to believe it when I tell him.

So I bend my elbows and let Upsurge build. "Now let's do this."

CHAPTER 37

Havanna

Calista, Malik, Keeley, and I form a united circle, our backs toward each other, and we're slaying like the powerful warriors we are. Dust lays a gray blanket on the entire field, turning our sweaty skin and hair into darker colors. A nasty gash on my cheek and bicep stings like nothing else, but I push onward. I've been under worse conditions and still fought for my life.

The smell of burning grass, sulfur, and old flesh assaults my senses with each slash of my sword. It's the epitome of a violent battle that I'd like to think we're winning. Bolt is helping the other soldiers fight as a gorilla, since his brute strength is a huge advantage. The Dormant King must know this, because he's relentlessly determined to get close to me. He reappears, then disappears the moment I have a chance to attack.

Quill's voice is soothing to my tired muscles and nervous heart. *Let me know if you need me.*

I will always need you, Quill.

I know. I'm irresistible that way.

I scoff as I twirl in the air and slash down on a Dormant. *The Dormant King is relentless. He's determined to get to me.*

Not if I have anything to say about it. I got you.

His protectiveness sends heat within me. I love that man so much it hurts. I will do anything to keep him alive. We owe it to ourselves to see where our lives take us after this is all over.

Koa and Quill dive from the sky, closing in quickly, then bank left to find a better angle.

I only have one arrow left. I'll try to use what I have.

Be careful. I force electricity into my blade, raise it to the sky, then spin in a circle. Lightning strikes a group of Dormants dead in one hit. *Be sure not to hit me or anyone in my circle.*

It's like you don't know me. I never miss, Zappy.

So I've heard.

A black hole opens in front of me—a sign of what is coming next. I break from the circle.

Right in front of me. Go!

Quill and Koa soar over us. A blade flings past my ear with a whoosh, aiming straight for the Dormant King, who just stepped out of the hole. He stops it immediately with Manipulation and flings it back in his direction.

"No!" is all I can scream as the knife hurtles toward him. I use Gridlock to freeze the knife in midair, just long enough for Quill to circle round and snatch it.

I turn back to the Dormant King and find his hand reaching for me, getting closer and closer.

"You're the last one—" he starts to say with a playful lilt. He's unable to finish his sentence, though, when a knife hits him in the right shoulder. He stumbles back, but doesn't fall. The affliction is vocalized in his obnoxious wailing, palming at the hilt. I watch, appalled, as he yanks the knife out of his flesh.

Koa swoops low and Quill hops off his back. Fury blazes in his chocolate eyes, an animal-like determination to kill as he forcefully pulls another knife out of a sheath from his thigh.

"Get away from her!" He growls.

This amuses the Dormant King when his face glows with a smug grin. "You lovesick fool," he hisses. "You were stupid to leave me. All because of her." He chuckles, then regards me. "All the more reason to take you for everything you have. He'll regret ever ditching me."

Quill leaves no room for anyone to think when he launches at the Dormant King with his knife ready to strike. He manages to catch Quill's hand by the wrist and kicks him in the gut hard enough to crumple him to the ground, then retrieves his knife and slashes at me with it. I dodge it, but not quick enough as he cuts my scar below my collarbone. I cry out, my head pressurizing with the effort of pushing air out of my lungs. So much so that I could explode.

Warmth trickles down my chest and into my shirt, followed by an unbearable sting. Just then, Quill grabs another knife and thrusts it into the Dormant King's leg. I use the opportunity to rev up Strike with my hand. He's been stabbed twice; it can't take much more than my lightning to end this once and for all.

Life changes in three seconds.

One. Lightning strikes next to the Dormant King before I can throw my hand down.

Two. The Dormant King stumbles.

Three. I turn around to see how lightning struck before I told it to.

And there, behind me, stands my mother.

Her palm still flickers a dim glow of yellow in the lightning bolt in her palm. She smiles brightly at me, tears brimming in her eyes, and her actions say three words that are a balm to my soul: *I'm here, Warrioress.*

She listened to me and my note. All the times she backed down in the past, she chose not to this time. My heart overflows with gratitude and my throat tightens.

She's here to fight with me. I get to see what this side of her looks like.

A new plan shines in the Dormant King's eyes. I know exactly what he's thinking. A step in my mother's direction says it all.

A man jumps in front of her, fully equipped in plated armor that digs up my childhood memories. He slashes his sword at the Dormant King with a triumphant yell, but he disappears before the man can get him. He turns to face me, and it's Papa. With the exception of his gray hair, he looks just as he did when he was a knight in Cal-léa.

Words choke in my throat. The anxiety of war, constantly wary of where the Dormant King will go, and seeing my parents has me inundated with emotions. I don't even notice when Quill gets up and comes to my side.

"Bolt gave us your note," Papa says. "It was time we redeemed ourselves for failing you for so long."

I can't help it. Their being here means so much to me that it brings tears to my eyes. "Thank you." I turn to Quill approaching my side.

"Now, Warrioress . . ." Mama steps closer to me, electricity sparking in her palm. "Let's finally change our history." She regards Quill. "And you can tell me all about him."

"Long story short, I'm adorable and I'll do anything for her," Quill says in a rushed manner and kisses me on the cheek before taking off. "I'm going to help Anara and Ender. They're on the

Tyranodrake. Ender's injuries are making it hard for him to fight and Dormants keep appearing."

Crap. He will need to heal Ender. Anara can't fight them off by herself without her trident, which I gave to Keeley for safekeeping. She'll run out of energy too early.

"No, I'll come with you." I turn to my parents. "They're the other Descendants."

Papa grips my shoulder. "Go," he admonishes.

Right on time, Koa swoops down to pick up Quill with his talons and makes his way to the Tyranodrake while I snatch the trident hitched on Keeley's back.

Bolt dives toward me as I hold the trident upright. He grabs each end of it with his talons and I grip on tight as he flies me to the Tyranodrake.

Dormants make their way up its legs like ants. It moves its legs up and down, causing them to lose their grip and making it easier for it to stomp on them. The horde of Dormants are nonstop, both on land and on the beast.

"Bolt, put me on your back!"

He flips me onto his back with a swing of his talons. A sword in one hand and the ruined trident in the other, I raise both tips to the sky. Lightning crackles in the dark clouds and connects with the weapons, a massive buzz vibrating along my arms. The flight gives me ample time to build up the power.

Quill lands in front of Ender and Anara and sees the Dormants climbing along the Tyranodrake's spikes toward them. Once we're low enough, I jump off Bolt's back with both weapons fully electrified. I land, throwing my hands down, and rain thunder so bright everything turns white. A dull ache forms behind my eyes that runs through my forehead. A throb starts in my temples.

I only have one Battle Elixir. I don't want to use it until I absolutely need to.

I inhale thick plumes of dust that make me cough. The Dormants have been cleared from the Tyranodrake, nothing but particles floating about. Anara is on her knees, her head hanging low as she catches her breath. Quill has a hand on Ender's chest as he uses Transform.

I crouch in front of Anara and hand her the trident. She examines it in a state of defeat, but turns around to Quill. His eyes are half open, beads of sweating running down his temples and his hands shaking.

She hands him her weapon. "Quill, fix my trident."

He looks up at her, exhaustion written all over him. "I'm a little busy at the moment!"

"But I need this in order to fight." She points to her empty water bottles attached to her hip. "I'm all out."

"I be fine, compo," Ender assures him. "I feel better."

Anara's countenance and voice are completely laced in desperation. "It'll just take a minute. Please."

She's not asking. She's *begging*.

Quill takes his hand off Ender's torso and groans. A few more rapid breaths hiss from his lips and he aims a hand at the trident. The prongs untangle themselves from each other and straighten out, free of all curves and imperfections. Within seconds, her trident is reverted to its perfectly straight form. The sleek, polished, blue metal shimmers in the daylight, and it somehow looks newer than it ever did.

"Thank you," is all she whispers.

Quill hangs his head, panting as if he had just finished running for miles. "I don't know . . . if I can finish healing you, Ender."

"Come on, you can do this." Anara drops to her knees to encourage him. "Take your Elixir."

Quill hurriedly retrieves the bottle from his pocket and drains it. He allows time for the potion to work through him as he takes deep breaths.

That's when it occurs to me.

I'm the only one who hasn't taken the Elixir. Once we've depleted our energy, we'll be done for.

We're going to run out of time.

When the Dormant King appears in front of us, we have even less time.

CHAPTER 38

QUILL

"All of you here at the same time," the Dormant King croons. "How convenient."

When he studies the Tyranodrake's head, which is dipped low and blowing more fire in the open field, I know exactly what he's planning.

I'm the only one that can intervene.

Whatever that other voice is telling you, don't do it. Listen to me. Keep fighting.

The creature lifts its head and releases a deep, guttural roar, then its back sways side to side roughly enough to make us stumble. The Dormant King no doubt is working his persuasive powers on the poor creature.

Just as I did with Koa, I keep talking to it.

Keep going. Breathe all the fire you have. Do not *listen to any other voice but mine.*

I repeat the same sentiment until it stabilizes, much to the Dormant King's chagrin. That smug smile of his never falters, though, as he calls on Blaze. His fists turn red at his sides, and I'm prepared to fight back with a hand on another knife. This time, I need to dodge his attack and get in closer quarters with him. I need to get him in the spot that keeps him alive: his cold, evil heart.

No fire pours out. Not a single ember sparks. From the expression on his face, he's making an effort. Punching, swinging his fists, centering his focus onto his arms with squinted eyes and knitted eyebrows.

Nothing.

He screams in utter frustration and moves in on Havanna with purpose and determination. I run beside the Tyranodrake's spikes, ready to collide with the Dormant King. I roll toward him, taking my knife out as I come back to my feet, and slash at him. He blocks all the moves, no matter how hard I try. Then he pushes me over with Manipulation, where my head lands dangerously close to a spike. He moves toward Havanna again, and she's ready to fight back with her electrified sword. The Dormant King stretches an arm out and uses Manipulation to keep her at a distance. She leans forward and slashes as far as she can, but to no avail.

What I see next makes me want to kill the Dormant King with every fiber of my being.

With his other arm, he reaches for Havanna's neck.

"No!" I scream, lunging over a spike without a second thought.

Anara throws a stream of water that wraps around his neck and tightens before he can do anything. Havanna takes that split second to lunge at him with her sword. The blade makes contact with a thick block of ice that forms on his arm within seconds. As she attempts to pull her sword away, he lifts her up and tosses her off the Tyranodrake like an unwanted cloth. I'm about to scream at the top of my lungs until I see Bolt dive to her rescue.

The Dormant King uses Upsurge to remove Anara's water rope that spatters on the Tyranodrake's skin. Havanna's not in his presence; now he can focus on killing the rest of us.

As I look up, flying Dormants dive toward the Tyranodrake's face, taunting and threatening. The creature shows its irritation with subtle growls. Everything changes when it rises onto its hind legs to snap its jaws at the monsters. The level of its spine morphs to a steep slant that has us tumbling down toward its tail. It keeps its balance with a couple steps that brings us midair as we're rolling. I scream and reach out desperately for something—*anything*—to grab onto. I hear Ender and Anara grunt in exertion, then I finally manage to make contact with a spike. I hang on for dear life despite the slick surface, my fingerless gloves being the only clothing on my hands that give any sort of friction.

I open my eyes at last. I'm met with a ninety-degree angle of the Tyranodrake's entire neck, as if I'm gazing at the sky from my back. Just feet above me, Ender has embedded his axe into the creature's skin and he's holding himself up by the handle while Anara grips his ankle for dear life. The Tyranodrake doesn't even notice as it swivels its head in all directions to chase the flying Dormants. Ender's grunts turn into cries of pain the longer he holds himself up and the longer Anara hangs onto his ankle.

I turn just enough to gaze over my shoulder to see how high we are above the ground. It would take about five seconds of falling to hit its barbed tail before falling a couple more seconds. Not a pretty ending for a pretty boy.

The Tyranodrake steps back to keep its balance, which messes with our grips on the creature. Anara's and Ender's bodies swing out and back against its flesh and I adjust my grip on its spike. I would tell it to get down, but it's helping kill Dormants in the air, something we desperately need.

Anara, I need to get to Havanna. Can you use Gateway?

Sure, just let me fall to my death first.

I'll get your Bennarus to save you. Just take me to Havanna.

She peers down at me with a pained groan. I use Transmission to call to Flame and Wave just as I feel something behind me.

I confirm there's a hole there with a peek over my shoulder and I let go, falling straight into the portal.

CHAPTER 39

HAVANNA

I'm fortunate enough to be caught by Bolt while I plummet to my death. He takes me to the general area of the open field where Calista and my parents are. Sabbian soldiers surround Calista and fight anything that tries to come after her. I see her hunched over, holding herself up with her spear, head hung low. She's losing strength, covered with dust so thick that it's changed the complexion of her skin.

The Mulhutna act as a wall that blocks any access to my mother. Their large frames are abnormally heavy enough to kill monsters in one hit; they're the best protection for Mama as she uses Strike on the Dormants charging toward them. I thank Quill in my heart for arranging for my mother and Calista to be protected. Bless him and his Transmission.

I raise my hands to the sky as Bolt dives lower toward Mama. Strike hums through every limb, every joint, every inch of my skin. Dormants close in on the Mulhutna guarding my mother, and I throw my hands down with a snap of my fingers. A storm crashes upon them, giving the giant trolls a chance to fight other oncoming monsters.

A sense of dread fills me when the dullness of my headache gets worse. After a couple more uses of Strike, I will have to take my Battle Elixir. Once I deplete that source of energy, if the war has not yet ended, I will have to push through it.

I find my father catching up to Mama from behind, putting his sword skills to good use as one Dormant at a time springs up and attacks. One slash of his blade, and that's all it takes. Bolt lowers me to the ground where I execute a running landing and catch up to my parents.

"All right, Warrioress, time to show me that you've lived up to your name," Papa says with a sense of pride. I can't help but smile. I never got to experience fighting beside my father. He was my teacher for the first few years of my life. I imagined showing him what I've learned over the years, but I never imagined it being under these circumstances.

"Happy to."

The Dormant King ruins that chance when he appears between us and my mother. Those dark, cold eyes aim directly at me as he grows an icicle out of his hand. Before he makes a move, Quill arrives out of nowhere and stands in front of me.

"You're going nowhere near her," he growls, getting his bow ready to use as a staff.

"Says who?" he replies in kind, stepping threateningly close to Quill.

"Us."

Thaeus and Aria march toward us with purpose, covered in dust and blood that I'm sure is not theirs. The way Aria's eyes shine with a hunter's glare of vengeance, her bow poised and ready, has me staring in awe. I haven't seen her with a weapon since the last target competition in Ketra. Thaeus's axe, donned with dust, gleams in the daylight, ready to annihilate anything in his path. Then, standing beside me are my parents. Calista, Keeley, and Malik gather behind me, scimitars in their hands and Calista's spear ready to throw in a heartbeat.

A resounding boom sounds close by, followed by an earthquake that brings us to our knees. The Tyranodrake finally lets itself down from standing on its hind legs, stomping on any Dormants in its wake.

The Dormant King takes in the scene with a blank face. A miniscule part of me hopes he will decide to just give up. That he understands that we will stop at nothing to bring him down. Then he says two words in the darkest, most haunting tone.

"Watch me."

He throws my father to the side, an unwanted rat contaminating his mission. With the help of his staff, Quill forms a wall between us and him with the thick dust blanketing the grass. The Dormant King claws around the wall with the violence of a rabid animal, gnashing his teeth and screaming out in annoyance, then uses Transform and blows the dust at us. I feel him at close proximity to me, although with impaired vision, and I slash my sword around me to keep him away. Rock and dust burst from beneath him and send him in the air with a quick motion from Quill, despite him rubbing his eyes with one of his hands. On a whim, I attempt to use Strike while he falls back to the ground. That does nothing but kill a Dormant that takes the hit for him.

With Gale, the Dormant King is able to lower himself to the ground without getting killed, which is right when my father charges at him with his sword. I turn to see Quill's eyes turn green toward the Tyranodrake, and it begins moving in our direction.

"I'm having it clear out Dormants over here so we can focus on him," Quill informs me as I help him regain his footing.

A measly flick of the Dormant King's hand, and Papa's sword bends out of shape, destroying it just as he did Anara's trident. From the rock that Quill formed, he takes chunks of it with Manipulation and throws them at him. I have my shield ready to act quickly enough that I can slide in front of my father and block the barrage.

There is a triumphant grunt the moment the rocks hit my shield. Calista appears out of nowhere and swings her spear at him. My stomach drops. She almost died at the hands of Backers; fighting the Dormant King will be the thing that breaks her.

I rush toward her, sword ready. Calista strikes as hard as she can with her spear, but the Dormant King dodges each hit with a maintained smug smile that says this is much too fun for him. I'm ready to slice my sword across his chest, but he blocks it when he causes a boulder to rise between us that uppercuts me on the jaw, then disappears. Calista and I recover quickly, and I turn to see Papa coming back for more, leaving his weapon behind.

"Here." I toss him my sword. My whole existence. The tool that helped me along this tough journey. A constant reminder of Jael always being with me. "I'll use my Strike. Be sure nothing happens to it."

He catches it by the hilt, twirling it around with his wrist. He gazes at me with understanding, as if he could already tell what my sword means, and gives me a subtle nod.

A black hole opens close to us. My hands clench into fists by default, getting electricity ready to stream through my veins, until I see Anara and Ender emerge through it.

"Thank Halivaara you're here," I say between heavy breaths.

"Where is he?" Ender asks through a low, guttural voice.

"Disappeared again."

Anara groans. "I'm so done with his *crap!*"

"Be on the lookout!" Calista warns.

That warning proves easier said than done when the Tyranodrake changes course. Instead of plowing through the masses of Dormants that won't stop emerging, its head and piercing orange eyes lock in directly on us. I'm positive it just grinned.

Then it charges straight for us at a frightening speed. Its jaws hang open in preparation to fit us all into its mouth. Its booming footsteps violently shake the earth beneath us and make it harder to maintain our footing.

"What's happening?" I ask Quill in a bone-shaking panic as I struggle to avoid falling.

"Freaking Dormant King!" He extends his hand toward it, trying to use Transmission to the best of his ability.

"Then he's in close proximity!" Malik shouts, his expression perfectly reflecting Quill's. His head whips to Calista, who happens to be in the line of attack for the Tyranodrake. He and Keeley dart for her, and I look back to Quill, knowing she will be taken care of.

Quill, on the other hand, is the most afraid I've ever seen him. Then I see why.

Underneath the Tyranodrake's body is a sea of Dormants charging forward, straight for us.

Oh please, Quill, make them stop.

His breathing quickens as he pales, eyebrows knitted and sweating profusely. He repeatedly falls to his knees and struggles to get back up while working to talk to the Tyranodrake. A vein pulses in his temple, giving his all to change the course of events.

"It's not stopping!" he shouts in a high-pitched voice that indicates strenuous effort. I witness him trying his best, and something squeezes my heart until it hurts. The Tyranodrake is slowing down, and lifts its head just a bit, listening to whatever voices are whispering in its ear. It's a short moment until it hears what clearly is the Dormant King's voice and continues charging. Despite the panic expanding and flowing through every part of my insides, I need to be there for Quill.

"Hold the Dormants back as long as you can!" I yell at the others. "I'll use Strike!"

Quill keeps his hand out, aimed straight at the Tyranodrake's face. It begins to waver in its course, lifting its head and chortling as its pace slows, then stops altogether when its feet stiffen at the same time. Then, it peers down at the monsters fighting our friends. My parents. Who are all largely outnumbered.

I cross my arms over my chest and crouch, electricity burning through me and heating up my skin. I make sure that the yellow barrier I produce only covers the Dormants, and I release. Bright white and yellow bolts crash down on the entire horde that effectively turn them all to dust. My headache gets slightly worse, but not enough to make it excruciating. The only thing that makes it mildly better is Quill's eyes, sparkling with pride as he smiles at me.

"Have I told you how incredible you are?"

I rise to my feet and bring him up with me. "No. But you'd be wrong, because you are far more incredible." I grab his face and kiss him, hard and brief. "Now let's kill some monsters."

We join the others as more Dormants rise from the ground. Seeing everyone's skills and talents working so well together, with little to no planning, is a sight to behold. Anara's Upsurge works wonders with siphoning multiple Dormants at once. Ender's fire burns in a perfect torrent from his axe, just as the Tyranodrake stomps again and shakes the earth beneath us, dust billowing in its wake.

Mama comes up next to me, electricity buzzing through her arms, just as it is mine. "Your power astounds me, Warrioress." She raises her hand to the sky. "I wish I had your bravery when I was younger."

Words I have been desperate to hear my whole life. Not from Jael, but my true, full-blood mother. I've made her proud—everything I could dream of.

I give her my prideful smile and extend my hand to the army without breaking eye contact. "Give yourself credit. You made it here."

I freeze a row of Dormants heading straight for me and Mama, and I wait for her to act. In seconds, she has lightning pouring down from the sky in a beautiful shower of light. In the blink of an eye, the light is gone and so are the monsters. I'm about to tell her how happy I am that we get to work as a team, but she cries out. She grasps at her temples and falls to her knees as soon as I come to her side.

"Kora!"

Papa's shout is laced with dread and concern as he leaves the others to come to her aid. We both kneel next to her and hold her.

"I don't think I can use Strike for much longer," she says. "The pain will be unbearable."

More Dormants spring up at the exact same time the Dormant King emerges from a black hole in front of the others. His eyes darken as they narrow directly at me. Suddenly, my body is suspended above the ground.

"Havanna!" Papa yells.

The Dormants head for me and my parents, but they skid to a stop just paces from us. They don't even touch us. Then they turn to face their master and aim to attack him instead. I fall back down when my friends distract the Dormant King enough for him to break his focus.

Quill's voice makes its way into my head as the Dormants cause chaos between us. *Please tell me I got them to turn around before they attacked you.*

Warmth envelops my heart. *You did. Thank you.*

I will do anything to make sure he doesn't go near you.

And I love you for it.

I return to attempting to bring Mama back to her feet. With her head hung low and eyes nearly shut, she's in more pain than I realized. Our friends are slowly getting outnumbered more and more, but they're still holding their own. It won't be long before we all run out of energy.

"I need to get her out of here," Papa says.

"I'm the one that started this war. He'll try to kill me before he tries to kill her." I point to a patch of woods off in the distance, just far enough away from the battle to not be detected. "Take her there and don't move."

He disappeared again.

I curse to myself on Quill's update. *Have Anara open a portal and take us to those woods. I need to tend to my parents.*

After a few seconds of silence, I help Papa keep my mother on her feet. As soon as we have stable footing, a portal opens.

"Where is this taking us?" Papa asks.

"Away from here. Hurry!"

We stumble quickly to the open hole that sucks us in and deposits us within a copse of trees in seconds. Mama falls to her knees, still clutching her head.

"Just stay here," I tell them both. "I have to go back out there."

"No!" Papa exclaims. "The Dormant King is clearly after *you*."

"I know." I point to my chest. "I need to kill him before he has the chance to kill me."

"You've tried!" he retorts, then scolds himself. "I knew we should have stayed in Paluso." He regards me again. "He's too conniving. He's going to best you—"

"I refuse to hide," I seethe. "I've done it my whole life. I've united the Descendants, and they're fighting the battle I've started." Tears well up in my eyes. "And I need to be there for the man I love. Just as you are with Mama. Just as you've *always* been with Mama."

Papa sniffs away his fear and breaks eye contact. Mama watches both of us in silence. Her gaze switches between me and him, no words of wisdom to interject with, the ache in her head most likely making it hard for her to think. The only thing she seemingly thinks to do, though, is bring her hand to his cheek and stroke it so lovingly. Her lips quiver with a hidden sob, a silent message to the man who's loved and protected her for so long. He gives her a subtle nod and lets the tears fall as he looks at me with regret.

"You've held back long enough," he says in a low voice. "And you've found a love worth protecting. You've come out the other side a stronger, more powerful woman who never sacrificed her loyalty and kindness." Papa turns to Kora with no effort to hide the love shining in his eyes. "Go. Fight for everything you love."

Then Quill's voice delivers a grave message.

Keeley's been injured. Anara is warping her with Calista and Malik to find a safe place to heal.

My heart drops to my stomach. *What happened?*

His voice is strained as he communicates while fighting. *The Dormant King said we can't stop him from finding you. He was about to use Gateway until Keeley intervened to keep him from reaching you. He took her scimitar and slashed her with it. He's gone and we don't know where he is.*

I forget how to swallow. I forget how to breathe. If he injured Keeley and disappeared successfully, then—

Go help Keeley! Heal her! I don't want her paying a price for trying to save me. Calista needs her.

Zappy, I'm near the end of my limit. I'm barely strong enough to hold off these Dormants.

"Havanna, what's wrong?" Mama asks through a pained tone.

"Are you all right?" Papa asks.

I can't hear either of them. I'm too devastated.

Anara used Gateway for them, and she's near her limit too. Ender isn't showing it, but he's slowing down. We're outnumbered, Zappy. And our Battle Elixirs are gone.

"My friends are getting tired," I whisper. "One of them is injured. And we're out of Battle Elixir." I swallow hard. "We're outnumbered."

A soft gasp comes from Mama. Leaves crunch under Papa's boots as he steps back. The air of hopelessness is suffocating. I don't want to believe that we're losing. I can't believe that this is how it ends. I refuse to lose any of them.

Not Calista.

Not my parents.

Not Ender or Anara.

Most of all, I'm *not* losing Quill.

I will think of something. Keep fighting. I will save all of us. Please don't give up. Please.

The only way I will willingly die is to save you, Zappy. I'm too pretty to die, so don't be getting yourself killed, all right?

I chuckle through the tears. Quill always knows what to say to break the tension, no matter how life-threatening.

"What do we do?" Mama asks, her tone laced with desperation.

"There's only one thing to do."

The Dormant King shows up out of thin air behind Papa. I don't have a chance to attack when I see Papa's eyes glaze over.

With an icicle protruding from his torso.

I don't hear myself screaming bloody murder. I don't hear Mama screaming either. The sounds around me are muffled by my own trauma and grief. Bile rises to my throat as I choke on my sobs and pure rage burns me to my soul.

"Stop fighting the inevitable," the Dormant King roars, and lets Papa collapse to the ground. Mama rushes to his side with some hope of helping him survive.

This is the exact scenario I was in months ago when Jael was dying in front of me. The ache blooming in my stomach is unbearable. I lost Jael, and now my father is slipping through my fingers too.

Screaming in pure rage, I use Gridlock on the Dormant King and throw him as hard as I can against a tree.

Hello? Havanna? Are you all right?

Quill's voice cuts in as the Dormant King stumbles to recover himself. Sobs break through, and I can't stop them.

My father . . . He stabbed my father.

Havanna . . .

I need you to save him. Please.

Whether he responds or not, I don't know, because I'm more focused on killing the monster in front of me.

I pick up my sword that I lent to my father. My breaths are vocal and angry as I send electricity from hilt to blade.

A portal opens behind me with Quill, Ender, and Anara rushing through it, charging straight for the Dormant King against the tree. Ender and Anara pass me without saying a word, and Quill evaluates the situation with Papa.

"Do whatever you need to do, just save him!" I beg. "Please! I'll do anything!"

"Havanna, I can't," he says with sadness. "I have nothing left."

"I don't care, save him!" I scream. Deep within my bones, I'm being selfish and irrational. Quill has told me multiple times he's out of energy. I'm begging him to nearly kill himself to save my father simply because I refuse to accept another loss.

Despite being near his breaking point, Quill lays a hand on Papa's torso. Mama is sobbing uncontrollably and Papa's breaths are labored. I already know we're too late. I know I would never forgive myself if we didn't try to save him. I also know I'm denying, with the marrow in my bones, that the Dormant King is winning.

"I can't!" Quill exclaims and releases himself from Papa. He shakes his head in defeat. "I'm sorry. I can't without killing myself."

With his sickly complexion, dark lines painted under his eyes, I know he's telling the truth. Seeing Anara and Ender fighting the Dormant King, he's overtaking them. She has trouble summoning Upsurge and Ender's constantly being thrown around and hitting trees, slower to get up every time.

I move to my father's side and reach for his hand while Mama holds his other. "I'm sorry, Papa. I'm so sorry I couldn't save you."

He shakes his head. "No. I'm sorry I failed you. I hoped this would make up for not being with you during the most important times in your life. I hoped for another chance in being a good father. I suppose I missed that chance."

I shake my head vigorously. "You didn't fail. You tried." I peer up at my mother. "You both did."

"I just hope . . ." He pauses every few words, his breath slowing down. "You look back and . . . remember how proud I am . . . of you."

I wrap his hand in both of mine, laying my lips against his skin, letting my tears drip onto him. "You got me started, Papa. I'm forever grateful for that."

"Never stop . . . fighting for what means . . . the most to you." His eyes flutter closed, growing heavier by the second. He lulls his head toward Quill. "Take care . . . of her."

Quill's eyes brighten unexpectedly with tears. He nods. "I will, sir."

His head sinks back onto the ground, eyes aimed straight above him. "I love you . . . Warrioress. I . . . always will."

His hand slumps from my grip, and he's gone.

Mama buries her face in Papa's chest, wailing with her loss. All I feel is determination and the fury that drives it.

His Backers killed Jael.

He killed my father.

My friends are out of Battle Elixir. Only mine is left.

Keeley is injured.

My friends are growing weak.

The Dormant King is winning.

I spring to my feet. Electricity surges through my sword, so much so that it might explode at any moment.

I'm done *losing*.

"What are you doing?" Quill calls from behind me.

I'm running full speed toward the Dormant King, ignoring his desperate calls.

"HAVANNA!"

The Dormant King sees me and smiles wickedly. I push harder, run faster. I give it my all to end him. I take my bottle of Battle Elixir with my free hand, yank the cork off with my teeth, and gulp it down forcefully. If no one else can be strong enough to finish this, I have to be.

He backs away, one step at a time. Then he opens a portal behind him.

Oh no. He's not getting away this time.

"You'll never catch me, Descendant."

He goes through the hole.

And just before it closes, so do I.

CHAPTER 40

Havanna

This is my second time free falling. The first time, it scared me beyond all reason because I knew I was staring death in the face. Except this time, the Dormant King is falling below me. I no longer care where we're falling to; I just want to make sure he'll die.

I straighten myself so I'm falling headfirst and dive faster toward him. His limbs splay out so gracefully as if he's done this his whole life. Which pisses me off even more. He just killed my father; he doesn't deserve to live out his days gracefully. He doesn't deserve to live at all.

Once I get close enough, I shove him, then slam a fist in his face when he turns to look at me. We shift so that we're falling sideways and I continue punching and kicking. He kicks me once in the shin and then my stomach. I refuse to show any signs of pain as I throw my fists in all directions, hoping they will land somewhere in his face more than the air.

"Insolent creature!" he bellows in annoyance when he shoves me away from him and kicks me again to seal the deal. Distance grows between us as we keep falling. I land on a sticky yet buoyant surface, and he's gone.

I can't get up. Whatever I've landed on is stuck to my back and legs, holding my arms captive. Squirming and trying to kick does nothing, just makes the surface underneath me bounce like a mattress. Somehow, I can turn my head to examine my surroundings.

Everything is dark and laced with purple mist. The dead silence is deafening—not a single sign of life. Even the trees are void of souls, stripped bare of leaves or woodland creatures. The grass in the distance is charred black with the mist dancing among the blades. Then, I notice what I'm stuck on.

An extremely large spiderweb.

A whimper escapes me as genuine fear takes over. Spiders make my skin crawl. The way they move is enough to make me yelp. And there's a Dormant version of it that exists somewhere.

A cold sweat breaks out as I thrash among the sticky substance. I don't know where the Dormant King is, and I'm stuck on a spiderweb to be feasted on in what I've concluded is the other dimension.

A hiss followed by a clicking sound makes me seize. A low growl makes its presence known, and more clicking, the way a tongue does on the roof of a mouth. The web bounces. Each step makes it move more. The shadow of the culprit darkens through the mist, and I see the tentacles waving in all directions in slow motions. From here, the Dormant is the size of Bolt as a gorilla, and only grows in size as it draws closer. Breaking through the mist is one leg as long as Ender's height.

A spider leg.

The end of its spindly limb slams down on the web. The next leg follows. Then another. And another, until all eight work in unison as it approaches its next meal. A head full of eyes of all sizes lock in on me, the clicking sound getting louder as its fangs move in and out of its mouth.

The pure dread rolling through me, enough to clench my bowels at the sight of the scariest thing I've ever seen in my life, has me screaming so loud that my vocal cords are on fire. Even when my throat is hoarse and beyond raw, I don't stop. No amount of thrashing makes a lick of difference. I have no way out.

Something lands on its back, and suddenly I'm not the one screaming anymore. The Dormant spider seizes, all its legs shooting straight up and locking in place. A dying cry squeaks out of the monster as it collapses on the web, everything going limp. A cloud of dust erupts, and I see my savior before me with a knife in his hand.

Quill.

"You came for me?" I ask breathlessly.

He runs across the giant sheet of web, but struggles when his boots catch on threads in their wake. "Of course I did."

He kneels beside me to cut me out of the web. "But . . . you're exhausted," I say, as if he needs a reminder of how he feels.

He chuckles with no trace of humor. "I wouldn't be alive if all it took for me to lose a battle was exhaustion." He narrows his eyes at me, vigorously ripping the blade through the web. "And you jumped through an open portal to chase an enemy." He winks. "I had no choice but to follow you."

Despite the seriousness of the situation, I softly laugh. "Thank—"

I fall through the web after Quill makes a decent dent in it and I land on a hard surface. A burst of sharp pain explodes in my shoulder. He escapes through the hole he made, hitting the ground beside me with a *thud*.

"You're welcome."

He helps me to my feet and I give myself a moment to slow my heart down. The last few minutes have been overwhelming to the highest degree, yet I can't give any of it thought right now.

Quill sheathes his knife back in his leg and reaches behind him for his staff. "I'm sorry about your father."

I swallow the lump in my throat, tears welling up again. "One more reason to kill the Dormant King." I gaze at him with cold, dark eyes. "Taking away any chance of having my father again."

He gives me a sympathetic look. "I know if somehow I had a second chance to have Indigo back, and he was killed again, it would rip me from the inside out." He sniffs, his jaw tightening as he fights back emotion. He only had one person by blood that loved him, and it was taken from him. It isn't fair.

None of this has been fair.

The only memories I have of my father are from my childhood, yet any dream I had of starting over with him for the last ten years just vanished out of thin air. Our chances of starting over with the people we love are nonexistent, and that enrages me.

I reach for him with a gloved hand, my fingers grazing his cheek in a featherlight touch. "Then let's fight for him. And my father. Together."

He turns to me with a sad smile, but everything else shines with pride as if he's glad he's finally not alone. He leans his forehead against mine, gripping my upper arms affectionately. "I never want to fight without you again."

His words invigorate me. Just as Halivaara made me feel when I needed it most.

"You won't. I promise."

He motions to the barren, lifeless land ahead of us with a new blade in his hand. "After you."

We tread the darkness for a minute, keeping an eye out for something to appear out of nowhere. The Dormant King may have gotten far away at this point. I'll look for him until I die if I have to.

"So . . . this is the other dimension, yes?"

I try not to smile at how awkward he sounds while still trying to break the tension. "How did you get here anyway? Anara would've had to know where to bring you if the portal closed before you got to it."

"Oh how you underestimate my quick thinking, Zappy." He races ahead to stay a few paces in front of me. "The portal was almost closed when Anara used her powers to keep it open just long enough for me to go through."

"Are they all right?"

"Yes. Ender's in a lot of pain, though."

Crap. He's barely had a chance to heal properly. This war has to end so he can get the rest he needs and deserves. And the rest of us can heal in peace from all the trauma.

The only sound that takes space in the air is our footsteps under crunching grass and dirt. The mist curls and twists to our cautious movements, in between trees, small hills, and rocky cliffs that are high enough to reach the sky, or ceiling, or whatever it's called in this dimension.

I lead Quill with hand motions in the direction my gut tells me to go. Each careful step helps me think through my remaining options as to what will officially end the Dormant King's life. All exterior attacks have done nothing. Perhaps the answer is *interior*. On the inside.

Greed is poison to the heart.

That's why he's been focusing so much on capturing me. If what Halivaara said was correct, that means owning all of our powers will be the poison to his heart. Considering that he has an abundance of powers already, I struggle to see how that is the poison.

When he copied Ender's powers, he acquired Blaze and Gale; he can use Gale, but he cannot use Blaze. And he can use Anara's Upsurge, though, which involves water.

Water is what hinders Ender's Blaze.

Water always puts out a fire. He can't use both because the water is dampening the fire within him.

There is always a limit to be reached.

The Dormant King hasn't reached his limit. I'm the only one left.

That limit, my beloved Descendant, will be what breaks him.

It all makes sense. Halivaara gave me the answer. I had it the whole time, and I didn't understand it until now.

Quill taps my shoulder and silently urges me to look where he's pointing. Off to the left is a decent sized body of water.

With ripples.

No breeze. No creatures lurking around. Not even a bird wading through it. Everything is silent. Which means something emerged from it recently.

I hold my sword tighter, more hyperaware than I was before. He must have landed in the water and ran off to hide. He knows we're here.

A figure in black matching the surroundings around him pounces from his hiding place and immediately slashes at Quill with a hammer made from ice. Quill manages to block it with his staff just before it meets his skull. The Dormant King's slow effort gives me an opening to shock him with enough electricity that sends him skidding a few feet across the ground. He uses Manipulation to send me airborne toward the pond, but fortunately, I don't meet the water. My utter weakness finally registers when I try to hold myself up with my arms. They quake so violently that I thud back into the dirt, and all I have the strength for is to lift my head.

Quill decides to go for the kill with a knife. The Dormant King beats him to it when an icicle shoots out of his palm. Quill moves, but he's too late.

It stabs him in the right shoulder.

The scream that rips from my throat fills my head with a pounding, intense ache. Grief seizes every bit of my heart, watching the man I love stumble back, eyes distant, and his hand acting of its own accord as he reaches for the shard embedded in his skin. He collapses to his knees, coughs coming out in puffs as he hunches over.

"That's what you get for not listening to me," he growls before Quill. "All you needed to do was stop fighting. Allow the inevitable. But no. You insist on proving how strong you are when what you truly are is *pathetic.*" He spits the last word in pure disdain.

Finally—*finally*—I know what I have to do.

Rage heats my blood until I'm hot to the touch. I have never felt so powerful. So strong. So ready to deplete everything I have and everything I am to do what I need to do. It feels as if something is controlling my movements when I lift myself to standing. Even more so when I run toward the Dormant King. I'm moving faster than I ever have in my life, and I push myself to speed up more. I use just enough Gridlock to slow his movements and plow into him with all my might. Just as I throw a fist toward his face, he stops it with his hand.

Just as I was hoping he would do.

"At last, you give me the final ability I need," he says with an evil smile. "My duty is complete."

Purple travels in tendrils through his hand, then along his arm. I nearly collapse on top of him as he takes what is left of me, but I force myself to resign to his greed. This is exactly what needs to happen. I'm more sure of that than I am of anything else.

He withdraws his hand from my fist, the purple dissipating into his body. He wiggles his fingers, acclimating to the sensation of his newly claimed power with a proud, giddy smile.

"I have won," he whispers at first. His voice rises in volume as he comes back to standing. "After five hundred years, I have won." He lifts his head to the sky to thank some invisible deity for accomplishing his lifelong goal. "I HAVE WON!"

A cackle follows his victorious pronouncement, one that grows in volume with each intake of breath. I stay down, watching closely, and wait for the results to appear. Then I see Quill before me, bleeding and beholding the scene playing out. I scurry over the pavement toward him in an army crawl and lift what I can of him onto my lap. His breaths become uneven and labored, and I have a dreaded feeling I'm losing him too. I swallow through the unbearable lump as I stroke his stubbly cheek.

"Please don't die," I beg through a choked sob. "Don't you dare die."

All he does is shake his head. *I'm not going to,* he says. *Just focus on beating him.*

"I am. But I'm not going to let you die in my arms."

He aims his other hand at the icicle sticking out of his skin. It wiggles in his shoulder before he yanks it out without touching it, leaving behind a bleeding hole. The bloody piece of ice lands beside us with a *clink,* then he sets a palm over the wound.

I'll use what little power I have left to heal myself, but it's going to be slow. He lays a hand over mine, limp and weak. *I'll be fine, I promise.*

A pained groan sounds from behind me. I turn to see the Dormant King's body convulsing, his arms spread out and bent at the elbows. Every bit of his limbs shake so violently that he falls down on all fours, but rises again. Crackling and snapping spurts from all over. The putrid smell of burning flesh assaults our senses as steam emits from his clothes and turns into smoke. Soon, they become embers at his feet, stripping him bare and revealing burn marks that tinge his skin an ugly black. His wails become louder and more drawn out as the burns turn his skin into a new charred color. Burning from the inside out.

The water interferes with fire, so he can't use Blaze. The electricity interferes with the water—an unsafe combination in any situation.

Greed is poison to the heart.

He poisoned himself by being greedy with the powers he claimed. I had to let him reach the limit of his greed by taking from me.

He has reached his limit. It's breaking him before our eyes.

You figured it out, Quill says in amazement. *You found his weakness.*

"You . . ." The Dormant King turns to us, his flesh nearly burned off now. Bits of what remains of him still clings to his bones. "You rats! I refuse to lose to you! I will rule this kingdom!"

Even through his dying breath, he refuses to accept defeat. His whole purpose in life encased his heart in black.

The cold, evil, unloving heart that happens to still be beating.

I gently lay Quill flat on the ground, slowly stroking my finger along his cheek again. His eyebrows knit in confusion, but finds himself too weak to stop me as I whip out my sword. One more hit and all of this will be over.

I come to stand, my legs shaky. The Dormant King's strength has declined, but he still manages to stay upright on his knees. He refuses to give up, even though his breathing is deeply strained. He's almost totally burned, and he still thinks he has a chance.

Wait.

Quill shifts painfully to his side and reaches for his staff. He cries out when he turns it back to a bow and hands it to me.

I have one arrow left. Use it.

"What? I can't do that!"

Yes, you can. Use my bow and deliver the last blow, just like you wanted.

I can't believe he remembered when I said that to all the Descendants.

"Quill—"

Please. I want you to. This is my lame way of helping you achieve your goal.

He believes in me. He always has.

That's the one thought I have as I hesitantly take the bow from his hand and slide the last remaining arrow out of the quiver. I take my time to nock it, squeeze my fingers around it, and get ready to pull back as I move one step closer to the burning enemy. And another. I focus on the spot I want to shoot for, then lift the bow, pull, and release.

The arrow strikes him right in the chest plate. The Dormant King's expression shifts to bewilderment, jaw going slack as he sees the arrow sticking straight out of his chest. His body finally gives up staying upright and he falls onto his back. The arrow stutters in time with his uneven breaths, although small.

I'm almost there. Everything I ever dreamed of is finally happening.

I drop the bow and grab my sword again. This time, I have the upper hand. This time, I have the power to control his demise.

I place one foot, then the other, on either side of his body, glaring down at him with all the heat and fire of Vulca Mountain. He's unrecognizable. The burns have turned his whole body into a blackened mass. Even his eyes have burned; the only evidence of their existence is the dim sparkle from the light of purple mist. He tries to speak with the tremble of his throat and cracked lips, but nothing comes out.

Despite how utterly exhausted I am, seeing him at his worst and completely at my mercy makes me smile.

I bring the sword in front of me, pointing the blade straight down, and hold the hilt with both gloved hands. I used to think about what my last words to him would be. Ones that would both prove that I won while also sending a message to future generations. I never came up with the right thing. Now, seeing him hanging by a thread, there's only one thing left to say.

"This is for everything your greed took from us."

Then I shove the blade into his heart.

He lets out a choked cry with no change in facial expression or anything to indicate how this last moment of his life makes him feel. That is, until I see a tear roll down his temple, then onto the ground.

Then, he takes his last breath.

The Dormant King, Alaric the Power Ancestor, is dead.

I finally did it. I killed the Dormant King. I ended the war. I changed our history.

I redeemed the people I love.

I loosen my hands from the sword and sit back on my knees. My gaze roams from the sword protruding from his heart to the arrow in his chest plate and to his face. The Dormant King lies completely still, yet I wait for the moment that tells me this isn't over. That he can never be killed and his rulership is inevitable.

Instead, the air fills with dust. So much dust that it changes the color of the mist around us from purple to a deep violet. It all floats upward, creating clouds in the sky, graceful as the lanterns of Cal-léa.

Killing the Dormant King kills all the Dormants. He was their source of life. And now, all of it will be gone.

A strained moan sounds behind me and breaks me out of my disbelieving state. I don't hesitate to spring to my feet and run to Quill's aid. I sit beside him and stare into his eyes. Neither of us says anything for a time. We just gaze at each other in awe. Years and years of living a life in hiding. Months of hunting down the Dormant King to kill him. Losing loved ones to him. Almost losing each other.

I bury my face into his chest, away from his healing wound, and sob with everything I have. Tears of joy. Of sadness. Of exhaustion, grief, and regret. I feel it all without holding back. Years and years of waiting, dreaming, hoping.

It's finally over.

"You did it," Quill says with pride as he rests his lips on my head. "You really did it."

I wake up to an enormous yet comfortable bed. From the feel of the sheets and the sandstone bedroom with open windows, I know I'm in Calista's room. I sit up, wondering how I ended up here.

"We're here, Warrioress."

I turn to the source of the voice, and smile brightly when I find the one person that invades my dreams every night. Jael takes my hand in hers with a soft smile. For once, she doesn't look troubled. She doesn't look like she's about to give me advice. She's not about to say something serious.

She looks . . . happy.

"You defeated him," she says softly. "You defeated *him*, Havanna."

I remember it all.

The Dormant King convulsing and his skin burning him from the inside out.

My last words before plunging my sword into his heart.

Crawling to Quill as he narrowly escapes death.

Crying out my entire soul into his chest.

I really did do it.

I avenged her. I saved Ketra, and all of Petros.

Yet, I'm crying.

"Why the tears?" Jael asks. "This is a time to be proud and celebrate."

I shake my head. "I had to do it all without you. I needed *you*. And it's my fault you weren't with me, and I'm sorry."

Jael takes on her most comforting tone. "You're wrong, Warrioress. You didn't need me to do this with you. You leaving Ketra and taking it all on your shoulders was proof of how strong you really are, and how strong you've always been. I simply opened the door of opportunity for you."

She did open the door for me. In multiple ways. Taking me in as her own, teaching me how to fight, how to control my power; giving me the freedom I dreamed of when she died.

I owe it all to her.

"You did." I pat her hand with a tearful smile. "Thank you."

"And if you're going to take anything away from this," she says, leaning closer to me on the bed, "I hope it's that no matter where your freedom takes you, I will always be there. Take this new life by the reins and live it the way you always dreamed of."

Her words bring me comfort. I feel so open and exposed. Now that nothing holds me back from doing anything, it feels wrong, but also beautiful.

Now, I can't wait to see where it takes me.

CHAPTER 41

ANARA

"What going on?" Ender asks, scanning our surroundings as he sits with his back against a tree.

I see it too.

Dust. Nothing but dust coating the air, thick enough for us to breathe it in. With dusk approaching, the dust makes it darker than it is as it floats up to the sky.

Movement. Sound. Voices. Screams. Clamor of weapons. All of it comes to a standstill. All that is heard is the wind taking the remaining Dormants away, as if they never existed in the first place. The ground beneath us also ceases movement, a sign that none will emerge. Even the flying ones that took space in the sky burst into plumes.

Beyond the confines of the woods we're hiding in, all the soldiers release a deafening cry of victory. Followed by cheering and whooping. No more bloodshed. No more fear.

The Dormants are gone.

The Dormant King is gone.

The war is over.

All that remains is peace.

"She did it," I say breathlessly. I smile wide at Ender and grab his shoulders. I can't help but scream and laugh ecstatically. "She did it!"

Ender's eyebrows touch his forehead. "She kill Dormant King?"

"She killed the Dormant King!"

Ender laughs in glee with me. I throw my arms around his neck and hold him in a tight hug. He hugs me back, so affectionate and loving, rocking me back and forth while his laugh booms in my ears. He lets me go, putting space between us, all so he can roar in glee. I watch his elated, wide smile as he resumes laughing with joy. And I see it for the first time.

Tears streaming down his face. When I touch my own cheek, I feel the wet streaks.

We're both crying. Together, for the first time. With unbelievable joy.

"I glad I do it all with you," he confesses through a sniffle.

I stroke his cheek, sniffing back my own tears. "I wouldn't have wanted anyone else by my side."

Then I kiss him.

I feel him hesitate at first, then he opens for me. Our mouths move in sync, my body heating with the contact as my hands slide from his cheeks to the back of his head. We part after a few seconds, our lips just barely touching as we gaze into each other's eyes. We chuckle at the same time, smiling at each other and still crying.

"Come," he says, groaning as he stands. He holds his enormous hand out to me. "We celebrate."

"Wait," I say once he pulls me back to my feet. "I need to bring them back."

I use Gateway and open a portal in the same spot where the Dormant King escaped and Havanna jumped through. I thought she was beyond stupid for doing that, but I suppose if any of us had a chance at ending this, it was her.

"I go with you," Ender says, leaving no room for argument.

I shrug with a side smile. "If you insist."

***

I don't think Havanna understands what is happening when we find her and Quill. Her face is blank, eyes red and swollen, and Quill is just clawing back from the brink of death. We see the Dormant King's dead body firsthand. It is disgusting. Traumatic, even. But it is the sign of new beginnings. He isn't capable of hurting us anymore. Being raised to be in constant safety, it is tough to accept this new concept.

At the same time, we are thrilled. Before fully accepting our victory, though, we need to find safer ground to heal and rest.

That place is back in Ketra.

I wake to daylight shining through the windows in Aria's hut, with Ender sleeping soundly behind me, his strong arm draped over my stomach. If I had to guess, we've been in Ketra for at least two days. I remember falling asleep on Wave's back on the way here, and I vaguely recall being carried to a bed. Everything else is blank to me.

I turn myself over gently to face Ender and examine his chest. He never got to fully heal before everything turned chaotic, and fighting made his wounds worse. I skim a finger over his bandage, a movement that makes him stir in his sleep and groan.

"Oh no, I'm sorry," I whisper, running my hand up and down his arm. "I didn't mean to wake you." I move to get out of bed. "I'll get you some more Healing Salve."

He mumbles something unintelligible, then goes back to sleep. I cross the wooden landing, then open and shut the door as quietly as I can. It's still early morning, and all is quiet, save the few people mulling around tending to outside duties. I cross the pathway to the beach and automatically gaze at the ocean a few paces away. The scene before me has me stopping in my tracks, and I smile.

Havanna sits between her mother and Quill, conversing and smiling. The love of her life and her mother, getting along as if they're distant relatives catching up. Despite losing her father, she can still start over with her mother, and start a fresh relationship with Quill at the same time. I accepted my situation long ago, but a part of me still ponders how different my life would be if I knew my parents. Sharifa and Masina filled the gaps where necessary, but the blood connection was missing, and I felt it. Perhaps I can find it in me to go back to Macaphin Village, just to thank them for sending me on my way. Where they knew I belonged.

Now I can't picture being anywhere else.

We stayed in Ketra for a few days. We gave Havanna's father an informal memorial service, with just the four of us, Kora, Aria, and Thaeus. David was buried where he died, so the service consisted merely of just memories of him and what he was known for. That night, Kora decided to make Ketra her new home. She missed out on living here with Havanna, and going back to Paluso Mountains was just a reminder of David. She felt ready to move on.

Kora and David loved Havanna, no matter how badly they screwed up. In the end, they showed up for her. My parents never came back.

But it's all right. Because I found a new family.

CHAPTER 42

Ender

The two months after the war ended are nonstop for us.

First, we had to start an initiative to rebuild Arythica, including the castle, and have the civilians vote on a new royal pair to act as king and queen. Queen Avela was so traumatized with Aldous's death that she stepped down from her throne and opted to live as a citizen. Since she's had many sessions with those trained in medicine, the people have taken good care of her. There was a funeral arranged for Aldous that happened to be a huge affair. The entire city wanted to be in attendance, but it was limited to those who worked for him in the castle. Why everyone wanted to be there is beyond me. I didn't think anyone liked him.

Since Ketra, Anara and I haven't slept alone. She has frequent nightmares about how Aldous died by the king's hand. One night, she woke up with a scream and struggled to catch her breath. On another night, she heard Havanna crying and went to her bedside. When the nightmares became unbearable, she went into detail about what happened in the throne room. She and Havanna were forced to watch as the Dormant King killed Aldous, and the sounds that came with it. The trauma was so intense as she retold the events that she vomited. I was more determined than ever to stay by her side, no matter what.

"I want you safe, always," I told her.

She always manages to fall back asleep, even though there's nothing I can do to help. As a chief and sole protector of a whole village, being at a loss in this way drives me mad. Quill told me that just being there with her is enough, which is something Havanna had to drill into him.

We returned to Killios soon after that. Some soldiers lost their lives, but Arthur was well. He was relieved to know of the Dormant King's demise, but was grieving the loss of his soldiers during the Dormant attack. Havanna suggested a memorial service, and the next thing we knew, we were gathering the entire camp. Arthur asked me to ignite every single candle that bordered the training grounds, and the ambience made the occasion more impactful. Anara drew in a shaky breath at one point. None of us knew the soldiers very well, but her heart has softened enough to be emotional for this occasion. Her attempt to brush it off as if it were nothing didn't work on me.

"Stop hiding," I told her. She knew exactly what I was saying. When her eyes filled with tears, I took her hand in mine. A silent understanding.

After two memorial services, I was done being helpful. I simply wanted to sleep for countless days. Havanna and Quill rolled their eyes at my incessant whining, Anara proceeded to call me a lazy troll, and that was that.

The one event that helped us forget about everything we dealt with was attending Aria's and Claeron's wedding on the beach just outside Ketra, crashing waves in the background. Seeing Havanna's best friend get married with Thaeus as the officiator was a sight to behold. Having Kane resting on Aria's shoulder as a shrew was even better. Earlier, it seemed the Bennarus were huddled together to say goodbye, because Kane decided to make Aria his owner.

The tradition of a Mulhutna couple wanting to marry is to journey to the very top of Vulca Mountain, an arduous and tough hike that goes straight uphill. When they make it safely to the top and they still want to be together, they exchange rings carved out of stone to solidify their commitment. I didn't think much about my own marriage in the future, and I never wanted to make that journey to the top. It sounded like a lot of work I didn't want to do.

Sitting next to Anara, though, it doesn't seem so bad. Making that trip together would be an honor.

The wedding festivities carried on to dusk. Musicians play a variety of instruments by the edge of the village while the guests dance. Laughter becomes its own music, roaring flames of torches dancing with us in the night. I'm brought back to the seeking party in Sabbia, only this time, I don't care about dancing with other women to feel desirable.

Neither Anara nor I know how to dance, so we pretend to know what we're doing when we hobble from one foot to the other. Her ankle-length dress brushes along the surface of the sand and sways in a ghostly yet angelic way. We laugh when our bare feet keep tripping over each other. Eventually, we find a good rhythm. Our bodies flush against each other, my heart thumps harder in my chest, the closeness so much more intimate than sleeping in the same bed.

"You no dance before?" I ask through laughter.

"My village did a weird dance where their bellies jiggled, but it was an excuse for the women to show off their impeccable abs."

"I show you impeccable abs, and you no like," I remind her as I run a hand over my stomach flirtatiously.

Anara rolls her bottom lip under her teeth. "Well, things have changed." She gazes into my eyes. "You're more than just impeccable abs."

"Yes. I have strong legs. Butt hard as rock."

She genuinely laughs, and I revel in the fact that she saves that musical sound just for me. Her hands reach up to my neck, her thumbs stroking the bottom of my jaw.

I peer down at her and smile. "And you more than emotionless human."

"You're the one who saw it first."

I knew, from the moment I met her, that I would wear her down. I also knew that she would see underneath the exterior of someone who was trying much too hard to win her heart. By some miracle, she accomplished both.

I shake my head. "No. I like irritating you."

She feigns annoyance when she replies begrudgingly, "And you succeeded. Thank you."

The question of what will now become of the four of us still looms in an uncomfortable bubble waiting to burst. We Descendants were so busy taking care of things, none of us talked about it. Things have settled in Petros, but the subject still hasn't been broached. I don't want to know everyone's answer to the question. I fear the answer will only bring disappointment. I don't want to be away from my compos.

Most of all, I don't want to be away from Anara.

The question is asked before I can stop it. "If I return to Vulca . . ." I swallow the lump in my throat. "You join me?"

Anara is slightly taken aback, eyebrows drawn together. "With the Mulhutna?"

"Yes."

Her immediate hesitation to answer makes me nervous. "I don't know," she replies with uncertainty.

My heart sinks. "You no want me around?"

She releases a shaky breath. "No, it's not that at all."

I brace for more squeezes and aches to my heart. She thinks carefully about her next words before responding. "We were hidden for so long. We went everywhere, all over Petros, but I don't truly feel I got to experience it. I didn't explore it the way I imagined I would while I was in hiding. I want to take some time to see everything. Take it in." She lays a hand on my chest. "The Mulhutna mean a lot to you, and I know you want to be back home. I know you've been worried about your mother, and the well-being of your tribe. I don't know how to feel about living on a mountain like that."

She wants to enjoy the land and I want to go back home. And, someday, perhaps we can make the trip to the top of the mountain together. Either way, I don't want to go back to my old life without her.

"What you saying?"

"I'm saying we both want to do different things. And I don't want to hold you back from what will make you happy."

Exactly the words I didn't want to hear. I don't want to be the reason she's unhappy. I want her to live her life the way she dreamed. I wish that for all of my compos. But I never imagined parting from the compa that has my affection.

I hang my head, squeezing her hips a little tighter. "I never like another compa the way I do you. I no like sleep without you no more."

She fights back her tears with all her might. "Me neither."

There has to be a way to make our dreams happen for both of us while still being together. I've left Vulca Mountain once; I suppose I can do it again. This time, none of our lives will be on the line, and it will simply be for pleasure and enjoyment. She's been to Vulca Mountain and has stayed for multiple days without much suffering—no doubt she can do it again.

The idea I come up with is a long shot, but I want to try anyway. "How about . . . join me to Mulhutna couple days, then we go away? See Petros together."

Relief fills the lines in her eyes. "You're saying I can come back with you, then we can travel?"

I nod once. "Way you always want to."

A laugh escapes her, full of relief and a happiness she never had. Leaping onto her tiptoes, she kisses me. "I can try that."

I smile so wide it hurts, and I lean down to kiss her again, longer this time.

This is it. The beginning of our future. Me and her.

My compa.

CHAPTER 43

QUILL

The Arbol Forest is quiet. I never thought I would be back here, in the exact same spot where I watched my brother die. I'm just staring at the spaces between the endless copse of trees, waiting for Backers to show up and destroy my life.

Two figures emerge from the darkness. I don't feel the urge to grab my bow, though. Deep down, I know who they are.

Indigo's arms spread out while he flashes a smile at me. "I knew you could do it, brother."

"I'm sorry it waited until after you were gone," I say, my voice thick.

"That was beyond your control." He steps closer to me, clapping my shoulder. "Don't ever feel that you somehow failed me. You didn't fail anyone."

"Speak for yourself."

Beside him is Nyx, glowering at me. "You asked everyone else to fight with you but me." She shakes her head, clearly hurt. "I would have fought with you in a heartbeat if you just asked. You're my best friend."

I had my reasons for not asking her to get involved, reasons I felt she would understand one day, even if it hurt her in the moment.

"I'm sorry, Nyx. I didn't think it was fair of me to ask since I left the village so abruptly. I was afraid you hadn't forgiven me for leaving."

I sit against a tree and fight back tears, apologizing repeatedly. We won the war, yet having them still missing from my life doesn't seem to make a difference.

I feel someone sit beside me, and an arm slides over my shoulders for a one-sided hug. "I know you were hurting. You always will. But you're free now. Be with the girl you love, and stop surviving. You need to live." She kisses my temple. "Just . . . don't be a stranger, all right? Don't wait too long to come back."

I hear Indigo sitting at my other side, dirt crunching under a pair of boots. "You leaving was the bravest thing you've ever done." His voice fills my ears. "You fought for the kingdom. You fought for us."

I did. I almost died for him, and I was honored to deliver the much-deserved revenge.

He brings my head closer to his chest, holding me tighter. "Thank you. Now go. Be happy, Quill."

I open my eyes to a blank ceiling at dawn. It takes a second for me to remember that we arrived in Sabbia yesterday, the day after Aria's wedding. We hadn't checked on the welfare of the town yet, and Havanna was missing Calista fiercely.

Keeley healed from her injuries, although it made her bedridden for a month and it drove her insane. Calista and Malik had to have Freya and Zena look after her, though, as they attended to other matters in town since they were absent for a time. The seeking party tonight will not only be about finding a mate, it will be about celebrating our victory and the fact that Sabbia's king and queen survived.

Whenever I dream of Indigo and Nyx, I wake up with a hole in my chest. A constant reminder of what I lost and why I never wanted to go back to Arbol Village. This dream was different. I don't wake up with heartache this time.

I feel . . . serene.

I roll my head to the side, Havanna lying beside me. She stares up at the ceiling, deep in thought. She sees me and smiles. "How are you feeling?"

Her question isn't about my physical well-being. She and I have similar dreams every night. Now that everything has changed for the better, the content of our dreams has been intermixed with positivity.

I hold up my head with my hand, lulling over the many emotions swimming within me. I redeemed my brother. I'm free. I can live the life I was meant to live. I've fallen in love. At last, things aren't bleak.

"Good," I say softly. "Really good."

She rolls toward me and kisses me. "Me too."

***

"So, I don't want to bring this up, but it's the bull in the room," Havanna announces, "so . . . what's going to happen to us? Are we going our separate ways?"

The seeking party is being set up, and the four of us decide to sit by the edge of the Reddawn Oasis and relax. Our feet are dipped into the water up to our knees while Havanna has to bring her knees to her chin to avoid touching it. Our Bennarus are having the time of their lives floating on the water in their bird forms. The frown on her face is evidence of how afraid she is of everyone's responses.

Anara and Ender give each other a knowing look, then turn to me and Havanna. "Tomorrow, I'm going back to Vulca Mountain with Ender for a few days, then he's coming with me to explore the land."

"You've already seen what needs to be seen," I note.

"Because we were trying to find the Dormant King," Anara retorts. "I want to see it in the eyes of someone who's not constantly wary of danger."

Havanna deliberates on this, bouncing her head side to side. "Fair enough." She gives Anara a side hug. "I'm happy for you."

"I suppose I'll let you hug me." Anara feigns relenting to her affection and hugs her back.

"Too late. We crossed that bridge at Snake's Canyon."

Anara chuckles and lets go. "What about you both? What are you going to do next?"

I direct my attention to Havanna. Neither of us had talked much about it since Arythica. Although she was unconscious, I promised I'd follow her wherever she went.

I have nowhere to be but with her.

"We might stay here for a bit," Havanna answers. "I want to visit my mother in Ketra at some point. It's time we rebuild what we should've had all along."

I think back to my dream and finally feel good about the idea I have. "I might be all right going back to Arbol Village to see my best friend." I nudge Havanna's arm. "I want her to meet you."

She leans her head on my shoulder. "I'd like that."

We sit in silence for a few seconds until Ender breaks it with an emotional statement. "I will miss you, compos."

Havanna waves a hand in front of her, shutting it down. "No no. We're going to see a lot of each other in the years to come. We've been through way too much to let that happen."

"Agreed," Anara says plainly. "We're heroes."

"Heroes that were in hiding," Havanna interjects.

Ender nods. "Hidden Heroes."

It's my turn to approve. A new name for us. "Hidden Heroes. I like it."

Anara sighs loudly. "Well, if we're not going to see each other for a while, let's make tonight count." She turns to Havanna's tightly curled form and motions to her whole body. "Starting with this."

Havanna scoots back from the water and straightens her legs. "What do you mean?"

"Hold that thought," she replies, getting up and walking back to Calista's house.

"Hey, that's what I say!" I yell at Anara's retreating back.

After a few minutes, Anara returns holding something in her hand. "I've been waiting forever for this moment," she says. "Doofus, remember when we were in Arythica and you wanted to buy that Swimmer's Repellent, but you didn't have enough money?"

Havanna rises to her feet. "Yes?"

Anara opens her hand and extends a bottle to Havanna. "Here."

She takes the bottle, her mouth hanging wide open. It holds a translucent liquid, closed by a cork, no bigger than an apple. "You didn't," Havanna says breathlessly, examining it like it's a dream.

"I felt bad that you didn't have enough money." Anara shrugs nonchalantly. "The look on your face when the potion maker told you the price was sad. I thought it was pathetic, but I started to think, 'what kind of life is it if someone can't enjoy something as simple as swimming? Or water?' So—" She motions to the bottle.

Havanna's lower lip trembles, followed by a sniffle. "I know you don't like hugs, but I'm giving you another one anyway," she cries, throwing her arms around Anara's neck. Anara doesn't seem to mind. In fact, she embraces it and hugs her back. "Thank you." Havanna sobs into her shoulder.

"You're welcome," Anara replies plainly and pushes Havanna off her. "Now drink it and go swim. Half the bottle is good for a whole day."

Havanna turns to me with the brightest, most cheerful smile I've ever seen. A simple pleasure in life she was denied simply because of her powers, and now there's a workaround.

She pops the cork off and gulps down just enough to leave half the potion left in the bottle. She wastes no time in rushing to the edge of the oasis, but then skids to a stop. "Wait. I don't know how to swim."

"For crying out loud, Doofus, that's what I'm here for!" Anara exclaims, walking ahead of her into the water, then holds out her hand. "Now hurry up and get in."

CHAPTER 44

HAVANNA

I can't believe this is happening.

I'm about to put my whole body into the water. And I'm not going to die because of it.

My heart pounds against my rib cage, taking one careful step at a time toward Anara's hand. She forms a kind of cushion out of water for me to lean my back on, then lowers me so that I'm staring straight into the desert sky. It's so warm, so comforting like a thick, soft blanket. The water drenches my clothes and my hair, and I don't care. I sweep my arms underwater and bring them back to the surface.

"How are you doing?" she asks.

A smile breaks on my face. My tears of joy drop into the water. I have much to be grateful for, and it's all overwhelming in the best way. "Incredible."

Anara takes us farther, toward the deep end, cradling my body along the surface. Ender and Quill watch in silence, waiting for my response to it all.

Anara warns me that she's going to bring me underwater and tells me to plug my nose. She does just that and I take it all in. The whooshing and rushing of water in my ears; the low, muffled hum of outside noise; the warmth coating my entire body; the heavy, yet soft feeling of it on my skin as my limbs move and I lift my head. I break the surface, droplets coming off my body in rivulets. I wait for the moment that my skin turns red and a burning feeling surfaces.

It doesn't come. I'm pain free.

I laugh. I laugh hysterically. I shoot my arms in the air and cheer loudly. Anara, Quill, and Ender clap for me. Soon enough, onlookers around the oasis are clapping, although not knowing what's so special about this moment.

"I wish I could stay in here," I tell Anara dreamily.

"Later," she says, bringing me back to the water's edge. "First, let's dance."

And we do.

I change into dry clothes, tie my wet hair to my head, the music starts, and we dance. I dance with Quill, just as I did at Aria's wedding. No serious conversation. No doubts or questions of loyalty. No romantic strain. Just us and the music. And the best sense of peace.

"Havanna!" Calista wades her way through the dancing crowd, making a beeline for me. The urgency in her tone has me wary, but she's crying tears of joy and smiling wide. "I have excellent news!"

I break away from Quill. "What is it?"

"I'm pregnant!" She sniffs and laughs. "I'm going to be a mother!"

A mother. A privilege that a miscarriage once denied her. Now, a second chance is building within her.

I scream in happiness and hug her with all the strength I have. "Calista, that's so amazing!" We both jump and keep screaming, and I turn to Quill. "She's pregnant!"

Quill raises his head to shout over the music, "Hey, everybody! Queen Calista is with child!"

The cheers and screaming that erupt is deafening, but it makes the moment all the more magical. More reasons to celebrate.

I go back to dancing with Quill while Malik comes to claim his pregnant wife, but not before winking at me and patting my shoulder. So much is happening, and it's fantastic. A nice reprieve from all the negative things that brought me down and nearly tore me apart. I can use my abilities for whatever and whenever I want without capturing the Dormants' or Backers' attentions.

Which gives me an idea.

The music has increased in tempo as I dance with Quill. I swivel my hips, raising my arms, all in a seductive manner. I spin in a circle and throw my arms down. Lightning strikes in the depths of the desert, and it's a spectacle. The Sabbians mumble to themselves. No Dormants on their way to attack. No monsters lurking in the desert. No Backers closing in to hunt down the one with abilities. Nothing but freedom.

When I jump and spin, I do it again, and they rejoice with cheers and applause, some looking my way, knowing it's me.

Soon after, Ender shoots a puff of fire out of his hands, one after the other. Anara giggles joyfully while she takes water from the oasis and creates a stream that weaves softly between people, further taking them by surprise. She brings it back to the oasis, shapes it into a person, and makes it dance. The Sabbians clap and giggle at what has turned into a talent show.

Quill causes a palm tree to lean forward toward a group of people and forces the fronds to tickle Sabbian faces. We Descendants cheer loudly, raising our arms, and the entire town joins in before resuming dancing.

This is happiness.

Quill picks me up from under my rear and spins me around. I throw my head back and revel in the moment. I don't remember a time I've laughed so much in a day, and it's the most wonderful, intoxicating feeling. He lowers me to my feet and kisses me, long and hard. I melt to his touch and kiss him like it's the last time.

"Thank you for being in my life," he says against my lips.

I will never tire of hearing those words. "I love you, Forest Dweller. I always will."

"I love you too, Zappy."

He kisses me again and the world melts into the background.

We dance the night away, letting it sink in that this is where our new lives begin. We can be happy, peaceful, and free. All with the ones we love and cherish.

The way it should have always been.

Thank you for reading *The Call of Freedom*, the final book of the Hidden Heroes series!

Want more of the Descendants? Subscribe to www.sarahblyn newrites.com and read an exclusive epilogue!

If you enjoyed the Hidden Heroes series, please rate and review on Amazon, Barnes & Noble, and Goodreads!

Follow me on social media:

Instagram: @sarahblynnewrites

Facebook: Sarah Blynne Writes

TikTok: @sarahblynne

Acknowledgements

Oh man, this has been a fun, amazing two years of writing this series. These books will always have a special place in my heart as being the first fantasy series I ever wrote. It's bittersweet: I'll miss my Descendants, but it's time to move forward.

I want to thank my parents, Francine and Alex, for being so supportive and open to discussing book ideas, and giving a listening ear to my venting sessions (there weren't a lot, but they did happen). I don't know what I would do without you.

I also want to thank my sister, Cameron, for also being a good support and inviting people to events where my books were being presented. You're the best.

Everyone I work with especially has been so amazing. You've all been wonderful cheerleaders, and I can't thank you enough for that.

I have way too many friends to list here, but you're all on my mind and in my heart. Thank you for being in my life.

To my editor, Kasey, and my cover artist, Velaya. You both are freaking phenomenal. Your input and advice have been a huge help. Thank you for following my journey for the last couple years.

And to my husband, Cody. You don't even like reading, yet you read my books just because. That means a lot. Thank you for being my biggest cheerleader. I love you so much.

On to other adventures!
Sarah

About the Author

Sarah hails from Tacoma, WA, where she began writing at the ripe young age of eleven, when she wrote her first fantasy story. She originally wrote her debut novel, Bloom, in high school, loosely based on her high school experiences, that she rewrote for publication in 2024. Her next novel to follow, The Call of Thunder, was published the same year. Now she has let those experiences, along with her wild music choices, inspire her writing, and expand her imagination.

In her spare time, she enjoys reading, cooking, drinking coffee, trying different restaurants and coffee shops, playing video games, going on walks, and spending time with her friends and family. And dressing up for Comic-Con.

www.ingramcontent.com/pod-product-compliance
Lightning Source LLC
Chambersburg PA
CBHW031959150726
47990CB00005B/1774